CRUSH

CRUSH

VIKKI MESSENGER

BENEATH THE KITE (PUBLISHING)

A catalogue record for this book is available from the National Library of Australia

ISBN: 9780648114703 (Paperback)
ISBN: 9780648114710 (Hardcover)
ISBN: 9780648114727 (Ebook)

Publisher: Beneath The Kite (Publishing)
Book Cover Design: Pickawoowoo, Laila Savolainen
Interior Design: Pickawoowoo Publishing Group

Printed & Channel Distribution
Lightning Source | Ingram (USA/UK/EUROPE/AUS)

With love

Les, Amy, Karen, Neil

...the seed of this goes way back in time and so do we

With gratitude

B Louden, J Munro

...double ticks from inspiring teachers are worth more
than a thousand words

Chapter 1

'Can you ride a bike?'

Clearly, the wrong bloody question.

Maddie pictured her boss lounging on the grass outside the smoko room, the question wafting from his lips.

Worse, her response. She mimed it, shrugging her shoulders, innocent smile. 'Course I ride.' Hardly a lie—her warm-up at the gym involved ten to fifteen minutes on the static bike, plus the odd spin class.

Madison Anderson, noob!

Poised on the rim of a limestone abyss, eyes wide, pulse ramped, the inadequate question pummelled her brain.

Lewis could have asked if she had a death wish, or if Evel Knievel was an inspirational figure in her life, either more relevant. Better still, he could have asked *someone else*. At least now she understood the upward creep of Roley and Westy's eyebrows and Bethany's amused expression as they witnessed the exchange. They might've let her in on the joke.

Maddie's hopes for a grace period to gently ease into the unknown had careened into the roadside ditch. The opening section, a long, steep gravel incline, had only served to broadcast her ability as the gears clunked disconcertingly all the way to the top. Lungs sucking, legs burning, she looked over the edge to the next section, a gnarly, pocked downhill run. Her heart switched from muscle to mallet, pump to thump, not wanting any part of it.

No biggie, except she was competing in the bike leg of an adventure race, approximately two kilometres down, another thirty to go. Gravel, sand, hills, single-track—berms for Christ's sake. Her 'riding a bike' experience didn't extend to those.

'On your right,' a competitor charging up yelled.

Maddie inched her bike from the path of the speeding rider and watched the Lycra-clad maniac manoeuvre expertly down the hill, hitting rocks deliberately to get airborne.

'Stay put, princess.' Another flashed by.

She pulled a face into his dusty wake. It was a lame place to park. Gloved hands squeezing grips, butt cheeks squeezing seat, she commanded jelly legs to action launching down the slope.

Christ. Another rider on her tail. Inching over the rocky ground of the narrow track she flinched as he yelled.

'Get your weight back. Look at the line you want, your bike will follow. Stop squeezing the friggin' brakes, you'll go arse over bars. Passing left when I can.'

Maddie's brow furrowed. Metres ahead the track widened enough for her to pull right. Gingerly lifting one hand in thanks, her guardian angel sped past, along with another hugging his slipstream.

Pressure lifted, she experimented. Shifting her bum back altered her centre of gravity giving her more balance for less effort. Nodding, she studied the track. Straight ahead was a daunting rocky drop and a little to the right, highly desirable level ground. She focused hard on the flat section and perceived a subtle shift as the bike followed the line of her gaze.

Holy crap it works!

Scanning ahead for the path of least disaster, jaw clenched, adrenaline coursing, she actioned her mentor's final wisdom, loosening her fingers off the brakes, and letting go.

As another rider sailed past, Maddie fought her instincts to slow.

'You're almost there, keep going.'

Thanks, sister. She rounded one last limestone cavity, a pothole of canyon-esque proportion, and finally reached the bottom.

Revelling in relief, the joy of even ground, her front tyre hit sand. The wheel bit deep stopping the bike instantly, leaving the laws of physics—as they apply to momentum—dangerously unsatisfied. The energy of acceleration had to go someplace. Barely registering the bike stall she flew from the saddle over the handlebars getting air Maddie style.

Air was over-rated Maddie decided, thrilled to be conscious before noticing the bike headed straight for her. She balled up her limbs. The rider deployed evasive tactics pulling-up centimetres from impact. Cursing vehemently he rebalanced and wheels churning dirt, took off.

Maddie was bogged. Struggling upright she dragged her bike through the dirty sand and assessed. Something had pierced her knee, the blood flow impressive for the size of the wound. Thankfully nothing snapped, popped or twisted. Confidence—hanging by a bike chain.

Maddie looked back and watched others plummet down the hill. Controlled plummeting. When they hit the pit of loose sand they pedalled hard, holding speed, maintaining control.

Taking a swig from her water bottle she noticed a course marshal shuffling down the track. Maddie raised her arm and yelled. 'I'm okay. I may be the only competitor without a hydration pack, but I refuse to be the first carted off in an ambulance.'

The marshal, an older bloke, broke into a broad grin. 'Often wondered what happened to Calamity Jane. She swapped her nag for a bicycle.'

Maddie gave him a thumbs-up before calculating a break in the flow of riders, pushing hard on the pedals. 'You can do this, Madison. Can't get any worse.'

She theorised, skills—crap, fitness—tick, attitude—everything. Keeping to the hard ground of the shoulder increased her pace. The track opened onto a fire road with room to pass allowing competitors to relax into their rhythm. Mottled sunlight rippling through green shady forest soothed and gradually Maddie found hers.

Pushing with the length of her legs, hugging the outside lip, she enjoyed the burst of speed. Assessing the wayward leaves of a tree overhanging the track she closed her eyes and ducked to the side, preparing for a swat.

Whumph!

Sideways in the dirt catching her breath she conceded a miscalculation of proportions—branch to leaves. On the positive, this time she was still attached to the bike.

'Okay?' Two riders slowed.

'Never better,' Maddie waved a hand at them. 'All good.'

As they moved on, she momentarily succumbed to the

unco mess of being horizontal on a bicycle, deciding survival may be the new black. 'Finish and survive' a worthy mantra.

But this was a race.

Clumsily she found her feet and dusted off once more.

The move to Margaret River was about making wine—great wine—at Beneath The Kite. How that translated to getting personal with the ground fifty clicks down the road in the wilds of Augusta was still to compute. It was fun, kind of—not falling off or getting sworn at. Perhaps challenging said it better, a Taser to her comfort zone, although her comfort zone had been taking hits for a month and was leaking credibility.

Just three weeks ago she'd packed up life in Victoria and driven west across the Nullarbor to park between the Capes in the southwest of Western Australia. One giant prod to comfortable life right there. She'd never driven more than a couple of hundred kilometres in one stretch; now she was licensed to claim taking on the road-trains, crossing the treeless plain. Fronting up to work in the temporary position of Vintage Winemaker, not knowing a soul, delivered another hefty slam.

Upright and moving, her thoughts landed unbidden on the image of Roley's hard bicep brushing her leg while stooping to clasp the timing band around her ankle. He looked good wet and tousled in a sleeveless wetsuit.

Whoa! The bike fishtailed violently, forcing her to slow.

Roley Douglas (team paddler), was the Vineyard Manager at Kite. The rest of 'The Flying Kites' comprised winery Cellar Hand, Westy (swimmer) and Senior Winemaker, Lewis Smith (runner). Enthusiastic and talented, each had performed admirably in their individual legs.

Suddenly Josh, her boyfriend back east, prickled in. He

wasn't happy she was competing. No explanation—just not happy. Maddie couldn't fathom the attitude. It was odd and disappointing. But she hadn't pushed, conceding his comfort zone also likely to be suffering under a barrage of friendly fire.

Determined not to be the weak link, to rise above Josh's negativity, she pedalled furiously recalling Bethany's words as they left work Friday: 'You're carrying the hopes and dreams of women everywhere Maddie—no pressure.' Maddie smiled at the thought of her new friend. *So many good reasons to finish this thing.*

Survive—finish. Survive—finish.

Cornering every curve revealed a new obstacle or welcome stretch for powering and overtaking. Maddie laughed out loud at one steep section of uphill—sand, roots, rocks and craters—nearly everyone off their bikes applauding the few with superior skill and endurance, determined to stay mounted and climb with everything they had. Admiration dissolved in trickling sweat as calves screaming, chest heaving, she pushed her own bike up.

As time ticked and kilometres clicked every exertion took a greater toll. Pumping hard on one section of road left her lungs searing, a dry tightness to her body inside and out. Maddie started to flag, vagueing-out over time and her location on the course. Her mind drifted. Bush passed in a mesmerising blur of greens with shocks of yellow, purple, orange and magenta. Grass trees on steroids, standing tall as she'd seen them, one blackened trunk holding three, sometimes four, spiny skirts. They headlined the landscape, skinny flowering torsos thrusting proud.

Survive—finish. Finish—survive.

Over a short steep downhill a competitor slid out with a yelp in a spray of gravel. Maddie uttered empathetic noises while a spectator rushed to assist. Further along a rider was off to the side with his bike upside down on its frame fixing a flat. *Crap!* She stared as she passed almost riding off the track. Then, a guy walking his bike, the front tyre miserably deflated. Maddie nodded, the 'patch kit' event organisers recommended suddenly made sense—tyre tube repair, not nicotine. Of course event organisers wouldn't indulge those unable to go the distance without a ciggie. She rolled her eyes. Next time someone asked 'can you ride a friggin' bike', she'd be ready. Do you mean one that moves?

She pushed on. Numb legs circling, her mind wandered. *Wasn't there a song, the wheels on the bike go...something, something.*

Finally, she registered an amplified voice and perked at the distant shouts and claps of spectators. The end was in earshot. Survive—finish, became finish, finish, finish. A marshal signalled her across a road into one last section of single-track through a tea-tree cocoon before she burst through to the grassy clearing of the transition. Slowing to dismount, willing her legs to hold, she caught sight of Lewis, Westy and Roley in the throng of bodies waving frantically. Smiling, she dropped the bike, fingers working to release the helmet buckle. *You bloody did it.* Grabbing her bottle, gulping the dregs, she shuffled towards the timing gate.

She checked the digital clock before exiting quickly calculating her time. Just outside two hours. Her shoulders slumped.

Lewis reached her first, pulling her in for a loose hug. 'Well done. Well bloody done,' he repeated setting her free. 'All we've been hearing is how tough the sand was this year. God Maddie, I didn't know the bike leg was so technical. We were worried.'

Her shoulders straightened. 'Yeah well, ignorance was my bliss,' Maddie puffed. 'Until reality hammered me—twice.' She bent forward resting her hands on her knees. 'Man, I'm happy to have finished. A little disappointed with my...'

Westy stepped close, one hand raised in a fist. Grinning, they punched knuckles. 'Sister, we're renaming you the be-spoke-n one.'

Maddie tilted her head and studied him until the reference finally clicked. She punched his bicep. 'Oh Westy that's cool. I love it.'

He eyed the ground, smiling. 'You did good.'

Roley stood quietly to the side. He pointed at her leg. 'Hope that's not as bad as it looks?'

Maddie's eyes followed his finger, and gaze, to her legs. Her knee was caked with dark dried blood running the length of her shin, staining her sock. Sand and dirt stuck to the blood in a grizzly fresh-from-battle scenario. Every bit of exposed flesh rendered with a sweaty, grit slurry.

Ignoring a pang of self-consciousness, she laughed. 'Wow. That would really be impressive except I know how it got there.'

Roley moved towards her but stopped as Lewis clapped, calling them to attention. 'Well team, let's finish this thing.'

'What?' Maddie looked from one to the other.

'God.' Lewis smacked his forehead. 'Maybe I never mentioned. It's a two-and-a-half kilometre team beach run to the finish.'

Maddie contemplated her options; collapse in a heap, or cry hysterically.

Lewis, reading her face assumed control. Putting his hands on her shoulders he yelled 'Westy feet, Roley hips', and together, to the amusement of spectators, they hoisted her horizontal and carried her across the sand. The shining knights dropped her in a giggling heap after a few uncoordinated steps but it was enough to jump-start her legs into a stumbling half-run and they started along the beach.

'My favourite bit of the ride was coming out of one nasty sandpit onto a main road.' Maddie panted. 'The marshals, two burly blokes, had parked their ute with the doors open and the stereo blasting ACDC's, *Highway to Hell*. Totally cracked me up.'

'Local support is awesome,' Lewis agreed. 'There were heaps of people lining the route of the run cheering and yelling. Sometimes it's just what you need to lift and dig deeper.'

'I had a stingray shadowing me for a bit,' Roley offered. 'That was pretty cool.'

'Was it cheering?' Westy inquired. 'Or telling you to watch and learn. No *barb* intended.'

Roley, Maddie and Lewis groaned as one.

Banter stopped as the track narrowed funnelling them into a rocky minefield bordering the cut linking river to ocean, eventually opening onto a riot of colour on the crowded river front. A minute later they crossed the line, arms linked.

Maddie soared. Surrendering the timing band to officials, posing for a team photo, satisfaction swelled. Moving with the flow of competitors she followed a trail of white plastic cups to a giant flask of sports drink. Chugging refills she absorbed the scene.

Lewis was standing near the organiser's tent beaming in the company of his family. He held his youngest boy on his hip and the eldest clasped his free hand while his wife, Mae, examined grazes on his elbow and calf. The boys looked engrossed as Lewis re-enacted the rocky tumble he'd taken during his leg, nearly taking them all to the ground. As Mae jumped clear the boys shrieked with laughter.

Maddie looked away. Excitement at telling Josh about the race somehow already marred.

Eventually she mooched to join the Smith clan as Roley and Westy arrived with watermelon slices procured from another sponsor's trestle.

The area surrounding the finishing chute was crowded with athletes; sweat-stained, salt-crusted, dirt-dusted, limbs-numbered, worn but happy. A degree of posturing was expected from this group of humans. Many trained hard, disciplined at every turn, to achieve the strong fit bodies essential to their quest. Overall the atmosphere held a subtle vibration of contentment, a communal Om, aftermath of mind-body exertion.

'Watermelon isn't sunscreen you two.'

All heads turned towards the boys. Their faces and forearms plastered in grainy pink chunks and dark seeds. They giggled and thrust the green smiley rinds at Mae.

Mae shrugged. 'Might be time to de-stickify. Paddle anyone?'

The boys slapped sticky hands together, each taking the hand of a parent, linking them like a little elephant family and Lewis led them through the crowd to the foreshore. Less than a hundred metres out of the event zone of milling bodies and droning loud speaker, they found lush grass under the shade of peppermint trees.

Maddie swiped at a dangling swatch of leaves. 'These things should come with a warning.'

Roley and Westy exchanged a quizzical look. 'Because?'

'Because, they have an aversion to bikes.'

Lewis appeared puzzled. 'Our karri trees are known to

throw branches on people's heads, cars, tents. Colloquially, they're the widow-makers. But peppies are generally regarded as pretty harmless.'

'We've got one at home. We built a cubby in it,' Lewis's son sounded defensive.

'It doesn't mind our bikes,' added the other.

'Yeah, and they're the favourite habitat of ringtail possums,' Westy joined the debate. 'We love our peppermint trees.'

Maddie raised her hands signalling surrender. 'Maybe it's an aversion to Victorians.'

Roley gently nudged her. 'Don't take it personally. They may multitask, but they're not too clever. I doubt capable of discrimination or other sinister acts.'

Lewis, Mae and their boys kicked off their shoes and headed to the shallow, lapping water of the inlet.

The soles of her feet were making noise about their own hot confinement. Maddie bent to release them, feeling the rest of her body twang, already stiffening. Shy of stretching in front of her teammates, she smiled broadly when Westy casually dropped into cow-face pose, and Roley sitting cross-legged started working his arms into eagle.

Barefoot, Maddie balanced on one leg taking the other behind to stretch out her quads. 'You realise, the energy coming from you two is restoring me on a subliminal level.'

Roley grinned, changing arms slowly.

'Sweet.' Westy acknowledged. 'Stretching is important, especially for a surfer Maddie. All that paddling can bind your upper body muscles into knots.' His voice adopted a Marvin Gaye timbre. 'Hard bulging muscles might be nice for the ladies,' his eyebrows danced. 'But long strong muscles mean we'll still be surfing when we're sixty.' He threw her a friendly wink. 'Some downward dog would be bliss after a marathon stint on a bike.'

Smile stuck to her face, Maddie positioned herself into downward facing dog; pushing up from the pads of her hands, lifting her bum to the sky, heels extending back to the ground. She groaned. 'Westy. Guru! I would totally salute you namaste style except—I'd fall flat on my face.'

Neither Westy nor Roley replied.

Bethany had told her of the two men's reputation for unofficially scrutinising all new Kite employees, fiendishly protective of its status quo. In her periphery, through a messy tumble of hair, Maddie caught their surreptitious wink and nod. Maybe she'd just passed. With difficulty, she crossed her fingers creating a neat variation; downward facing hopeful dog was born.

Chapter 2

Endorphins gone three days post-race, the high persisted. Lying on the sand, bathers wet, skin prickling cold with crusting salt, Maddie stretched her toes to the sea, fingers to the dunes. Soreness hit her muscles a day after the event and was gone again within twenty-four hours leaving her mind and body live. This place was stimulating. For twenty-eight years whenever the morning sun skimmed the ocean it touched her face. Here, drawing up cross-legged looking to the waves, its warmth was at her back. The universe was pelting her with changes, turning a lifetime of familiarity on its head. Poised, Maddie was catching them, spinning them on her fingertips like a pro.

Warm getting warmer prodded a phone check. Time was moving on. She gathered her things and walked lightly across the sand pausing in the dunes for a last look back at the sea. 'Later,' she promised, blowing a kiss before following the scrubby track home.

She smiled as her shack came into view. Calling this place home for the length of her contract was the cherry on top. It nestled into the landscape at the foot of a hill, the untreated boards and bush poles faded to a soft grey and lots of glass opening to the north-west. Approaching from the beach, a set of stairs led to a raised deck at the rear of the house, the wooden stumps sitting high enough for the single storey dwelling to catch sea views without being subjected to the blustery south-westerlies. Of all the new or refurbished architectural monsters peppering the street, the humble shack was Maddie's favourite.

Shell grit crunched as she crossed her backyard. At the edge of the deck the grainy weathered planks were still cool under foot. She flung her towel over the railing turning on the hot tap. At this time of morning the water was heated just enough to rinse and warm. She stripped off her bathers and tilted her head, offering her face to the tepid flow.

The house offered immersion in beachside life without feeling exposed. The sounds of the ocean, a remix of wind and tide, were a background track on continuous loop and just as songs affect mood, Maddie felt hers respond to its booming swells and profound stillness.

The spring in her step had little to do with the sea today. This morning the Kite team were tasting eight-month-old Cabernet barrel samples. No ordinary day at the office; tastings were occasions, opportunities to learn. As she drove over the ridge her mind was already ticking through a preparation checklist.

The tasting room at the top of the stairs was part lab, part office. Sun shining through the streaky webby windows lit the glasses arranged in four settings around the table. She'd taken the samples first thing, running them up the stairs. Now eighty-odd medicine bottles with little white dot stickers coding their barrel of origin lined up for assessment.

They were grouped according to vineyard and when the grapes were picked. Three groups from one vineyard alone picked at different times over a ten-day period. The differences in flavours, acidity and other technical elements could be noted, even within days. These sessions allowed them to see the results of their picking decisions and to select which barrels would make their premium Cabernet.

Maddie saw it in simple terms. Today the wines were given their mid-semester report cards. Smelling and tasting each sample determined how the wine and the barrels were getting along. They would vary from positive—blossoming, developing, showing great potential, to the dire—lacking promise. Tasting these wines required concentration, stamina to deal with the chewy cheek sucking tannins and foresight. They still had a way to go, at least another ten months in barrel to soften and flesh out.

Never dull, four individual palates ensured discussion would be lively.

The late spring sun in the pale sky promised enough heat for polar fleece to take a day off. Milky limbs appeared poking from shorts and rolled sleeves.

Lewis walked into the room, his dog Taxi, padding behind. 'Hiya Maddie. All set?'

'Just finished,' Maddie smiled, bending to rub Taxi's temples. He dropped a saliva-coated bung at her feet.

'Not in here Taxi,' she admonished. 'You know the rules.'

Taxi tilted his head to the side not taking his eyes from the bung.

Maddie laughed. 'Oh, what's that Maddie? I can't hear you. Too much fur in my I-can-hear-the-lid-of-my-biscuit-tin-from-a-kilometre-away ears.' She stroked his head. 'Sorry mate, I'm not buying it.'

Lewis used an old exercise book to record his notes. He sat and began hand-ruling rough columns.

'Still four of us tasting?' she asked.

Lewis nodded, scrawling headings. 'Roley's been held up. He'll join us when he can.'

Maddie looked through the window to the vineyard, wondering what was keeping him.

Westy sauntering through the door brought her attention back.

'Hi Maddie.'

Taxi flashed to drop the bung at his feet.

'Dude! You trying to get us both kicked out?'

'Ever hopeful,' Maddie laughed. 'How was the surf?'

Westy stuck out his bottom lip, nodding slowly. 'A nice little four-footer out at Ellensbrook. Offshore. Sets consistent. Did you swim?'

Maddie smiled, narrowing her eyes. 'I did. I'm thinking of challenging for the swimming leg next year.'

'I dunno Maddie, me and wheels. Could be ugly,' Westy grinned.

'Well, *me* and wheels wasn't exactly pretty.'

'Ah, come on,' he teased. 'You looked cute covered in sand and blood. I'd just look scary.'

Maddie rolled her eyes. 'Okay, maybe I'll save for a kayak.' Pulling a laptop from her bag, she frowned. 'Water felt cold this morning. Is that my imagination?'

Westy turned solemn. 'We were discussing that in the surf this morning. Currents changing, water's getting colder. Happens this time of year. The south-westerlies start howling and the Leeuwin Current loses heart, leaving our toes to turn blue.'

'Ready when you are,' Lewis stated evenly, looking up.

Westy and Maddie took their places organising their tablets to record notes.

Maddie had already poured the first bracket. Without introduction they started working through the wines.

There was a moment of quiet before tasting sounds took over. Glasses chinked, bumping neighbours in the line-up. A stream of wine hit a spittoon with a ping. Whirring from the ventilation unit, soft tapping on keypads, the gentle suck of air through a mouthful of wine. A heavy sigh of resignation from Taxi—no one was throwing the bung anytime soon.

Gentle stirring marked a break in concentration and Lewis led discussion through the bracket.

During the second bracket Taxi jumped to attention, dutifully picking up the slippery bung before disappearing.

Within a minute, there was a heavier footfall on the stairs.

'Roley!' Maddie exclaimed aloud before reddening, dropping her nose back into the glass.

Lewis looked over his glass at her, expression neutral, before turning to the door as Taxi led Roley into the room.

'Sorry I'm late,' Roley addressed the group taking the spare seat at the table. 'Found a couple of blown solenoids this morning. Just got the sparky sorted.'

As Lewis talked him through proceedings, Maddie lifted her eyes the very second Roley looked her way.

She grinned stupidly, feeling fresh colour rise to her cheeks. *Crap.* She quickly looked down trying to channel composure but drew blank. Composure had left the building.

Fleeing seemed a good alternative. Fingers flying, she tapped out notes on the last sample and excused herself.

Taxi, quick to recognise an opportunity, seized the bung and followed her out.

In the soft sunshine Maddie wiped the silicon plug on the grass before throwing it haphazardly for the spring-loaded dog. A vague notion of Roley creating flux menaced her brain.

'I have a boyfriend,' she announced as the dog returned.

Taxi, care factor zero, didn't take his eyes from the bung.

'Although things aren't fabulous there,' she theorised, picking it up, lobbing it again.

'We haven't spoken properly since the race.' This time Maddie held the bung so Taxi would at least have to look. 'Sure there's a three-hour time difference with daylight saving…still.'

Taxi cocked his head, empathy or indifference. Maddie pitched the bung again.

Deep in thought she watched him emerge from the bush around the dam, a length of reticulation pipe replacing the bung. He trotted closer, within metres, before she realised; not pipe—snake!

The creature clamped close to its head between Taxi's jaws, writhed, properly pissed-off.

Thinking fast, Maddie yelled 'give' loud and gruff. Taxi obeyed, opening his jaws, releasing the spirited plaything.

One eye fixed on the snake she lunged, grabbing Taxi's collar, yanking him to her. Taxi yelped. She took a big step back as the snake raised its head to strike.

Maddie screamed and backed up another step watching

horrified as the snake kept moving towards them. Without averting her eyes she swooped up the startled dog.

Alerted by the cries, Lewis charged down the steps with Roley and Westy on his heels. Bethany and visitors at cellar door registering the commotion moved outside to observe from a distant huddle.

By the time Lewis reached her the snake had reconsidered its options. It slid across the grass to the scrub down by the dam.

Westy, hot on its disappearing tail, cupped his hands yelling back. 'Tiger. Cool markings. It's gone.'

'Good boy. Good dog.' Lewis reassured, taking Taxi from Maddie's arms, setting him down to scan for puncture marks.

Maddie reached to rub Taxi's ears, exposing two raw scratches on her arm. 'Oh.' As she straightened, she stumbled.

Roley reached for her arm. 'Here. Come and sit down.' He led her gently towards his ute, sitting her in the passenger seat before retrieving the first aid kit from the tray.

'How're you doing?' he asked, wiping the scratches with an antiseptic swab.

Maddie rested against the seat and closed her eyes. 'It happened really fast,' she blurted. 'I thought it was some old reticulation pipe, washed into the creek. I wonder what happened to the bung? God, I hope Taxi didn't get bitten. Tiger snakes are really poisonous, right?' Maddie rabbited all the thoughts her brain put on hold as the drama unfolded, eventually clearing the backlog.

Roley tied off the bandage. 'How're you feeling now?'

'Better. Thanks.' Maddie moved her arm back to her side. 'Felt a little weird for a while.'

Roley smiled. 'You'll live.' His eyebrows rose as distant movement caught his attention. 'Human geyser?'

Maddie followed his line of sight to see Bethany racing towards them, water splashing from a glass.

'My God, Maddie! Are you alright?'

'You're wearing my water,' Maddie joked as she neared.

Bethany ignored her. 'My customers were uber impressed. Girl saves dog and all that. Then someone suggested they form a vigilante to seek out and kill the snake. I had to stop them from arming themselves with courtesy umbrellas and storming the bush. I explained snakes were protected but it took me ages to calm them.' Bethany dropped her voice. 'In the end I told them due to safety regulations I had to close up so they all had to leave immediately.'

Bethany worked in cellar door and studied wine marketing at the local college. The friendship was new, but didn't feel that way. Wavelengths and humour in tune, they bonded over their love of wine and practically everything else.

Maddie let out a crazy laugh. 'Maybe I was wearing earplugs when they passed that legislation. You know I quite like snakes. But this one was possessed.' She shrugged. 'Then again, I suppose being pinned between slobbery canine jaws is enough to make an unsuspecting snake cranky.'

Maddie reached for the glass and Bethany gasped at the bandage.

'God Maddie, you didn't get bitten?'

'Not fangs or teeth, claws of the frenzied dog.'

'And it's not that bad,' Roley interjected. 'I didn't have any smaller bandages.' He left to put the first aid kit back in the box on the ute's tray.

Bethany ducked her head. 'Cute nurse.'

Maddie smacked her with her good arm. 'How's the bear-clawed hound anyway?'

'Yeah, let's go check,' Roley suggested, walking back around.

'Wait. Wait.' Maddie implored. 'I'm desperate for hydra-tion.' Tilting the glass above her lips, the un-spilled water dripped out.

Roley snorted, cracking Maddie up too.

'Ha, bloody, ha!' Bethany screwed up her nose. 'It's the thought that counts. Wrangling reptiles obviously doesn't affect humour.'

Maddie took her arm and they walked back together to find Lewis outside the smoko room.

Lewis draped his arm around Maddie's shoulders. 'You didn't list snake charming as an interest. Anything else I should know?'

She smiled. 'How's Taxi?' At the mention of his name, Taxi rounded the door from the smoko room.

Lewis laughed. 'He's bored, looking for his next adven-ture. Wants to know what you're doing later this arvo?'

Maddie leaned down and Taxi nuzzled her hand.

'God, are you okay?' Lewis pointed at her arm.

Westy appeared around the door. 'Roley's first aid instruc-tor was an Egyptologist. What happened mate? You run out of bandages?'

'Saving one for your mouth mate,' Roley replied. 'It's too big for the back of my ute though.'

'Seems like everyone's recovered,' Lewis declared, hands on hips. 'Still plenty going on in the lab. Another fifty-sixty samples at least.'

Maddie handed the glass back to Bethany with a wink. 'Thanks mate.'

They resumed tasting and an hour quickly passed.

As they finished samples from the eastern boundary

vineyard, Roley talked them through the challenges particular to the site. 'It's notorious for uneven ripening, which is why we pick so many batches. The terroir is so variable, we have to be sensitive to the fluctuations.'

Maddie nodded. 'For me there's a distinct rose petally, rosehip character across the palate of these wines. What're the major variables of the ecoscape?'

Roley, Lewis and Westy looked at each other, shifting in their chairs.

'What do you mean by ecoscape? Is that even a word?' Lewis asked.

'Not officially, but I think *The Macquarie* should consider it for the next edition.'

Lewis shook his head, raising his eyebrows. 'I'm almost afraid to ask. Define ecoscape?'

Maddie launched. 'It's the Australian equivalent of 'terroir'. Or at least the one I use, the rest of the industry hasn't caught on. But, given time...'

Lewis and Roley both slowly shook their heads.

'Seriously!' Maddie cried. 'I don't speak French and my accent is crap. Every time I say 'terroir' it comes out differently. If I'm speaking in public, I have to repeat it because I say it wrong and people look at me blankly then it sounds like I'm stuttering. My friend, a speech pathologist, has forbidden me to use it.'

'Oh Maddie,' Lewis sighed. 'Really?'

'She's got a point,' Westy weighed in. 'You know there are websites dedicated to its pronunciation, even a YouTube vid.'

'That's right,' cried Maddie, adding surreptitiously to Westy, 'actually I didn't know about the video.'

Maddie glanced up and was suddenly struck—Lewis looked older. Could people age over the course of a conversation? Roley appeared amused. Cute and amused.

'It's a great English alternative. Eco, from ecology—the relationship between organisms and their environment; and scape—a view or expanse of a particular location. It's perfect. A year from now wine writers will be all over it.' Her tone dropped soulfully. 'The ecoscape of eastern boundary block.'

Lewis and Roley reclined in their chairs, legs splayed, shoulders broad, chests forward. It was a man thing, dismissing her entirely. When Lewis entwined his fingers, placing his hands behind his head she knew she'd lost him—for now.

Maddie drifted. One day they'd remember this moment, celebrate her inventiveness.

Late afternoon during the final session, excitement tiptoed through the door, charging the room.

Jupiter Rising was a pretty vineyard, separated from Kite by a couple of properties, close as the crow flies. Kite made their Cabernet under contract. Into the third year of the agreement the vineyard, shaping up under their direction, was showing marked results. The samples brought the group to attention.

'You didn't mix this up with the cordial in the smoko room did you?' Westy asked.

'Um. No. But I know what you mean. It's blackcurrant elixir.'

'So intense,' remarked Roley. 'If someone gave me this outside of a tasting, don't know if I'd even recognise it as wine.'

Lewis smiled. 'It's outside the box. But you know what? It's exactly the sort of wine that will stand out in a line-up. It's going to show well.'

'And, to be fair, while the flavour profile is one-dimensional it has great balance,' added Maddie. 'The mouth-feel is lush and it has beautiful length.'

'Yeah. It's way more complex than cordial, now I've gone back to it,' Westy teased. 'Pretty bloody fine actually, as long as you're into blackcurrant.'

Roley nodded at Lewis. 'Jeff's got to be happy?'

'He will be. He's in the States for another month or two, hasn't seen it for a while. But he'll love it. He's all about fruit concentration and expression. This is exactly what he's been aiming for.'

Maddie was on her feet organising the final bracket. 'These are the samples from 'Wedge'?'

'Pet name for our vineyard on the western boundary,' Lewis explained.

The group lingered over the wines sniffing, swirling, tasting over and again.

'Wow!'

'These are amazing.'

Lewis and Roley shared conspiratorial smiles. 'Wedge' was their best Cabernet block, the samples a reward of faith.

Maddie looked from one to the other. 'I've never seen anything like it at this stage of its life. I'm getting dark berry fruits. There's blackcurrant, but there's a backbone of ripe blackberry and some lighter, brighter notes. They're exceptional—awesome character and complexity.'

No response.

Maddie's head bobbed. 'They don't look like eight-month-old wines.'

Nothing.

'Oh, come on guys. No holding out. Tell me everything.'

Lewis raised his eyebrows. 'Every year we try to keep the

24

balance tight. Yields lean. Canopy in check.' He signalled for Roley to continue.

'We've spent years trialling cover crops and monitoring irrigation levels. Four years ago we changed the whole trellis altering the way we prune. One budget-blowing decision after the next.'

Lewis laughed. 'He's not kidding. The owners have been very accommodating with our dreams for this plot.'

Westy had been quiet. 'Then you get a wine that says 'told ya'.'

Lewis eyed the faces round the table. 'I believe we have two contenders for the Fine Young Cabernet Awards this year. Jupiter Rising and Wedge, both deserve a guernsey.'

Every head around the table nodded, even Taxi's, as he drifted in sleep at Lewis' feet.

'Good tasting?' Bethany enquired as Maddie entered the cellar door with a tray of dirty glasses.

'Awesome! I learnt so much about the wines, the vineyards, contractors—the wines are bloody solid.' Maddie's hand shot to her mouth as she quickly scanned the room for customers. She lowered her voice. 'So impressed.'

Bethany laughed. 'All clear. It's been a quiet last half hour.' She took the tray and loaded it into the glass washer.

'Great. Can you chat while I polish?'

'God yes. Usually the boys dump and run.' Bethany handed Maddie a polishing cloth.

'By the way, there are a few samples still in the lab. Lewis wants to run you through them.'

'Really?' Bethany gripped the counter. 'Think I'm feeling faint.'

Maddie smiled. 'Harsh, Bethany. He knows you're

studying. Anyway, working on the front line, you need to know the wines you're selling. Lewis gets that.'

'Yeah, I know Lewis gets it, but he's never included me at that level before. Sounds like a Maddie initiative to me.'

Maddie kept her expression neutral. 'Lewis knew you'd be keen.'

Bethany smiled. The glass washer beeped. She lowered the door and pulled out the steaming rack.

'How's study going anyway?' Maddie asked, reaching for a glass.

'I'm enjoying it. Funny what a different experience study can be when you love the subject.'

'You've just finished for the year, right? What was on last semester?'

'Sensory evaluation, mainly,' Bethany answered screwing up her nose. 'I enjoyed it, but I suck.'

'Going through the barrel samples will be great training. What makes you think you suck?'

'I think my nose is lazy,' Bethany complained. 'I only identify smells and tastes once someone else has suggested them. Then it's like oh, yeah, raspberry, duh.'

Maddie laughed. 'You know that's really common right? It's that power of suggestion thing.'

'Lewis has told us you have an amazing palate.'

Maddie rolled her eyes. 'Only because I worked really hard.'

'Oh.' Bethany's curiosity prickled. 'I thought it was all down to genetics. You know, you either have three billion taste receptors or three trillion?'

'Don't get me started on the science of wine—pyrazines, esters, terpenes, thiols—I'm one of those chemistry nerds who read technical books in bed. But sensory evaluation was just hard slog. Fun, but hard slog.'

'You trained your palate?'

'God yeah,' Maddie nodded emphatically. 'And it didn't happen overnight.'

Bethany reached for another glass.

'I was always gobsmacked with what people saw in wine. I used to put it down to creative imaginations or guesses based on grape variety and stuff. But it never explained people who could taste without knowing anything—and work it out.'

Bethany nodded. 'So how did you train your palate?'

'I started paying attention.'

Bethany rolled her eyes and performed her favourite political impersonation. 'Please explain?'

'I started putting my nose into things. I'd pass a flower stall at a market, literally stop and smell the roses. In the deli, scrunch leaves on herbs, especially the ones I didn't know. I followed bees to blossom, orange, lemon, lime and tried to smell the differences.'

'That simple?' Bethany asked.

Maddie nodded. 'Then,' she rubbed her hands together, 'I started on taste.'

Bethany laughed as she closed the glass washer door and hung up the cloths.

'I thought about everything I put in my mouth. I'd try to identify and differentiate between flavours; black pepper from white pepper, orange pith from orange rind,' Maddie pulled a face. 'Not all of it was fun. The Asian spices were my favourites. Fresh—chilli, ginger, garlic—or processed paste. Coriander or cardamom?'

'Right!' Bethany exclaimed. 'I can eat, drink and pay attention. It could be my new project.'

'Love a project. I'm happy to help.'

'Unreal! You can be my coach.' Bethany was psyched.

'Tomorrow's Friday, right? Why don't you come over after work? We'll get Thai.'

'Awesome.' Bethany's enthusiasm was contagious. 'I'll bring some spices from home and test you.'

Bethany tilted backwards raising her hands and eyes to the ceiling. 'This'll be brilliant. Thanks.'

Maddie smiled. Swim, tasting, close encounter with wildlife, social invitation…life here was hectic.

A man stood poised at the open door of a battered van in the driveway.

Maddie studied him as she cruised to a stop at the verge. Stepping out of her Subaru, she could feel him watching her. Womaniser, gay hipster or hippy dude? Maddie, with the rundown from Bethany on her housemates, couldn't determine. The vehicle suggested not gay hipster. His attention was intense. Employing her best defence, she walked tall straight towards him and thrust out her hand.

'Hi, I'm Maddie.'

'Strobe, dude,' the man drawled, clasping her hand, drawing it to him. 'I'm guessing you're here for Bethany. She's inside,' he said inclining his head towards the house.

Maddie gawked at the large, milky-pink stone hanging on a leather strap around his neck. 'Thanks Strobe. That's a wicked rock.'

'Pink tourmaline crystal. Off to see my lady.'

His slow smile suggested the two were related. Maddie made no reply.

Strobe elaborated. 'Pink tourmaline, purifies the heart chakra.'

'Oh.' She nodded.

'Crystals man, healing light. You should come by the shop sometime, follow your vibration to its source.' Strobe leant back to examine her. He held up two big hands, palms facing outwards and closed his eyes, his body swaying in a smooth arc. 'Your aura would really sing with a little…aquamarine.' His body came to rest and he slowly opened his eyes. 'But right now my business is love.'

Maddie's shoulders dropped, his voice was hypnotic. 'I like blue. Why aquamarine?' Her head lolled to the side.

'Cleansing,' Strobe nodded slowly. 'Liver in particular.'

'Oh!' Maddie's head snapped back. 'Thanks Strobe. Good to meet you. Hope business, um goes well.' Maddie backed up around the bonnet, heading for the front door. Turning round, she bumped smack into…

'Well hello sister. That's a friendly greeting you've got going on. BTW you smell good.'

Gay hipster?

'Hi Evan, I'm Maddie.'

'Get out! Am I wearing a nametag?' He tilted his quaffed head. 'Gotta run. My friend's hosting a superfood cocktail party—spirulina, goji berries, vodka—the possibilities. Strobo's giving me a lift. Ciao.'

Maddie smiled as he was absorbed by the van. Waving them off she turned back to the house half hoping 'womaniser' hadn't left for the evening.

'Hello,' she called through the flywire door.

'Hey Maddie. Come on in.' Bethany met her in the hall. 'You've just missed Strobe and Evan.'

'Nah,' Maddie laughed. 'I got 'em. How much fun is this house?'

'God, wait 'til you meet Rick. He left a while ago, but if you look carefully, you can still see an oil slick.'

Maddie laughed as Bethany wiped a hand along the wall. 'Makes my beach shack look abandoned.'

'Do you get lonely out there?' Bethany led Maddie down the hall.

'I've lived in share houses since I left home.' Maddie rolled her eyes, still smiling. 'A mix of experiences, but as an only child, I'm enjoying my space—for now anyway. Does my aura look okay to you?'

Bethany studied her. 'Not sure about your aura but I like your top. Only child, eh? Does everybody ask if you wish you had a brother or a sister?'

'About one in two,' Maddie shrugged indifferently. 'We're a curiosity. It doesn't bother me.'

Bethany extended her head. 'So?'

Maddie was thoughtful. 'Sometimes I guess, when I was growing up. But I'm sure all kids question their circumstances. Wished they lived by the beach, or next door to their best friend, or had famous parents.'

'Or wished their sibling dead,' Bethany laughed. 'I did my share of that.'

'Please tell me you get along famously now?'

'Yeah! I've got an older brother and a younger sister. We love it when we get together. So, did your folks only ever want one child?'

'My dad died before I turned two. I guess they just didn't get there.'

Bethany froze. 'Shit Maddie. I'm sorry. I'll stop interrogating now.'

Maddie put her hand on Bethany's arm. 'All good. It was a long, long time ago.' She smiled, continuing evenly. 'I didn't even know my dad. He died in a car accident. My mum is a rock. I never knew any different.'

Bethany still looked struck.

'You know I have this aunt, Aunt Bling. She's been an amazing part of my life. If my dad hadn't died I don't think I'd have the same relationship with her—and that's something I can't image.'

'Drink?' Bethany asked meekly.

'Let the training commence.' Maddie fished a bottle of wine and some little packets marked A through J from her bag.

'God! I'm half expecting a scout from the Australian Institute of Sport to come and recruit you.'

Maddie pointed to the suspicious looking packets. 'Or the police to call a raid and arrest us.'

Bethany organised glasses while Maddie sorted and opened the fragrant bags.

'Do you want to try it blindfolded?'

Bethany raised an eyebrow. 'Now that's something I'd hear through Rick's wall.'

'Eeew!' Maddie screwed up her nose.

'Seriously, do you think it helps?'

'I sometimes close my eyes when I'm tasting. I think it helps my nose to focus.'

Bethany fetched a scarf and they sat at the table in the small kitchen. Maddie tied the scarf into place and started handing her the opened packets.

Bethany nosed them, sniffing tentatively and then inhaling deeper. 'Vanilla. Cardamom. Ginger.' On a roll until star anise and clove unravelled her.

'That's crazy.' Bethany announced, removing the blindfold. 'Star anise is one of my faves. I can't believe I got that wrong.'

Maddie shrugged. 'Interesting, isn't it? I'll test you again

31

this week at work—without the blindfold, might look a little weird. I reckon you'll get them next time.'

'Can we drink some wine now?' Bethany twitched her nose dramatically.

Maddie laughed as she poured. 'That's not a good look if the law comes to the door.'

'Thai?' Bethany asked as their conversation slowed.

Maddie nodded. 'My mouth's been watering with the thought of green chicken curry since yesterday.'

'Too easy.' Bethany grabbed her phone and rang through their order, chatting happily with the person at the other end before disconnecting. 'I'm a bit of a regular. One of the temptations of living so close to town. Shall we walk?'

Crossing neat quarter-acre verges they made their way down Bethany's street.

'One more wine question?' Bethany asked shyly.

'Sure. I love it. Ask away.'

'Are you one of those people that can taste a wine and name the vintage and producer and what you were wearing when you tasted it at such and such restaurant two years ago?'

'No way,' Maddie shook her head. 'Wish I could, but my memory doesn't work like that.'

Bethany raised her eyebrows.

'I could remember the characters of the wine and the region it was from, but I'd struggle with producer and year. Definitely wouldn't remember what I was wearing, unless I spilled red wine and ruined something. Lewis has surprised me a few times. I think he's pretty cluey like that.'

Bethany was quick to agree. 'When he and Annabel talk wines, it blows me away.'

'Annabel?'

'Annabel Estelle. Her knowledge is amazing.'

'Annabel Estelle is a bloody legend!' Maddie cried, suddenly animated. 'How do you know her?'

'She's a really good friend of Lewis. I thought he must have mentioned her.'

'Nope. I'd remember. She's one of my heroes. Hope I get to meet her.'

Bethany tilted her head to one side. 'Well she and Lewis are tight. Trust me. I'm sure she'll be around.'

'Sounds like you're suggesting someth…'

'Bethany. Maddie.'

The girls stopped and looked around. They had reached the main drag. Simultaneously they spotted Carmel, perched on a stool through the open window of a wine bar fronting the street, waving madly. Bethany and Maddie crossed.

'Hi Carmel.' Bethany leaned awkwardly through the window for a hug.

Carmel beamed. 'Hi girls. What are you up to this Friday evening?'

'Maddie is helping me study—sort of.' Bethany grinned. 'Do you know each other?'

'Course I know the lovely Maddie.' Carmel gushed. 'She came out for my Italian wine and pizza night. You'd only just arrived in town hadn't you? Brave girl.'

'Hi Carmel.' Maddie leaned in for a hug. 'It was my first week at Kite. Roley invited me along.'

'That's right,' Carmel nodded. 'You guys teamed up.'

Bethany's eyebrows rose.

'Steady Eddie,' Carmel looked at her with rebuke. 'It was an options night, people were on teams…although they did seem to get along very well.' She winked overtly.

Colour rose in Maddie's face. 'We were just getting to know each other,' she blurted.

Carmel and Bethany laughed. 'Relax,' Bethany reassured. 'We're just messing with ya.'

Maddie smiled. 'It was a great night. Thanks for having me along. Awesome wines.'

'Oh, you're welcome. Drop by anytime you're at a loose end, for a cuppa or a vino. I love people dropping in.'

'Maybe we'll give you a call next weekend, see what you're up to,' Bethany proposed.

Maddie nodded. 'We could meet at mine and walk to the cafe?'

'You're on.' Carmel agreed.

'Now we're off to pick up yummy curry. I'm starving!' Bethany started pulling Maddie away.

Carmel laughed. 'Give Maddie my number will you? And text me Maddie, so I get yours.'

Maddie nodded and waved as Bethany led her down the street.

'I love this movie.' Maddie squealed as Bethany fiddled with the remote.

They plonked onto the couch balancing steaming bowls and wineglasses.

'Really?' Bethany tilted her head. '*The Devil Wears Prada*. I wouldn't have picked that.'

'I'm sure my daypack's a Prada.' Maddie quipped. 'I dunno why. Imagine going off to work looking like that every day?'

They pulled faces at the screen in unison.

'I really like Emily Blunt in this. And what's his name— Simon bonk-worthy Baker.'

Maddie looked at her sideways. 'No man in your life at the moment?'

Bethany stuck out her bottom lip, shaking her head. 'I split up with my last boyfriend around the time I started studying. Just haven't got back to it.' She smiled. 'It's not like a conscious decision or anything. I guess my lifestyle's just changed a bit.'

'Makes sense.'

'I've got lots of male mates,' Bethany held up an arm. 'I haven't gone off them or anything, just no one calling my name.'

Maddie smiled and forked a mouthful of curry.

'And you and Josh?' Bethany probed.

Maddie chewed thoughtfully, before opening her eyes wide. 'God. There's a good question.'

'You don't have to answer,' Bethany added quickly.

'No. It's good for me to talk about it. Honestly, Josh is a really nice guy...'

'Uh, oh!'

Maddie's head dropped theatrically. 'That's not good, is it?'

'Opening clarification says it all girlfriend...honestly, nice guy—nope, not good.'

Maddie's eyes met Bethany's. 'I should've called it before I left. There! I've said it.' Maddie looked down. 'Things happened quickly once I got the job. Josh hadn't wanted me to apply at all, and I get that, but I was also a bit mad about it. I felt like he should've been more supportive. Such a good opportunity.'

'Absolutely!' Bethany affirmed. 'It's not cool to put yourself before your partner when opportunity knocks. That's Relationships 101. Good on you for not caving in to that.'

'Gawd, you can be my relationship coach. I suck

at it. I didn't want to hurt him, now I feel like I am anyway, and I feel guilty and mad for being in this stupid position —and selfish because I'm here having a good time.'

Balancing her bowl with both hands, Bethany fell backwards on the couch. 'Shit! You don't need a coach you need a bloody intervention.'

Reaching for her arm, Maddie pulled her up. 'Seriously. I always get myself into these situations. Drives me fucking crazy.'

Bethany laughed. 'I think you and Roley would be sweet.'

Maddie groaned, falling back. 'Stop. You're meant to be my relationship coach not devil's advocate leading me astray. Have you forgotten his lovely Genevieve?'

'Have you met her?'

Maddie struggled up. 'Yes. Lovely and gorgeous.' She placed her empty bowl on the floor and cradled her wineglass.

'I'm just messing around.' Bethany hesitated before raising a hand in the air. 'But can I just say one thing?'

Maddie hid behind her glass. 'Go on.'

'I think Roley *fell* into that relationship, more than *put* himself there.' Bethany looked pleased with her revelation.

'And? So?' Maddie probed.

'Nothing sizzles there. That's all I'll say.' Bethany closed her eyes and put a hand to her chest. 'Just my humble observation.'

Simon Baker's close-up on screen caught their attention as he shot Anne Hathaway a pelvic-melting smile.

Bethany moaned. 'Now he calls my name.'

Maddie's phone's ringtone started playing. Juggling her shopping, she pulled it from the back pocket of her shorts, quickly checking the time and calculating the difference. Four o'clock Saturday afternoon, Josh time.

'Hi Josh.' She plonked the bags on the grass and crossed her arm to grip the bicep supporting the phone at her ear. While Josh talked, one of her neighbours walked by with her two silky terriers. Maddie couldn't tell the cute hairballs apart. She smiled, raising her supporting hand in greeting.

Josh sounded low. Maddie tensed. She watched a beetle climb the curb. Then, looking up at the clouds, her ponytail swung like a pendulum between her shoulder blades as she slowly shook her head.

'I don't really understand,' Maddie cut him off. 'I saw the photos Jeremy posted. You were out with them Thursday night, last night. So when are you 'bored, not doing much'? And 'feeling like you've been kicked', really Josh? Maybe it's a hangover. I'm not sure you can put all this on me.'

'I'm not putting anything on you and what do you expect me to do?' Josh backpedalled with volume. 'It's okay for you—new job, new friends, new place. Your life's sweet.'

'Were you going to tell me you're all off to Lorne next weekend?' Maddie scoffed.

His response didn't register. Her brain was busy translating his previous comment. *How would you know what my life was like? You haven't asked anything about the adventure race or what happened in my week.*

The next time he paused, Maddie sighed. 'I have to go.'

'I miss you. It wasn't my idea you move across the country.'

Maddie disconnected, slipping the phone back into her pocket. She picked up her bags and continued walking home. His argument was flawed. Replaying the conversation teased her brain like a cipher; Maddie felt confident interpreting the signals but damned if she could crack the code.

'Kettles on?'

The invitation rained down. Maddie raised her head to see Stubbsy waving from his balcony.

'Perfect,' she yelled. Turning into the steep driveway Maddie marvelled; Stubbsy's kettle either possessed intuitive properties or he had an urn with a thermostat.

Chapter 3

Maddie felt a gentle tap on her shoulder. Her head shot up.

'Roley.'

'Hey Maddie. Sorry. No way to get your attention without scaring you.'

'Sorry. No worries.' Maddie struggled to sit and bring her brain up to speed. She removed her earphones. 'Just been down to the Riptide. Hope you weren't standing there long, cos I would've sung the words wrong,' she finished to the tune of the song.

He smiled.

It was late Sunday afternoon. Maddie was on her back deck enjoying the sunshine cat-like, spread out on the day bed listening to tunes. She must have dozed for a minute.

'Tea?' she asked, picking up her unfinished stone-cold cup. Maybe more than a minute.

'No thanks. I was going to send you a text, but I've just been down the beach and since I was passing, thought I'd call in.'

'Great. What's up?'

'Lewis and I are meeting down at Southers first thing tomorrow to check out the Malbec. He suggested you come along.'

'Really?' she asked, straightening. 'Definitely. That would be unreal. Can you draw me a mud map? I haven't been down that way.'

'Probably easier if I swing by and pick you up. Seven?'

Maddie nodded, smiling. 'So much hype around this Malbec. I can't wait to see it.'

Roley, hands on hips, looked suddenly awkward.

'Beer?' she fired quickly.

'You having one?'

'Yeah, drinking tea makes me thirsty. I'm ready for a beer,' she smiled, standing up. 'You in a hurry? We could take them down the beach?'

'Sure. I had a wicked surf this morning, just been back for a swim. Wind's dropped, bit of cloud about. Sunset should be joy.'

Roley's voice stretched into the kitchen. Maddie fanned her face with her hands in front of the open fridge, willing bravery into her being, her heart rate to chill. Roley's good company, a friend, she reasoned grabbing a couple of beers.

The sun tracked its trajectory for the horizon. Random clouds hindered its rays, softening the bright light to a gilt-edged, late afternoon mellowness. Maddie and Roley sat below the dunes, digging toes into warm sand.

'Have you always surfed?'

'Pretty much. Though I'm not as diehard as a lot of the crew down here.'

'Like Westy?'

'Yeah, Westy's hardcore.' Roley buried his beer in the sand freeing up both hands to demonstrate. 'Surfing is his world and other things in life are just little moons circling round what the swell is doing.'

Maddie laughed. 'Are all surfers poets and philosophers? I'm starting to see this connection.'

'I'm no poet,' Roley affirmed. 'Not like Westy.' He took a swig from his stubby. 'Guess you have time to think about things bobbing on a board waiting for sets.'

Their workmate was safe ground. Maddie shy of firing personal questions at Roley. 'Westy grew up here, didn't he?'

'Born on the hill.' Roley turned to face her. 'You know you're not a local if you weren't born on the hill?'

'There are no hills in Margaret River.'

'Shhh,' He put a finger to his lips. 'You could be deported for dissing local folklore. Besides, try telling that to Westy's mum. She probably walked to the old hospital to give birth while his dad was out surfing.'

'Probably feels like a hill when you're nine months pregnant and in labour,' Maddie mused. 'The old hospital's that group of buildings where the soup kitchen lives?'

Roley nodded. 'They held the markets there before moving them out to the college campus. The Wine Association had its offices there too, going back a few years. They were in the old infectious diseases wing, call buttons still on the walls. I think they stored their archived records in the morgue.'

'God, that's gross,' Maddie squirmed.

'Pretty sure the bodies had been moved before they took it over.'

She tucked her elbow and bumped his shoulder. 'What about you? When did you move to Margies?'

Roley tilted his head, giving her a questioning look.

'That's what Stubbsy calls it.'

Picking up a dried strand of seaweed, he started popping the brown balls between his fingers and thumb. 'From Perth, originally. I moved to Margies four, coming up five years ago. Time flies.'

Maddie nodded, alternatively raking patterns in the sand with her fingers, erasing them with the flat of her hand, hoping he would continue.

'We used to come down this way as kids. Close friends of my folks had a holiday shack in Busso, right on the water. I think nearly every holidays we headed south. Whole family loved it—though it was just me and my sister, and the other family had two girls so I was out-numbered.'

'How did that work?'

Roley shrugged. 'We all got on. Being right on the beach there were always heaps of kids. We'd swim, play cricket, frisbees, footy. We'd go out in the boat fishing or crabbing. God, we had kayaks and boogie boards.'

'Is that where you learnt to surf?'

'Yeah.' Roley smiled. 'A neighbour two houses up was a surfer. When I was old enough he offered to teach me. The whole tribe came along to help push me onto waves or watch. I remember them all cheering from the beach the first time I stood up on my foamie. So, what about you?

Maddie, transported by Roley's happy memories, was momentarily startled.

'Have you always loved the beach?'

Picking up fistfuls of sand, letting it run through her fingers, she contemplated. Telling people about her dad was tricky. She felt detached from the tragedy of her history until it was shared. The empathy and emotional responses of others could unsettle her more than the facts of her circumstances.

'My dad died in a car accident before I was two,' she blurted quickly.

Fingering a piece of driftwood, Roley made no response.

'My mum worked really hard.' In the nostalgia rich atmosphere, the words registered sharper than Maddie had ever experienced. Choking tears suddenly welled. She stopped talking.

Roley, eyes on the sea, leant his shoulder into hers.

A single tear splashed Maddie's cheek. She took a sip from her beer and swallowed hard, waiting for the wave of emotion to ebb. 'I have an aunt, Aunt Bling. The most amazing woman on the planet. Every school holidays she would try to get us away somewhere. Sometimes it was just her and I, mum would have to work. But when it was possible all three of us would head to the coast. Sometimes we camped and sometimes we'd hire a house. I loved the beach because everyone relaxed. No rushing to get up and be someplace or chores or routine. The beach felt like freedom. Mum was different at the beach. She'd read and we'd play music, watch movies if there was a telly.' Maddie stopped. As she turned towards Roley their shoulders parted. 'Listen to me drone on.'

Roley looked at his half buried feet. 'So for me the beach is surfing, for you, peace of mind. Both balance related, eh?'

The sun dipped below the level of the ocean sending pink and gold streaks across the darkening blue.

Maddie slapped at a mozzie on her leg. 'Bloody things just wait for that sun to go.'

They stood, rubbing sand from their limbs, the tide changing silently before them.

Darkness descended quickly once the sun was down. As they made their way inside Maddie flicked the lights and pulled the bi-fold doors half closed behind them. The fan spun slowly in the high ceilinged space.

'Dinner?' she raised her eyebrows with the idea.

Roley hesitated.

'I'm making a really simple pasta,' Maddie added quickly. 'There will be leftovers for a week if you don't help me out.'

'Sure. Why not? Actually, I've got a bottle of wine in the car you may be interested to try.'

'Weren't you on your way home from the beach?' Maddie quizzed.

'Yes Madison,' Roley feigned rebuke. 'Ben's mate Solly gave it to me in the carpark, thought Ben and I might like to try it. I think he'd just ducked down for a swim after work, happened to have it in his car.'

'Just curious,' Maddie smiled.

Roley ducked through the door to retrieve the wine.

An hour before she'd stood at the fridge willing herself to be brave. Now, pulse racing, she addressed her reflection framed in a glass pane. 'It's dinner, not a date. And you're cooking.' She'd planned on a toasted sandwich but hastily rethought the options. Thank God for the Saturday markets. There was good olive oil from a local grove, fresh rocket, free-range prosciutto cured by a wine making legend turned farmer and a round of organic sheep's cheese. Opening the pantry she found hand-made fettuccine from the previous week's foray. Sorted.

Roley reappeared, brandishing a bottle of unlabelled red. Ben's mate Solly made wine at another local estate. It was an unusual bottle, giving nothing of the variety away.

'Oooo! Tell me everything.' Maddie filled a pot with water.

'No way,' Roley teased. 'Think you're up for some options?'

Maddie embraced wine options with irrepressible excitement, like she had Christmas when she was eight. Suspecting that was tragic and uncool for a winemaker of her experience, she tempered her froth. 'Sure.'

Maddie would be given the wine and Roley would ask a series of questions. She'd make educated guesses to narrow down when and where it was made and the variety of grape. So far, she knew the wine had been given to Roley by Solly but that didn't tell her anything.

Roley crossed into the kitchen making for the top drawer.

'Corkscrew?' she quizzed intrigued, her mind racing through possibilities. Maybe the wine was made and bottled overseas. Or, maybe a garage production; a small quantity made by someone without easy access to a bottling line.

Maddie handed him two glasses. Roley turned them delicately in his hands before setting them on the bench. His lips twitched a wry smile. She wasn't bothered. They were a prestigious brand—so what. Wine was her passion, investment in good quality glassware, mandatory. Like her mother's choice of sensible underwear—some things a girl couldn't compromise.

'What?' Maddie demanded.

'What?' he countered, cheeky grin widening. 'Nothing. Just most of my mates have eclectic collections of jam and honey jars for special bottles or special company,' he teased.

She threw a tea towel at his head. 'It's something you should know and accept about me. I can drink wine from plastic tumblers. I'm no snob. God I've drunk wine from Disney cups in a McDonald's car park. But, given a choice…'

'Let me hazard a guess, you're not a fan of stemless glasses?'

'Are you teasing me?'

'Yes. I suppose I am.' His smile morphed to mock indignation. 'But I'm also interested.'

'Right. Well allow me to put your mind at rest. No. Not a fan. I don't like fingermarks clouding up a glass of wine and if you don't have a stem to hold onto, that's what happens. I particularly don't enjoy them when finger food is served. They may serve some practical purpose at picnics but then half the fun is trying to balance your glass, especially at the beach.' She was just getting started. When she looked up, Roley was openly grinning. 'Bloody lucky I'm out of tea towels. I do have this knife though,' she turned it menacingly in her hand. 'I could do you up a fact sheet if you'd like? That's how much I have on them.'

'I'm good.' Roley raised his hands.

'Are you a fan?'

'Hell no! Hate the things. Really hard to cheers with them. Fingers get in the way and drinking a chilled wine—well, my hand gets all cold and damp.' He wiped his hand on his shirt theatrically, totally embracing the performance.

Maddie lobbed a ribbon of prosciutto.

He caught it, stuffing the whole thing in his mouth, offering a glass in return. 'North or south?'

The question related to hemisphere and was a good start to the game, narrowing the wine's origin by half the world in one guess. Maddie studied her glass, taking in the rich ruby colour. Holding it to the light she noted its brightness before angling it over a white note pad sitting on the bench to see the colour of the wine's rim. It had a bright, reddish hue.

The wine was clear suggesting filtration and youth, not old enough to throw sediment yet. The brightness suggested youth too, older wines were often deeper and darker. The ruby colour Maddie associated with Cabernet more than Shiraz, but this wine could be anything. The nose and palate would determine any guesses at grape variety.

She gave the glass a strong swirl and the wine moved in a molten garnet wave. Bowing her head in a fluid, practised motion alerted her nose. A deep inhalation and there it was, bliss.

Wine and the ocean refract light in tricks of movement and colour. One smells of salt, the other smells of everything. One tastes of salt, the other tastes of the essence of life. She could never explain it but wine and the sea wove the fabric of her soul. It was as close to spiritual as she got.

Roley was openly studying her.

'It's interesting,' she offered, slightly flustered.

'North or south?' he repeated, leaning forward, resting his elbows on the bench, not taking his eyes off her.

The relaxed mood developed a shadowy edge of intensity. Maddie started to prickle under Roley's gaze. It had nothing to do with the game.

'Well, I'm getting some lovely cherry notes, plum and a little herbaceous character, maybe sage. It's opening up. I like it.' She swirled the glass again, this time closing her eyes to savour her first taste. As she took it in, noting flavours and assessing texture, she opened her eyes and watched Roley do the same.

He mirrored her actions, swirling, head bowed before taking a good long draught from his glass. With the wine in his mouth he parted his lips and slowly sucked air through his teeth, aerating the wine. In two steps, opposite the sink, he pursed his lips and in one deft release a stream of wine left his mouth hitting the centre of the drain-hole. 'North or south?'

Holy crap! Maddie spluttered, choking on her wine. Her internal thermometer had just spiked, shattering into a thousand dazzling fragments. She checked Roley's chin for signs of dribble, the sink for stray red droplets. Nothing! She clumsily wiped her mouth with the back of her hand, mesmerised.

'You okay?'

Maddie knew people could spit accurately. She'd witnessed it many times. Hell, she was reasonably competent herself. Years ago, after months of spitting on her own boots in the winery and dribbling her way through tastings, she'd embarked on a spitting in the shower training regime. Eventually it paid off.

But OMG, she never expected it of Roley. Maddie loved being surprised. And this surprise was good. 'Sexy' was such a personal thing. For some it was tight, low riding jeans or a smooth, rippling six pack. For Maddie it was a controlled, perfectly executed suck and spit. She knew it was goofy, kinky, whatever, but she found it tantalisingly erotic. Ludicrous or otherwise, she was aroused to hot and bothered status, bordering on dangerous.

The water boiled on the cook-top.

Turning her back to Roley she raised her eyes to the ceiling. 'I'm thinking south,' she managed, adding salt to the pot.

If Roley sensed her agitation he didn't acknowledge it.

'South it is. Anything I can do to help over there?'

Way too many things sprang to mind. 'No! Thanks. I told you I'm keeping things simple.' She bit her bottom lip. 'So where'd you learn to spit like that Roley?' Immediately, she cursed the cheesiness of the question, or her delivery—both.

Roley laughed. 'Impressed, eh?'

'I don't think impressed is the word. Although it's kind of impressive,' Maddie stammered.

'Most people find it absolutely impressive,' Roley teased, playfully. 'And I really can't say how it evolved, maybe from running. You get pretty good at spitting when you run with other people. No one likes it when you spit on their shins.'

Maddie laughed and a little anxiety seeped away. 'Well, I know winemakers who dream of spitting so beautifully. Skills Roley,' she tipped her glass towards him. 'But, enough about spitting. And really, why are you spitting anyway? Options please.'

'Good question. Habit. Showing off my hidden talents,' Roley hurried on. 'Shiraz? Cabernet? Tempranillo?'

Maddie picked up her glass and swirled and sniffed. There were black cherry and plummy notes and some mustiness, not fragrant like spice, more leathery. The savoury characters could come from the oak, so not helpful in determining variety. She concentrated on the fruit notes. Black cherry she associated with Shiraz and Tempranillo rather than Cabernet. She withdrew the latter from the mix.

Another swirl, sniff and taste. 'Got it!'

Roley's eyebrows rose.

'There's a delicate note of tomato. It has to be a Temp.'

Roley's eyebrows crept higher. 'Are you kidding me? Tomato? What the hell does a delicate note of tomato smell like?' he shook his head, swirling and sniffing his glass.

'It's more on the palate than the nose,' Maddie stated factually. 'And, like I said, it really is pretty delicate. Not obvious like tomato leaf you sometimes see in Sauvignon Blanc, it's more the fruit. And it's ripe, kind of sweet and savoury at the same time.'

'Lewis tells me you've got an amazing palate. Skills Maddie, a Temp it is.' Roley tipped his glass towards her.

Maddie suddenly felt self-conscious. 'Well, all I really

know is that it's going to taste bloody good with dinner. Shall we eat inside or out?'

Roley walked outside to check the conditions and Maddie smacked her forehead, feeling like a smitten teen.

'Do you have any mozzie coils?' Roley called. 'Too nice out to eat inside.'

'Try the rack under the barbie.'

Roley organised mozzie coils and citronella candles before topping their glasses. Maddie plated the pasta into deep bowls, finishing with a grind of pepper.

They fell quiet making a start on dinner. Above the chime of forks chinking bowls, outside sounds drifted on the still evening—the shrieks, laughter and deeper adult tones of families heading home after a barbeque at the park between the beach and Maddie's place. They could make out the darting shapes of kids running with head torches and flashes of reflectors as bikes were lifted into utes. The slam of car doors and friendly goodbyes. Winding down, waning momentum of a sun-kissed day.

'Thanks Maddie, this is really good.' Roley finally pulled up after attacking his bowl. 'Didn't realise how hungry I was.'

'Sorry it's a little on the lean side. Stubbsy's been promising me home-grown cherry tomatoes, but they're either not quite ripe or his resident lizards keep raiding them.'

'So you're on good terms with Stubbsy, eh?' Roley quizzed. 'You know he has a reputation as a ladies' man?'

Maddie laughed. 'He's been nothing but a gentleman to me. So kind and generous. I've learnt a lot about this place care of Stubbsy and his balcony.'

'Stubbsy's a legend. Westy went to school with his daughter.' He looked up and found her eyes. 'Seriously, he's a good person to have in your street. He'd be a good guy to turn to if you ever felt worried about anything down here.'

'Thank you. You know he insisted I have his landline and his mobile, and made me promise to call him about anything, anytime.'

Roley nodded. 'I mean, you could always try me too,' his gaze dropped to his bowl. 'Just Stubbsy's close and wired to the local network.'

His quiet offer was touching. 'The only scary thing about this place is the swooping birds. Stubbsy says they'll get over it once their babies have left the nest.' Maddie steered the conversation back. 'So, how is the Malbec looking?'

Roley finished his mouthful. 'At the risk of sounding like an old farmer, I'm quietly excited.'

'Go on, old McDonald.'

'At every turn it's been easy. It was easy to establish, easy to grow, and now, this year, it's flourishing. I'm sure if it could speak it would say, *merci beaucoup* in an Australian accent,' Roley added laughing. 'It's a resolute immigrant that's packed up life in France to begin again here, without looking back, determined to make this new life, the best it can.'

'Nice analogy,' Maddie nodded. 'You're sounding a little like Westy though.'

They both laughed.

'So, promising then?'

'You know this is the fourth year it's fruited. First year we dropped the crop on the ground, couldn't use it. The last couple we've done fairly selective harvests. I'm sure you've seen it?' Roley asked.

Maddie shook her head. 'No. Lewis blended last year's with the Cabernet. It was blended before I started.'

'Bugger.'

'Yes—bugger! It's so topical. Lewis and Westy both rave about it. And this may sound out there, but I reckon I can see it in the Cabernet. There's a whole other spectrum to that wine which I reckon comes from the Malbec.'

Roley winked. 'This year, eh?'

She squeezed the brake on her bristling curiosity. 'More?'

Roley sat back laying his hands on his stomach. 'I thought you'd included seconds in my first bowl. That was a huge serve and I loved every…'

Maddie's mobile sang from the kitchen bench.

'Grab it,' he signalled. 'I should make tracks anyway.'

Maddie's smiled tightly. 'No, it's okay. It's just Josh.'

Roley ruffled. 'So, don't you want to talk to him?'

'That didn't come out right. What I meant is, it's Josh home from the Sunday session. Not riveting conversation.'

Roley's scrutiny was unnerving.

'It's all good. I'll call him tomorrow.'

'Sorry Maddie,' he raised his hands. 'Not my business.'

She picked at a fingernail. 'So, you didn't catch up with Vieve this weekend?'

Roley stood and collected their bowls. 'Perth. She worked all weekend. She had time off during exams. Now she's repaying the guys who covered her shifts.'

'Was she happy with her exams?'

Roley's head bobbed. 'She thinks she passed everything. She's no honours student. She'll just be happy not having to repeat anything. I should really head. Can I give you a hand with these?'

Maddie stood, picking up their glasses. 'It'll take me no time to clean up.'

He placed the bowls in the sink and walked to the front door. Hand on the doorknob, he hesitated, turning slowly back to face her. 'Maddie, can I ask you something?'

Maddie's heart stalled mid-beat, her head nodded automatically.

'Would it be reasonable to quote 'beautiful spitter' on my resume?'

She narrowed her eyes, unable to mask a smile. 'Night, night Roley. See you in the morning.'

'Ha! Night Madison. Thanks for dinner,' he called, half turning on his way down the steps, a dumb smile breaking over his face.

Maddie pulled the plug from the sink and watched the foamy level fall leaving little bubbles to burst on her arms. Washing the dishes, she'd replayed the whole scene, afternoon through after dinner without reaching a conclusion.

It was a really nice evening. They'd both seemed to enjoy it. The food, the wine, getting to know each other a little better. They hadn't said or done anything out of turn. So why the feeling like she'd just done something wrong?

She dried her hands on her shorts and picked up her phone. Josh hadn't left a message and it was too late to call back.

As Maddie remembered her reaction to his call, she blanched. *Yeah, nice one Madison. What could Roley possibly read into that?*

Shaking her head she switched off the lights and padded to her room.

Roley's ute pulled into her driveway right on seven o'clock the next morning. She pulled the front door closed and walked across the yard.

Barely glancing at Roley, she opened the car door and climbed in. 'Morning.'

'Hi.'

She reached to plonk her daypack on the floor of the back seat, suddenly self-conscious of her bare legs. Staring out the windscreen she tugged at the hem of her shorts, trying to think of something to say.

Roley seemed to share her predicament. They drove over the ridge in silence. Ellie Goulding's new single started playing on the radio.

'Mind if I turn it up?'

'Sure.' Roley adjusted the controls on the steering wheel and the volume rose.

'Did you surf this morning?'

'What?'

'Surf?' Maddie yelled.

'No,' Roley shook his head. 'Slept in. You?'

Maddie frowned and leant closer.

'Did you get to the beach?'

'Oh. Yeah. Water was freezing.'

Roley's eyes were fixed on the road; Maddie's trained on her side window.

Suddenly, an epiphany—Roley was trip-wired. Around Westy and Bethany she was uninhibited and spontaneous. With him, reserved and measured. It seemed absurd. Yesterday afternoon they chatted and laughed, sharing personal history. Less than twelve hours later, it felt like starting from scratch. She rolled her eyes at the passing scenery. If her head turned any further left, she'd resemble the possessed chick in that horror movie classic.

Twenty minutes later they pulled up at Southers. Maddie leapt from the car like it was on fire.

Chapter 4

Maddie looked up from the barrel to see Lewis striding purposefully towards her. She shut the water off.

'What's up?'

He ran a hand through his hair. 'I just got off the phone to Steve down at Rock Ridge. He thinks he's stuffed up the sulphur additions on his Chardonnay. I have to head down and check it out.'

'That's fine,' Maddie nodded. 'I'll be okay with the tanker.'

'It should've been here by now.'

'Really Lewis, it's all good. I know what to do.'

'Yeah, that's alright but…' Lewis's mobile started ringing. He checked the display. 'Shit!' He turned his back to her. 'Lewis here.' He nodded, pacing. 'Steve don't do anything, I'm on my way.' He looked back at Maddie, shaking his head. 'Just don't touch it 'til I get there.'

He disconnected and refocused. 'When I was talking

to Steve in the office I found an old email. Samples for the Young Cabernet Awards should have been sent last week. Don't know how I bloody missed it. I've rung them. We have until five o'clock today to get them there.'

Maddie hadn't experienced Lewis flustered. 'I've got this Lewis. I'll organise the samples. I'll deal with the tanker.' She flashed a confident smile. 'You go and get Steve sorted.'

Lewis put his hands on his hips. 'All had to happen the day Westy's not here. Sure you'll be…' His mobile sounded again.

Maddie mouthed 'go'.

Lewis spun on his heels raking fingers through his hair. 'Lewis here.' He snapped his fingers and Taxi appeared, falling into line as he marched to his car.

Maddie prioritised. Samples first, barrels can wait.

Inside the cellar she stopped for a few beats letting her eyes adjust to the darkened room. Everything she needed was at the workstation. Maddie grabbed a wine hose and three sterile bottles. She knew where the wines were stored, but methodically checked the code on the Jupiter Rising barrel before taking out the bung and syphoning wine to fill the bottles. Replacing the bung she took them back to the workstation, using the benchtop screw-capper to seal them.

'Thanks Warwick. Love your work.' Maddie smiled every time she laid eyes on the machine's nametag that Westy had sticky-taped in place.

She repeated the process for Kite's Wedge Cabernet.

Maddie was reaching for the sticky labels when John, the tanker driver, appeared around the door.

Maddie's hand shot to her chest. 'Oh John, you surprised me.'

'Sorry Maddie. Couldn't find anyone outside. I'm in a hell of a hurry today.'

John was a gentleman. He wore the usual uniform, work shorts and shirt, but John wore his with style. Most of the industry threw on faded, frayed or holey mishmashes of shirts, pants and shorts. John's were ironed crisp, shorts belted, shirt buttoned.

Maddie dropped the stickers. 'Let's go. What's happened?'

'Caught two lots of road works this morning, cost me twenty-five minutes, then the pump at the last place played up. I've got to get back to Perth to unload, then out to the Swan Valley for another job.'

Maddie took control. 'I've got this John. Do you want to grab a cuppa?'

'No thanks love.'

Maddie chatted about nothing in particular, moving fast and efficiently.

The transfer took just over an hour and John seemed less anxious when he left. Leaning through the window he saluted Maddie as he pulled the heavy tanker out.

Maddie smiled and waved. Even through the open window of the cab his hair remained impeccable.

Maddie didn't stop. As the tanker moved down the road she was unhitching the hose from the pump when the courier flew around the corner, dust billowing in a violent cloud behind.

'Shit! The samples.'

Waving at the courier she ran across the concrete pad, jumping wine hoses and power leads, agile and fast to the cellar.

'Not waiting today Miss!' George bellowed, hot on her trail.

Reading his angst Maddie hurtled towards the samples. She was at the workbench when he stormed through the door.

'George I know,' Maddie rabbited, furiously writing a consignment note, 'you have the patience of a saint. You don't have to wait and yet I know you will because I really, really, have to get these samples off today.'

No response.

'And I know that's not your problem, and I won't even tell you about having to drop everything to fill up that tanker that just left because that's not your problem either.' Maddie babbled appeasements, eyes down, scrawling madly.

She handed the book to George and started scribbling labels for the samples.

George carved his signature into the consignment note, tore his copy from the book and slapped it hard on the bench.

Maddie moved fast, George's aggression tangible. If she didn't need him to take the samples so badly, she would happily tell him to pull his head in, knowing from Bethany he instilled terror in his customers around the district.

Maddie didn't like bullies. Today he was a menacing bundle of pent-up anger, threatening to blow. It wasn't acceptable. She remembered Bethany's story of one girl who hid in the toilets every time his van pulled into their drive.

Sticking the first label on the bottle Maddie jumped as George, issuing a series of expletives, turned on his heels for the door.

Bastard!

Maddie ripped at the labels slapping them on the bottles, bundling them into a Styrofoam pack. Balancing that with one hand she grabbed the tape-gun and black marking pen with the other and blundered out the door after him.

George slammed the back door of his van. Maddie dropped the package on his bonnet and manoeuvred the tape-gun, possessed.

He sat heavily in the driver's seat. Maddie could feel his contempt drill into her.

She threw the tape-gun to the ground and bit the lid off the marker pen, frantically scratching the address.

George revved the engine.

Maddie slammed her fist on the hood, and met his eyes in a challenging glare.

To his credit, he didn't run her down. Instead he leapt out of the van and stood terrifyingly close.

Maddie could see pressure pulsing behind his eyeballs. She flinched as he grabbed the package, throwing it through the open door onto the passenger seat.

Maddie stepped back as he gunned the van into reverse. She watched the red-dust tornado rage down the driveway in his wake.

Reaching to retrieve the tape-gun Maddie noticed her shaking hand. She sat heavily on the concrete crush-pad and hugged her legs to her chest. She would speak with Lewis. Lodge a formal complaint.

'Never, ever gonna be a driver for a living.'

It was after three in the afternoon when Lewis and Taxi reappeared.

Maddie waved as she forked the last barrel back into the cellar. She parked up the forklift and found Lewis in his office. Her throat felt scratchy as she perched on a chair at his desk.

'How'd you get on?' Lewis turned from his computer to face her.

'No worries with the tanker,' Maddie's voice wavered. She cleared her throat. 'John was behind in his schedule but he was cool. I've sterilised the tank and updated the board.'

'Cheers,' Lewis nodded. 'You're thorough.'

Maddie's face remained passive, she swung slightly left to right in the ergonomic chair.

'Samples?'

Maddie stopped swivelling. 'That's what I've come to see you about.'

Alarm rose on Lewis's face.

'They've gone,' Maddie reassured. 'Just…George was a pig today. Actually, that's unfair on pigs.'

'Out of sorts today, was he?' Lewis asked. 'George can be a grumpy bastard.'

'No Lewis, he crossed a line today.' Maddie held his eyes. 'I'm no pussy, but today I felt scared. I don't like being a dobber but his behaviour was so out of line, beyond acceptable. I want to make a formal complaint.'

'Right. Tell me.' Lewis took off his glasses and entwined his fingers on the desk.

'He yelled, swore. He was abrupt. He invaded my personal space.'

Lewis nodded.

Maddie raised her hands. 'It sounds so lame out loud. But seriously, I was still shaking for about twenty minutes after he'd left. It was a bit of a nightmare.'

Lewis nodded again, with what registered as more conviction.

'How about you document it in writing and I'll email it through to his boss? This won't be the first complaint Hazel's had about George.'

'Okay,' Maddie nodded. 'Just, I'm sticking to my guns on this one. It's wrong. He shouldn't get away with that kind of behaviour.'

'Fair enough,' Lewis agreed. 'Just be aware, Hazel might want to talk with you directly.'

'I'm okay with that.'

'Did you just finish the racking?'

'Yep. All done.'

'Why don't you go and write it all down while it's still fresh in your mind. Do you have your laptop?'

Maddie nodded.

'Do it from home if you like. We'll deal with it in the morning.'

'O-kay,' Maddie said slowly.

'I'm not fobbing you off Maddie,' Lewis held her eyes and picked up his glasses. 'You did well today. I'm sorry I wasn't around to help you out. Get the incident out of your head into an email and I'll speak with Hazel in the morning.'

'Okay,' Maddie gave a decisive nod. 'How's Steve's Chardonnay?'

Lewis rolled his eyes. 'Bloody self-taught winemakers. Love the enthusiasm but we don't do four years study for nothing.' Lewis shook his head and looked at Maddie with a cheeky smile. 'His Chardonnay has almost recovered. I may take a little longer.'

Maddie read through her account of the incident. Dot points were wicked for sticking to the facts. The exercise smoothed her emotional flurry, leaving George temporarily filed in the back of her mind.

Company would be good. She picked up her phone. It was still before six o'clock. Her call went to message bank.

'Hi Stubbsy. Maddie here. I'm just whipping up a frittata and wondered if I could invite myself up for dinner? Oh, and I've got a nice bottle of red.'

Halfway through cooking the frittata her phone pinged a message.

'Fritty what-what? Sure to be good. Wander up anytime. I'll see what's in the garden for a salad.'

Maddie smiled. She finished cooking and jumped in the shower.

'G'day neighbour,' Stubbsy opened the door, taking her basket.

'Hi Stubbsy. Thanks for letting me invite myself over.'

'Your message made my day. You know my balcony loves company. Gin?'

Maddie smiled.

'So what's a frittyatta?'

She pulled the plate from her basket. 'Ta, da.'

Stubbsy's bottom jaw dropped and he sucked in his lip. 'Egg and bacon pie without the pie.'

'Pretty much,' Maddie laughed.

He mixed the drinks and handed her a glass.

'Here, I haven't picked the salad yet. Come and I'll show you the garden.' He led the way through a beaded curtain to the backyard.

The block sloped steeply up the hill. Terraced beds were brimming with vegetables, flowers and fruit trees. One side was dominated by a green tin shed and a good sized greenhouse that appeared to be made from old windows.

'You don't have kids next door who play footy and cricket?'

Stubbsy stood with his hands on his hips. 'It's my own design. I have spare windows in the shed. If one gets broken, I just remove the whole thing and slot another one in.'

Maddie moved for a closer look. 'It's ingenious.' She peered inside.

'Best thing about being a builder, all the recycled materials. I've been retired a few years now and my shed's still groaning.'

The greenhouse was alive with plants in various stages of growth. One whole shelf dedicated to an array of pretty orchids, their flowers dangling on arched stems, vibrant with detail and colour.

'I didn't think you could grow some of these things so close to the ocean?' Maddie asked, taking in the netted fruit trees and the thriving beds.

'Just takes a little more care and attention, Maddie girl. Gotta be selective too. Some things just don't like the salt. It's been a long learning curve.'

Maddie gave Stubbsy a sideways look. 'And here I was thinking you only left your balcony to make tea.'

He handed her a bowl and a pair of secateurs. 'Here, what do you think will taste good with no-crust quiche?'

Maddie stood in front of a burgeoning bed. Snow peas hid in tendril nests, tomatoes hung from cane pyramids and clumps of spinach formed a carpet pocked with herbs and carrot tufts. Maddie smiled and started snipping. 'Everything.'

The sun left the sky in a garish display, intent on blinding anyone daring to look. In comparison, the frittata disappeared quickly with less fuss while the red wine gently slipped away.

Over dinner, Maddie vented.

'Slammed your fist on his bonnet, eh?'

Maddie pulled down the corners of her mouth. 'Where

did that even come from? Surprised myself with that one.'

'Good girl, calling his hand. Not something I'd usually recommend with a two-tonne truck involved. But good for you.'

Maddie dropped her head into her hand. 'God, I really wasn't thinking was I? Pure reflex.'

'Well Maddie girl,' Stubbsy reached out his hand to her arm. 'You stood your ground. It's over now. Time to let it go.'

Maddie raised her head, smiling weakly.

'And bloody time the man retired. Sounds like he should go bush; work out what's really messing with his mettle. Running wild with feral camels for a bit would soon have him hoicking it up, spitting it out of his system.'

Maddie shook her head. 'I wouldn't wish it on the camels.'

They sipped on their wine and nature raised its voice in the pause. Beyond Stubby's balcony the sky hung like an indigo curtain studded with stars, the roll and slurp of waves drenching its hem.

'Ah. And there's the night kite reminding us we're right where we should be.'

Maddie's eyes wandered the sky. 'What?'

Stubbsy let out a heavy sigh. 'Maddie girl, you're not telling me you don't know the night kite?'

Stubbsy sounded mortified. 'Um, is it some kind of satellite?' Maddie guessed.

He took a deep breath, blowing out a loud whistle.

'Bird? Although, I didn't think kites were nocturnal.'

'Maddie girl. Here I was all this time thinking you were bloody Australian!'

'I am bloody Aust-rail-yan,' Maddie accentuated the syllables.

'Better show me your birth certificate, cos if you don't

know the kite is the Southern Cross constellation, then I don't bloody believe ya.'

'Oh. I suppose it does look a bit like a kite.'

Stubbsy crossed his arms on the table and sank his head for a breath. 'So, that place where you're workin', Beneath The bloody Kite, what did you think the name was referring to?' His accent more ocker with every word.

'Um, sorry Stubbsy. I guess I haven't thought about it.'

He groaned.

Maddie talked quickly. 'I've never heard the Southern Cross referred to as a kite, or night kite, so I guess I would have thought it had something to do with the bird of prey.'

Stubbsy looked at her like she was speaking unintelligibly. She rambled on. 'I mean both have a mythical sense, beyond the reach of mortals in the Australian landscape.' She stole a quick look sideways, hoping for appeasement. Stubbsy only shook his head. 'Does it really matter?'

'If you were my daughter, I'd wash your mouth out with soap.'

Maddie raised a hand and clamped her lips. Eyes wide, she shook her head.

Stubbsy laughed. 'Of course it bloody matters. Kites, the raptors, are weak-footed birds.'

Maddie's look betrayed her lack of comprehension.

'Think of the first Australians padding about this land, almost beyond our imagination's reach in time. The soles of their feet slapping this raw crust from one edge of the country to the other—condemns weak-footed to an absurdity, don't you think?'

'Oh. When you put it like that.'

'Maddie girl, the Southern Cross is our compass. Indigenous Australians, well some groups anyway, used it to navigate laws and customs, changing seasons and food sources. And for us whities, we used it to find our way here.'

Maddie nodded. 'I only really know it from studying Australian history at school. They flew a flag with the Southern Cross at the Eureka Stockade.'

'The Southern Cross has been shining for ten to twenty million years, burning above this land. It holds its place in the sky while down here, we spin our lives away.' Stubbsy shifted forward in his chair. 'Whenever life leaves us reeling we only ever have to look up. Beneath the kite we centre and ground. We're home.'

Maddie's eyes opened wide. 'Wow! Feels quite special, the way you explain it.' Picking up her glass she swirled the wine, taking a long inhalation before setting it gently down. 'I think your balcony could be one of its moons.'

Stubbsy looked at her awhile before closing his eyes, resting back into his chair. 'I miss my daughter.'

'Will you see her at Christmas?'

Stubbsy's eyes twinkled as they opened. 'Yeah. I'm heading over.' He smiled slowly. 'Queensland never seems as far away when I know she can look up and see the Southern Cross too.' He shifted in his chair. 'Imagine, light from years across a universe keeping us connected.'

Maddie felt the weight of starlight on her skin as she trailed her hands through space. 'This place is one revelation after another.'

The sky was alive with light, twinkles, beams and glittering pools.

Stubbsy looked at Maddie and smiled. 'Wouldn't live anywhere else in the world for quids.'

Chapter 5

During the week, Roley and Maddie saw each other every day at work. Each convoluted meeting they oscillated between talking like old friends and falling awkwardly shy. On Wednesday, en route to smoko Maddie stopped in her tracks. It wasn't coffee she was looking forward to. Hands on hips, she one-eightied and headed back to the cellar. She pulled out her phone and punched Josh a text. A short, nothing text about nothing. She signed off with her usual two kisses, deleting them before hitting send. The kisses felt wrong, her heart didn't back them. Her heart and her head were having some kind of Mexican stand-off.

Somehow she'd developed a sixth sense knowing when Roley's ute pulled up. Lifting her head, he walked through the door.

'Hi. Missed you at smoko,' Roley walked close. 'Are you

doing one of those giving up caffeine for a month things? No-toxin-vember or something?'

Maddie pulled a face. 'I'd be better off having a go at Mo-vember,' she petted her top lip and the sides of her mouth. 'I'm seeing a full, black gringo moustache.'

Roley raised his eyebrows.

Maddie shook her head and laughed. 'Don't mind me. Cellar confinement makes me crazy. What's up?'

Roley handed her his phone. Open on the display was a photo, a jewel blue streak of a bird. 'I came across this little guy this morning.'

'He's stunning,' Maddie zoomed in on the picture. 'I can't believe his colour.'

'I know. You guys don't get them in Victoria,' Roley smiled. 'I looked it up. You get the superb blue-wrens. This is our splendid wren, and at this time of year they're iridescent.'

Maddie handed back the phone. 'Thank you.'

Roley nodded. 'Better get back to it.' He slipped the phone into his pocket. 'Later Maddie.'

As the door closed behind him, Maddie dropped her head into her hands. The cedar smell of barrels cloyed her nose chasing oxygen from the room. Mexican stand-offs didn't have happy endings, someone always had to die. Maddie crouched as a wave of light-headedness threatened to pull her under, waiting for the bullet.

The Tavern was heaving.

'It's going off!' Bethany's face was live.

'What?'

A bouncer had cracked the door and Maddie couldn't hear a thing over the thudding beat of the band.

Bethany angled her head at the open door, raising her eyebrows, Cheshire Cat grin.

Maddie placed her hands on Bethany's shoulders and gently pushed her through.

Instantly imbued with the beat, they signed 'drink' to each other and smiling and bopping worked their way through the jam of bodies to the bar. Maddie wondered if they would make it as Bethany stopped every second step for a hug or kiss, or to wave at someone across the room. She tried introducing her to some crew but words drowned in the soundwaves. Reading lips, nodding and smiling, names were exchanged with swaying shoulders and hips; unheard and irrelevant. The moment belonged to melody and beat. Maddie surrendered to the vibe.

Westy was leaning against the bar. She noted his surprised, happy expression when Bethany touched his arm, and was thrilled as his face lit up all over again on seeing her. Westy added their drinks to his order, passing them over as they arrived. They each took long sips before weaving away from the bar to find a spot large enough to huddle. Turning towards each other they raised their beers, Westy holding two. 'Cheers.'

Maddie grasped only the odd word Bethany shouted.

'Who...with?'

Westy bent in to hear before straightening to look around.

Maddie knew who the other beer was for before her eyes followed Westy's nod to Roley, making his way back from the Men's.

Something zinged through Maddie's system. An image flashed, a cowboy and a Mexican facing each other at thirty paces, squinting eyes, hands poised at their hips.

'Loaded guns at dusk,' the words slipped out.

Both Westy and Bethany turned and leant close. 'What?'

Maddie was shaking her head as Roley joined them. Westy handed him a beer and they clinked cheers again.

Bethany addressed Roley and as he leant across to hear, Maddie's nose, unaffected by the noise level, took full advantage of his musky spice aroma. Roley laughed and her brain flashed another image—Josh in Jeremy's latest Instagram post, his head back, arm around a mystery blonde, enjoying a joke. She blinked the vision away.

Mostly, Bethany's attempts at conversation were answered with furrowed brows, ears pressing close and shrugs. Eventually Maddie took her hand and mouthed 'dance'. They found a ledge for their drinks and moved towards the stage, joining the throng of bodies moving to the beat.

Their circle widened as Bethany found friends on the dance floor. Maddie couldn't think of the last time she'd danced in such an intimate venue, remembering only that she loved it. They stayed on the floor until the last note died on the neck of the bass player's guitar; Maddie and Bethany shadowing him all the way on air-guitars. As the final applause eased, the bass guitarist flicked his plectrum towards them. Bethany caught it, tucking it seductively into her bra. Their faces ached with laughter as the bass guy mimed jumping off the stage before raising his guitar to the crowd, throwing her a wink.

As the band disappeared the lights came up and security and roadies moved in. Ushered outside they caught sight of Westy and Roley.

'Hey Maddie, you should come along,' Westy sang out as they neared.

Maddie still couldn't hear a thing. She pointed to her ear. 'What?'

Westy smiled. 'We're surfing in the morning. A break near the Wilyabrup cliffs. You should come along.' He looked thoughtful, hands on his hips. 'The place has a special energy. I reckon you'd love it.'

'Sounds awesome.' Maddie enthused. 'How do I get there?'

'You need a four-wheel-drive,' Roley said. 'I'll swing by and pick you up.'

Maddie pointed to her ear again, leaning closer.

'I'll pick you up,' Roley spoke loud and slow, miming the actions.

Maddie laughed. 'Great.'

'What about you Bethany?' Roley asked. 'Plenty of room.'

Bethany put her hand on his shoulder. 'Well thanks for thinking of me…eventually,' she leaned in closer, laughing. 'I'd love to but I'm working at cellar door tomorrow. I'm gonna have to pass.'

Westy said something.

Maddie pointed to her ear again. 'What?'

Bethany grabbed her waist and started pulling her away. 'Cinderella's ears are turning into cauliflowers,' she teased. 'I'm taking her away before I have to pack her into a vegetable crate.'

As Bethany pulled, Maddie waved. 'See you in the morning. I'll put in a request for good conditions.'

Westy and Roley both pointed to their ears. 'What?'

Maddie and Bethany laughed all the way across the carpark.

The next morning, Maddie was rugged up on the deck, sipping a cup of tea when her phone pinged a text.

Pick you up 6.30?

It was six fifteen. Maddie had been up almost an hour. She thumbed one back.

Sweet. Have packed food. Fare for locals' tour.

Arriving home in the wee hours, Maddie whipped up a batch of raspberry studded brownies before finally falling into bed. Drifting off to sleep she mocked her bizarre behaviour, the self-discipline of not ironing her bikini.

On waking, she made ham and salad wraps and packed all the food into an esky. Water bottle, beach things, hat. She closed the front door as Roley pulled into the drive.

Westy sat cross-legged, arms raised, emphasising his point.

'The ocean and the land don't meet at an edge. The notion of a coast 'line' is simplistic.' He shook his head slowly. 'Typical example of humans having to define things, break them into digestible chunks like Lego blocks, to make sense of the world. The crazy part is, while simplifying what's going on around them, they distort and overcomplicate what's real.'

'How do you see it then?' Maddie dared.

'The ocean is a liquid coating over a solid mass. It's the sauce, the mayo if you like, sandwiched between earth and air. Land doesn't end and the ocean doesn't just begin. They co-exist and, in places, one reaches higher than the other. There's not enough mayonnaise to cover all of the filling.'

Maddie and Roley exchanged a look while Westy rambled on.

'It's not a bloody aquarium. Some separate vessel that exists against a rocky edge or sandy beach. They're intrinsically connected. The sea penetrates beneath its floor which isn't solid at all, soaking deep into sand. Rivers are tendrils of the ocean and the ocean, collective spills of the sky. Land is…'

'Urrgh! Westy my head hurts. I get it. I get it. I really do, but all of this big picture stuff stretches my brain, makes me hungry.'

Roley laughed, catching the ham and salad wrap Maddie threw.

Westy grinned as he chewed, looking out across the water.

'Westy?'

'Yeah Maddie.'

'I don't want to alarm you, but a tsunami is headed for your chin.'

Westy wiped his hand below his lip catching a thin glob of mayonnaise snaking its way from the corner of his mouth.

'You're classic, Maddie,' he wiped his sticky hand across the rock. 'There, universal harmony restored.'

After lunch, Westy and Roley laid back on the rocks. The morning's surf had been long and, she suspected, hugely satisfying. Neither seemed in a hurry to move.

While they were in the water, Maddie had swum and explored to the north. Keen to cover more ground, she slipped on her daypack, looking south.

On one side the ocean slammed into rocks sending frothy plumes of spray high into the air. On the other, the rocks rose in towering cliffs.

Hold the mayo, Maddie thought to herself as she stared up at them. With nothing uniform about them, the rocks did resemble blocks. Heavy, hard blocks of granite wedged in an inky creviced grid. Lines cut so long and deep in places it was hard to imagine what kept them from tumbling toward the earth.

As if Westy could read her mind she quickly acknowledged

the physical forces at play. They didn't stand by chance. They were marvellous.

It was a pretty day, radiant with sunshine. Bright blue chiffon sky wafting above clear water, stars of sunlight tripping its surface.

Earlier, she jolted with alarm, spotting a fin in the swell beyond the group of surfers waiting for a set. Her body tensed before recognition brought relaxation and joy. Dolphin—not shark. There had been a pod of five, hanging together, catching waves. She watched as the surfers found them too, pointing and turning their boards to watch.

Rock hopping south, crabs feeding on the slippery spray covered surface scrambled for cover; flashes of orange and purple scurrying on pick-footed black legs. Memories flooded in. As a girl fishing with Aunt Bling she tried to catch them, dangling line with baited hook between the rock gaps waiting for hungry crabs to grab before yanking them up. The clever crabs always let go. Time had flown as she lured and teased. Maddie wondered if her aunt ever fished now, or was it something she did with her, in the absence of a father. She made a mental note to ask.

'Good luck,' she bid the oystercatchers. The pink legged birds with their long red bills looked the same as the ones in Victoria. They were well equipped but their prey was formidable, the birds needed every tool evolution bequeathed if crabs were to feature on their menu.

Nearing the next jutting headland she stopped to look up. This must be the place Westy referred to. The energy was tangible, emanating from deep within the rock's layers of age and event. Maddie was humbled; here footsteps were a breeze and breath a silent reflex. The cliff had a dark shadowy eye where a rock had dropped, leaving a nose protruding from the face. An ancient sentinel looking seaward, bearing witness to the sun melting on the horizon, stormy waters reaching to sting its cheek as time hung weathering. An old man's smile, his bottom jaw had dropped and smashed. Studying her feet, Maddie moved with reverence between the granite molars.

The next bay was wider, tall cliffs marking the points either end gave way to scrubby slope in-between. High on the hill, the wind had shredded the leaves off the small trees that clung to the sides, exposing their grey skeletons. The scrub lower to the ground appeared lush, a palette of greens parted roughly in the middle of the bay by a freshwater stream.

Transition from slabs of granite to smooth-skinned boulders to dank earth and rooted life was dynamic. Birds shrieked alarm warning neighbours of intrusion. Fresh water and dense bush, tiger snake paradise. A sudden vision of Taxi with the snake in his mouth made her shudder; from there on every rustle made her jump, followed by a reflex laugh.

The booming sounds of the ocean surrendered to the sharper noises of the land. Like closing her eyes to smell or taste, Maddie noticed she could hear more keenly what held her eyes. Senses so connected, gathering information, feeding into her. Maddie couldn't remember being so aware of them. Somehow this place amplified sensation.

She had walked thirty odd metres from the sea. Looking back it was framed on each side by the blocky cliffs. She took a long, deep breath, absorbing, thinking of Westy and Roley dozing on the rocks, the handful of surfers still in the water. Maddie knew spectacular coast. It had been part of her childhood. This place touched her differently.

She followed the creek as far as she comfortably could, reality being, green didn't equal soft. Only resourceful plants thrived in coastal extremes; hard, woody support and bristly, spiky leaves. She reached a point where a crude track crossed the stream discovering a Cape to Cape track marker. Stubbsy had told her stories of the walk, having hiked from Cape Naturaliste in the north to Cape Leeuwin in the south in one hit, over six or seven days. His knowledge and whimsical storytelling conjured it to life. Maybe post vintage she could con Stubbsy into an overnighter on the track, explore another section.

As she meandered back, the wavering belt of horizon teased her imagination. From this coastline or edge—bloody Westy—this bit before getting your feet wet, it was a long swim to South Africa, with little chance to rest along the way. A vast, rolling wilderness that infused this place with possibility.

Roley's form came into view, wetsuit peeled to just below his waist. Cushioned on a towel, one hand supported his head, accentuating the curve of his spine. Her bikini shrunk a size beneath her beach shirt, pulling on the skin of her breasts. Neither boy stirred. She spread her Turkish towel sitting legs forward, hands crossed at her ankles, simpering in the transfer of heat from the rock. She laid her head on her knees and her eyes studied the bands of muscle resting beneath his skin, the dry, fullness of his lips.

Roley's eyelids opened. Their eyes held, fixed for a second too long; the language of look firing primeval paths long buried beneath diffident drifts of words.

Blinking couldn't undo it. Maddie closed her eyes. Blue, red and yellow dots danced behind the thin skin curtains. It was time to woman-up.

'Maddie. Hi. I was just about to call you. Do you have some time? We should talk.'

He's breaking up with me. Ego prickled sending her reeling into fight mode. Wounded pride swelled into a bubble of incredulity before—pop!—she remembered why she'd called. She almost laughed. 'Hi Josh. Now's good. What's happening?'

'I can't do this Maddie.' His voice strained. 'This distance thing. It's not what I signed up for.'

And I didn't realise our relationship was an Australia's Got Talent audition; army service; an anti-fracking petition. Response scenarios whizzed through her head before she answered simply. 'Uh, ha.'

'I just…I don't know.'

Maddie braced.

'I just don't understand why you took the job.'

She took a long breath. 'I know,' she crossed her legs beneath her. 'You know it wasn't personal. It's a really solid opportunity for me.' She paused, pulling thoughts together. 'I don't know what else I can say. You know how serious I am about winemaking. Working in other wine regions was always part of the plan.'

'I know. I just figured, when it came to it, our relationship would be worth more than a casual job.'

It was a whine. Maddie almost let it go but changed her mind. 'And I would have thought, if our relationship was worth anything, we could survive five or so months apart, while one of us pursued their dreams.'

'Oh crap, Maddie. What? So you could come back for a month or two before heading off again, following the next one.'

'God,' Maddie sighed. 'You make me sound so unreasonable. And, truth is, I think you're being unreasonable, looking at my big opportunity as some casual gig.' Maddie's chin dropped to her chest.

Silence.

'You don't want *me* Josh. You want a girlfriend that's convenient. The girl could be anyone. She could be blonde.'

'If you're referring to the Instagram post, it's not…'

Maddie shook her head, cutting him off. 'Sorry Josh. Let's not even go there. That's not what this is about.'

Silence.

'So how are things going over there?'

Maddie looked up at the sky. It took breaking-up for him to ask.

'Fine. Job's great. People are great. It's a beautiful place.'

'Sounds like you could stay longer than vintage?'

Maddie softened. It wasn't a whinge or cloaked in sarcasm. 'Early days, who knows? I guess anything's possible, now I'm single.' She quickly bit her lip.

Josh responded calmly. 'Will you text me when you're back?'

'Sure,' Maddie acquiesced, knowing it wouldn't happen.

Silence.

It dawned, Josh couldn't, or didn't know how, to end the conversation. Maddie stepped up. 'I'm glad you called. Not easy, but good to talk about things. You know, lay it out.'

'Yeah,' he paused. 'I hope vintage goes okay. You know, lives up to your expectations.'

Disconnecting from one awkward space, landed her in another. No tears, no whoops of joy. Maddie lay back against the cushions of the day bed, absorbing the end. She'd thanked him for calling. She grabbed her phone to check who had rung who, knowing it didn't matter. It was done.

My place. Beach walk for coffee. 10?

Maddie sent the text, leaving the phone on the kitchen bench while she headed to the bathroom. Brushing her teeth, her phone sounded two messages received.

Hanging out the last of her washing, the slam of car doors announced their arrival, followed by Carmel and Bethany's chatter as they made their way round to the back deck.

'Hi, coming,' Maddie yelled, picking up the empty basket.

'Hello, hello,' they exchanged hugs.

'Great morning for a walk,' gushed Carmel.

'Great morning for coffee,' Bethany groaned.

'Uh oh,' Maddie studied her. 'Did you party hard last night?'

'Worse,' Bethany looked dumbfounded. 'I stayed up playing some stupid board game with Evan and his friends.' She stuck out her tongue. 'They made this disgusting antioxidant punch which was great cos I didn't get pissed but I didn't get to bed 'til after two this morning.'

Carmel and Maddie laughed.

'So it wasn't sex keeping you up either, if it was Evan and friends. Or was Rick home?' Maddie teased.

Bethany punched her arm. 'Already you know too much about my crazy life.' She put her hand to her cheek. 'Not sex or drugs—board games, with gay friends,' she mimed hitting her head on the wooden railing.

Maddie laughed. 'What about you Carmel? Any Saturday night board game action for you?'

'No Maddie,' Carmel put her hand on Bethany's arm. 'I have a life.'

'Ha, ha.' Bethany mocked. 'But actually it's true.' She turned to Maddie conspiratorially. 'Carmel went to a dinner party at a friend's place and the guy she's got her eye on just happened to be there.'

'Ohhh,' Maddie clapped her hands. 'So how did it go?'

Carmel smiled. 'Dinner was lovely. Actually the whole evening was lovely.'

'And Brendan?' Bethany quizzed.

Carmel's smiled broadened. 'Lovelier than ever.'

'That sounds encouraging,' Maddie enthused. 'So, progress?'

'I don't know,' Carmel threw up her hands. 'I think he likes me. Hard to tell. He did ask if I was planning any more wine tasting nights.'

Maddie pieced things together. 'Oh. Is that Brendan from the wine supplies agency in Cowaramup?'

'Yes, that Brendan,' Carmel smiled.

'He's pretty shy,' Bethany offered. 'I reckon he's warming up slowly.'

'Meanwhile, I'm going to self-combust,' Carmel fanned her hands in front of her face. 'Anyway, enough about my desperate situation, what did you get up to?'

Maddie took a deep breath. 'Quiet one for me. I broke up with my boyfriend yesterday, so I wasn't up for much.'

Carmel and Bethany froze.

'It's okay,' Maddie shrugged. 'I'm okay.' She felt a prickle of sweat under their scrutiny. 'Honestly,' she grabbed her cap and sunglasses off the table and tried to sound upbeat. 'Come on. Let's walk.'

They moved in single file down the stairs. As they scrunched across the shell grit Bethany asked mildly: 'So do you want to talk about what happened?'

'Yeah…you know, I think I already told you it was inevitable.'

The narrow bush track opened onto a limestone path and the girls spread across its width, Maddie in the middle.

Bethany flung an arm around her. 'Still crappy though. Why didn't you give me a call?'

Maddie looked ahead. 'You know I just…was alright. I opened a 2012 Beneath The Kite Cabernet and snuggled up on the day bed and just thought about things.'

They walked a few metres in silence.

'Sometimes it's good to let the dust settle,' Carmel pitched. 'Reflect on things. See what we can learn—hopefully to take forward into our next relationship.'

Maddie and Bethany looked at her.

'God, we should consult you for relationship advice.'

Carmel laughed. 'God no. Just been through the wringer a few times. It's good to look at things objectively. Look for patterns so you don't keep repeating them.'

'Yeah, I was kind of doing that,' Maddie said slowly. Blue water blurred past as they walked. 'I decided I don't want to be responsible for another person's happiness.'

'Deep,' remarked Bethany.

'Insightful,' added Carmel.

'Just the best I could come up with under the circumstances. I think I'm pretty independent and I need a bloke who has his own stuff going on, not rely on me for everything.'

'Was Josh a bit needy?' Carmel asked.

Maddie thought for a beat before answering. 'Kind of. It's like I was his focal point and when I moved over here it upset his orbit.'

'So you want a bloke who ignores you? Who like, just checks in for the occasional dinner and sex.'

Maddie looked at Bethany. 'No. Not like that. Although…' she smiled, winking her eyebrows. 'I want someone who's interested in what makes me tick. It's hard to explain.' Maddie's hands worked overtime. 'Like one eye can follow me around, checking me out while I do my thing,' she smiled. 'But the other eye needs to keep looking ahead to its own path, moving forward to realise his own dreams and potential.'

'God. No wonder I'm single…so complicated,' Bethany mused.

'I think I get what you're saying though,' Carmel ventured. 'You don't want to be the centre of someone else's world. That a relationship should be more like a partnership, two people contributing equally.'

'Yeah, I think so. It doesn't seem practical that one person relies on another for their happiness or balance or whatever. We should be taking care of that for ourselves.'

'Woah. That sounds a little lonely, doesn't it?' Bethany asked.

Carmel reasoned. 'I actually think you're onto something, Maddie. You've had one of those big things-falling-into-place moments.'

'Yeah, cuddling my Cabernet last night, a few things became clear. I don't know how my thoughts led to this, but I was thinking you wouldn't give your brain to someone to look after the night before an exam. Or I wouldn't anyway. I wouldn't trust my revision to anyone. Only I know what I need, to do well. And I reckon it's the same with happiness.'

'I'm drowning over here,' Bethany moaned.

Maddie looked across at her and shook her head. 'No way, Bethany. I was thinking about you last night too.'

'Uh oh,' Bethany hid her face behind her hands.

'You could have a boyfriend if you wanted one. But you've made a choice. You're concentrating on your course and there's no one on the scene that really interests you.'

'That's more the point,' Bethany exclaimed.

'Either way, it's not fate or chance, you're making choices.

You're taking responsibility for your happiness whether you like to think so or not.'

'I'm not some sad person? Shouldn't consider re-homing cats?'

Maddie tilted her head and looked at her sideways. 'Nothing sad about you, Bethany.'

'No,' Carmel assured. 'And you don't want cats. You're a dog person.'

Traffic on the path increased closer to the cafe. Fluffy puffs of cloud sped across the sky. They stopped at the first set of steps leading down to the beach.

'Anyone want to get their feet wet?' Carmel asked, already bending. She slipped off her shoes and made her way down to the beach.

Maddie and Bethany crouched to deal with their footwear.

Bethany nudged Maddie, taking a punt. 'Anything happen on your surf trip yesterday I should know about?'

Maddie hesitated before raising her eyebrows. 'I've fallen in love.'

Bethany's head jerked and she overbalanced, falling backwards on her bum.

Laughing, Maddie reached for her arm, sprawling backwards with her into the path of a golden retriever.

'Sorry,' Maddie fended off the licking dog, struggling to her feet.

The dog's owner tugged on the leash, gifting Maddie an annoyed look before moving on.

Maddie brushed at the white powdery sand, offering Bethany a hand up. 'I've never grovelled around on the ground so much as I have since moving here.'

'What are you two doing?' Carmel called from the beach through cupped hands.

As they made their way down the stairs, Bethany punched her arm, urgently whispering. 'So, do I know him?'

Maddie leant close. 'Not a him, a what. I've fallen in love with Margaret River.' Pulling away, she caught Bethany's eye-roll. 'Honestly. My spirit hardly knows itself. It's like I'm reinventing me.'

'Holy crap, Maddie. No more drinking Cabernet on your own, contemplating life. Makes you fucking loco.'

As their feet sank into the sand, Bethany pleaded. 'Sure there's nothing on the horizon I should know about?'

Maddie raised a hand to shield her eyes as she looked across the ocean. 'Blue sky and calm seas.' She ducked just in time. Bethany's slap, aimed squarely at the back of her head, only caught the air.

Chapter 6

Mesmerising was one way to describe Annabel Estelle. It went beyond individual features—skin, eyes, hair, beauty in every part creating a stunning whole—to a presence so captivating, people turning for surreptitious second looks found themselves openly staring, unable to take their eyes away.

It was the biggest pain in the arse for her at times.

Her early years were rife with frustration. Nobody listened. She would have people's attention, some wouldn't take their eyes off her, but still on occasions it was apparent they hadn't heard a word.

Through her formative years, believing the fault lay within, she embarked on becoming interesting. Following sports, dabbling in music and the arts, reading widely, nothing off limits, she explored. But her goal, to create intrigue and attract friends, was never realised. Peers kept their distance. If anything, the more she blossomed, the further they retreated.

Majoring in physics at university, her intelligence shone and a sense of humour, as dry as her looks were bewitching, surfaced, giving her an attribute triple whammy and an even greater exclusion zone.

Finally, as first love struck so did the understanding people weren't bored by her lack of amusing anecdotes. In fact, she was told, they were simply entranced watching her mouth, the play of her lips as she spoke, the flick of silky hair resting on high cheek bones, the fine veil snagging on the dark bank of lashes holding the green-grey chalk of her eyes—or some such bullshit. It had never occurred to Annabel her appearance was a barrier just as it never registered as leverage she could apply to advantage. The concept that her looks held such power was a bizarre reality she was loathe to accept.

Disbelief tinged anticipation when Heath, the best looking guy on campus, asked her on a date. It was a mild, pretty day and time slipped by quickly as they lunched lakeside, before walking through the grounds finding a place to sit under leafy shade. Annabel's initial nerves were squelched by the first flash of Heath's warm smile. Conversation flowed, building from steady stream to uninhibited torrent.

Annabel finished her sentence, putting a hand to her chest. 'I swear I don't normally talk this much.' Her mouth closed round a shy smile.

Heath put his fingers to her lips.

'What?' Pulling her head back she felt around her mouth with her own fingers. They'd not long finished smoothies. 'Is there something there?'

'You have no idea do you?' he shook his head.

'I have ideas. I have great ideas for anyone who bothers to listen.' It came out terser than intended. Annabel deflated, thinking she'd blown it.

'Oh no, don't be mad. I only meant you don't have any idea how beautiful you are.'

'Nice recovery.'

'Seriously,' he sat up, and took her hand. 'You are, without exception, the most beautiful woman I've ever gone out with.'

Annabel answered with an eye-roll.

'I'm not kidding. You're quite possibly the most beautiful woman I've ever seen.'

Heath's demeanour appeared earnest. More utterances of disbelief could mean he'd just keep oozing. Instead she sat passively, waiting for an opportunity to change the subject.

'You really don't know it?' Heath was insistent.

She dropped her head, feeling the sting of colour forming in her face.

Gently he reached out and raised her chin.

'I'm sorry. I don't mean to embarrass you.'

Heath hesitated. When she met his eyes he continued.

'Don't you notice everyone, and I mean everyone, stops to look at you? Walking through the park just now, that couple walking their dog both stared, openly. The guys kicking the football all stopped to check you out and at least one or two of those cyclists turned back for another look. Nearly took the whole pack down.'

Annabel looked sideways into the distance. 'People have always done that. It's just the way it is.'

'For you maybe. But not for the rest of us. I walk around in a fog of anonymity.'

'That's so not true.' Annabel gushed. 'You're the best look-ing guy at uni.' Her head dropped and her shyness returned.

'Well, like all things, there are degrees. If I'm good look-ing, you are drop-dead-gone-to-heaven'. It's not normal for people's jaws to gape when they look at someone.'

'You're making me sound like a freak.'

'Freaking good looking.' Heath was adamant. 'It's not a bad thing.'

'I guess I really haven't thought that much about it,' Anna-bel said plucking at the grass. 'I've been busy the last few years.'

'But I've heard people ask if you model. Doesn't that tell you something?'

Heath's persistence was wearing. 'People have asked that question since I was a girl. Literally all my friggin' life, people have asked that inane, bloody question.'

He raised his eyebrows. 'One hundred per cent, people mean it as a compliment, right. Why would you get upset about that?'

'Remember, you started this,' Annabel warned. 'Now you're going to listen to my side. Better get comfy.'

She looked into the distance, the core of these feelings was elusive, difficult to contextualise. She began slowly. 'When you were a kid, were you ever really good at something?'

'Um, yeah, I guess cricket was my thing for a while.'

'And how did you know you were good at it?'

'Well, I won trophies; fairest and best and for bowling.' Heath answered thoughtfully. 'Bowling was really my thing.'

'Did you get a lot of attention being a good bowler?'

'Yee-aah! People used to tell me I'd probably play for Australia one day; lots of references to the baggy green and the Ashes, trophy cabinets. Funny what you remember.'

'Hilarious,' Annabel stated flatly. 'So what happened to this cricket career?'

'I probably enjoyed daydreaming about taking a hat trick in a test match, but truthfully I knew it was never going to be a career for me. I was good for our club, district even, but it didn't go beyond that.'

Annabel turned a page of an invisible reporters pad, retrieving a pretend pencil from behind her ear. 'So what put an end to your cricket aspirations?'

Heath smiled. 'Well, I guess as I got older, I just wanted to do other things. I think some of my mates started playing basketball. They'd shoot baskets in the park after school and on weekends and competed on Saturday mornings I think.' He paused, thoughtful. 'I wanted to hang with my mates and it all clashed with cricket training. We had Saturday games too.' Heath shrugged. 'One season I think I just chose basketball. It really wasn't a big deal.'

'Did people pressure you to keep playing cricket?'

'No. My folks thought it was great that I try different things. Quite honestly I think mum was happy not to have to sit around a ground watching the grass grow waiting for me to bowl, soaking my whites.'

Annabel smiled. 'Did you never get hassled out for giving away such a great opportunity?'

'Not really. My grandfather was disappointed when I stopped. He loved cricket. We used to watch games on telly together. He took me to a couple of games too.' Heath rubbed the back of his neck. 'I guess some of the old guys from the club saw me around and told me what a shame it was I'd given it away.' Heath suddenly straightened. 'Actually, my coach was the worst. Every time I saw him, anywhere, he would shake his head and tell me I could've really been something.'

'And how did that make you feel?'

'Funny, I think I got really pissed off with him in the end. It was like, let it go. I'm doing other stuff. I think I even avoided him when I could, just so as not to have to deal with it.' Heath looked at Annabel. 'I haven't thought about any of this for ages.' He sounded rattled. 'What's your point?'

Annabel didn't back down. 'Imagine when you chose to move away from cricket if the people involved in the club and all your friends kept saying you should stick with it. You could be a test player for Australia. Imagine people telling you that cricket is your calling. Your future was in the game; good money, travel, lifestyle.'

'I reckon I would've had to tell people to move on. Not really their business, right.'

She looked at him intently. 'What about people who didn't know you? People meeting you for the first time or who just started talking to you at a train station. What if they said you would make a great cricketer? You look like a cricket player. You should consider making your future in the game.'

Heath took a while to respond, he seemed to journey back from some faraway place to re-engage the thread. 'Do people do that to you?'

'Only all the friggin' time. Strangers actually take it upon themselves to tell me 'oh, you must be a model', 'you really should be a model', 'you could be Australia's next super model', model, model, model, model, model.' Annabel punctuated every phrase with exaggerated animation, finally leaning forward out of breath. Leaning back, she motioned throwing the reporter's pad and pencil over her head.

Heath leant back on propped arms. 'So, am I understanding, catwalk walking or posing for photo-shoots are not what you want to do with your life?'

'Nice work Sherlock. I've never, ever, in my life considered it. I would rather dismember bodies than model. More than that though—it's my business.' Annabel was incredulous. 'Nobody bothers to ask what I want to do or be or where my interests lie. People look at me and think they know better, feel entitled to make these insane presumptions.'

'Coroner? You do mean dead bodies I'm hoping?'

Annabel pushed on one of Heath's arms, sending him toppling onto his side.

'You'd look great in a lab coat.'

She removed the cap from her water bottle and splashed him.

'You could be the next face of *Death Examiners Weekly*.' Laughing, he pulled in his limbs.

'You're right to be scared,' Annabel moved towards him. 'First I shall examine the chest cavity,' she placed her hands on his ribs, digging hard with her fingers.

Both laughing, Heath fell back, taking Annabel with him.

The first date going well became the first of many. Heath was good for her; finally someone to talk through all this stuff. Friends had rarely been sympathetic. Most assuming if her greatest frustration involved being asked about modelling, she was too precious for words. Not that close friends were plentiful.

Heath listened and observed and over time seemed to understand what a defining factor her looks were—the assumptions others made, literally on face value.

One day he took on her battle. They were sharing the Sunday paper over coffee in a sunny cafe when someone literally ran up to their table and blurted.

'You're so beautiful, you're like a princess. Do you have a sparkly crown?'

Heath channelled his inner thespian. Smiling kindly he gently waggled his finger at the star-struck admirer. 'No, no. This woman is not a princess, model or beauty queen, spending hours fussing with make-up or clothes all *mirror, mirror on the wall...* This lady doesn't care about those things and doesn't have time to spend on that stuff because she's really smart. She's studying physics at university and one day, she'll complete a PhD with honours and probably win a Nobel Prize...'

Annabel's hand on his arm acted as a brake. She bowed her head to whisper.

'I think women are too busy doing fabulous things to mess around with tiaras, and besides, imagine all the magpies that would swoop in for a look.' Annabel ducked her head. 'They would give me a big fright,' she smiled after the girl who ran to share the news with her mum.

'Really Heath,' she whispered. 'Spinning my story like a fairy tale—and telling fibs. I don't *not care* about the way I look, it's just not a priority. Funny, but I think four-year-old girls get women can be whatever they want to be. It's as we get older we tend to over-think it.'

As months passed, Heath's discomfort over the attention she attracted somehow allowed her to take a step sideways, releasing some of her own. It was a liberating catharsis with a sad side-effect. As Annabel became lighter, darkness descended into Heath. Tension mounted, cooling the warmth of his humour. Possessiveness brought a hard edge to his usually relaxed nature. Even his generous empathy seemed to retract.

One evening, walking through the city after a movie, they spied a group of Heath's mates in the courtyard of a pub.

Heath dropped his head and quickened his step. Annabel, registering his intention mirrored his actions, but the invisibility gene didn't exist in her DNA. Heath's mates, already half-cut, started calling out her name. Reluctantly Heath steered them over, dropping her hand on the way. Annabel's presence fuelled testosterone levels and the group became louder, jostling for her attention. Discomfort growing, Annabel turned to Heath for reassurance to find him standing some distance away, hands in pockets, jaw set.

It came to a head on their six-month anniversary. Heath had asked her to dinner and Annabel was beyond excited. The restaurant he'd chosen had a fantastic reputation. She'd found a stunning dress in the op shop and fossicked in the wardrobe for her rarely worn heels, putting more effort than usual into her appearance, making up her eyes and lips to maximum effect.

She was brushing her hair when the doorbell rang. In the mirror her face came to life, eyes open wide, smile dazzling. Clapping her hands she flicked off the light and ran for the door.

Heath, looking hot in the doorway, provoked her to twirl spontaneously.

He stood expressionless before his mouth moved in a twisted smile. 'Great. I can already see how this will go. The whole restaurant will come to a grinding halt. The sommelier will forget what wine I ordered. The waiter will ask you three times if you'd like pepper and forget to bring my food. When I return from the Men's, the chef will be sitting in my chair running you through dessert options personally.'

Annabel deflated, biting her lip to stave off the tears.

Heath's head dropped. Raising it slowly, he found her eyes. 'Sorry Annabel. You look amazing.'

It was the final act in a disturbing paradigm that moved her, with more than a little sadness, to leave him to mend.

Sound evaporated instantly as the chairman of judges walked through the door. Unfazed, Annabel Estelle, continued into the room smiling warmly, engaging as many pairs of eyes as she could. Some stewards looked positively rattled in the presence of her trademark burgundy lab coat. She empathised, knowing they'd get over it. It was always like this on the first day of judging. The steward's bravado would return along with their banter as they poured hundreds of wines and polished hundreds of glasses over the coming days.

Glen, the chief steward, was watching over his charges intently. Finally, he met her gaze and she flashed an almost indiscernible wink.

Annabel was over the moon to see him. They'd worked together at the previous two Fine Young Cabernet shows and he'd preformed impressively both times. On the first occasion he'd been a rookie, but the chief steward had proved utterly incompetent. Glen, still getting his head around proceedings, managed to salvage what could have been a disastrous event. The following year he was chief steward, excelling in the role.

Many protocols existed around wine shows to ensure accuracy of results and impartiality of judging. Importantly, each was observed to ensure: producers had entered their wine in the correct class; judges were never given anything identifying a producer's wine; and accurate recording and summation of results.

Lab coats signifying roles were worn by all attendants. Judges wearing white coats were permitted on the tasting floor and in the smaller laboratory to the side where they met to retaste and discuss medal winners of the classes. Stewards wore royal blue. They were the only ones permitted behind the heavy panel screening the cool room where the show wines were stored.

The only exceptions were the show's director and chief administrator, effectively representing the owners of the show. Often they didn't wear lab coats at all, having free rein of the venue.

Annabel would happily wear white, but her burgundy lab coat had become an unwritten tenet in her wine show contracts. When accepting a judging role, the proviso was her signature lab coat was also expected to attend. Annabel had forgotten it once and the resulting disappointment was enough to ensure it was now the first item packed, and always into her carry-on should her luggage be lost.

It was the closing session on the last day of judging. The stewards had completed the re-pours on the final selection of wines. Glen called the judging panel to assemble one last time to decide the trophy winner.

Five sets of four glasses stood lined up against masking tape guides marked A through D. In the brightly lit room, three judges assessed the wines once more, and this time Annabel tasted with them. The associate judges shared a set of glasses, their role was to taste and observe and reflect on their sensory observations alongside those of the experienced judges.

These wines were gold medal recipients of their classes. The judge's task now, to decide which would receive the trophy for wine of the show.

Four glasses of hope. The juice of decisions made one after another. The wine would continue to evolve beyond today's judgement until ingestion molecularly restructured its form from liquid to memory; the spark of a synapse evoking its essence, like the snap of a screwcap in its previous life.

Memory held the waft of violets, a luxurious velvet palate or the shock of intense fruit flavour. Often memories extended beyond the contents of the bottle. To friends who savoured it and what happened when, after consuming another bottle or switching to beers, they jumped on a skateboard and took off down a hill into their young adult bliss of no regard for consequence. The friends who sipped it, sharing thoughts and dreams, progressing to lovers as the bottle emptied. Plans made, business secured, delicious food shared.

Annabel owned the room. She swirled each glass checking colour up against the light and down against the white surface of the bench. Intensely focused, she worked methodically through the line-up, aware of every move the judges made. Glen was still on duty, but the other stewards leant passively against the walls of the room enjoying the spectacle, the climax of their wash, polish, pour week.

Annabel assessed the wines with unique flair, pausing after each to subtly bow her head. People likened her technique to a mini-meditation. It was the quiet reflection that allowed her to mentally record and file samples without the need for notes.

Swirling and spitting stopped. Every pair of eyes trained on the conductor in the wine coloured robe.

'I'd like each of you to give me your two most successful wines.' With a nod, Annabel deferred to the chief judge.

'A and D.' The flick of his head and confident tone suggesting the outcome was obvious.

Annabel eyed the next judge.

She smiled. 'Definitely A and D.'

Across the table the third judge took his cue. He leant back, raising both hands.

'A and D. No question.'

Annabel gave a soft laugh. 'Well, we're making easy work of this. Our bookends are shining.' She hesitated, then explained. 'The highest pointed golds of their class, these four wines are superb examples of Cabernet. Pulling out these wines to assess them again, standout against standout, is the only conceivable way of judging them further. Associates, how did you rate them?'

They answered in unison. 'A and D.'

Murmurs and gestures affirmed the judge's confidence in proceedings.

'Please push wines B and C back. They are no longer in contention.'

On her cue, around the bench the judges pushed samples B and C back, leaving A and D in the front line.

'Let's look at A and D again. One of these wines will be taking home the trophy.'

Around the bench, the weight of responsibility was tangible. The judges swirled, observed, sniffed, sipped, spat. Deeply focused, a range of habitual gestures surfaced; raised eyebrows, small head bobs, quirky, monosyllabic sounds as they assessed.

Quiet, stillness descended once more.

'I think I'm detecting a house style in these two,' Annabel looked around the judges before noticing Glen, bristling with alarm. In his position as chief steward, he was not at liberty to confirm or deny her observation. She flashed her eyes, quickly adding. 'And that's not a question Glen.'

His shoulders relaxed.

One of the judges looked quizzical. 'When you say house style, do you mean in the fruit or the winemaking?'

'Fantastic question,' Annabel shot back. 'The most striking quality in each of these samples is finesse. They both have great concentration with extraordinary balance which is what makes them the two wines that have risen to the top of the class. You all know that concentration and balance—well, it's difficult to achieve both—yet these two samples have it in spades. To my mind it's in the winemaking that I'm seeing similarity and that's the house style I'm referring to. The characters of the Cabernet itself are showing quite different qualities to me here.'

The judges nodded perceptible agreement. Annabel continued.

'Wine A has lashings of berry fruit.' Picking up the sample she swirled and sniffed. 'There's blackberry, blackcurrant and a little note of something my nose is chasing but can't quite catch. Mulberry, I think.'

The judges laughed.

'Thank you,' the judge on her left smiled. 'I couldn't grasp that light, fruity note long enough to identify it. I kept thinking raspberry but you're right, mulberry.'

'Agreed,' the chief judge weighed in. 'We have a mulberry tree in the backyard but the bloody parrots think it's theirs. Don't think I've tasted a ripe one in years.'

They all laughed again.

Annabel drew their attention back. 'Wine D though, is remarkably pure in its expression of fruit. In another wine it could look linear or simple, but here it looks incredible. Is incredible.' She paused, looking around the faces in the room. 'If you took the ripest, most juicy, delicious blackcurrants and squashed them, the juice would look like this.' She smiled. 'Almost. Of course here there is length and complexity.'

'I'm also getting a cooling character in this wine,' the chief judge added. 'It's not coming from the alcohol and it's not minty or green. It's telling me that this wine is going to age beautifully.'

There was a murmur of agreement.

'I've never seen blackcurrant so intense in a wine before. It's gobsmackingly good here. You know blackcurrant is one of the major fruit characters we get in our Cabernets, but I've never seen anything quite like this. Sometimes those ripe, singular characters can be cloying on the middle palate but, maybe because it's Cabernet, this one fleshes the middle palate with freshness and vibrancy. It's generous yet restrained at the same time.'

'This wine has X factor. I can see the oak influence, detect it in the structure and complexity, and yet there's not one character I can pull from the flavour profile that says oak. Even on the nose I'm struggling to pinpoint it.'

Annabel nodded towards the associates.

'It's stunning,' stated one.

'I'm getting in quick to buy a case for my cellar,' added the other.

Speculation began around its cellaring potential while marvelling they'd happily drink a bottle with dinner that night. This sentiment expressed through dark tannin-stained teeth and lips from long days of tasting was high praise indeed. Usually, at this stage of proceedings, most judges craved sparkling water or beer, red wine the last thing on their wish-lists.

'Okay, let's make it official. Round the bench with your most successful wine please?'

One judge after the other declared 'D' without exception. 'Associates?'

'D,' they chorused.

'Unanimous!' Annabel declared, turning to Glen. 'D is our trophy winner.' A slow smile spread across her face. 'If my palate's on the money, I have a feeling a friend of mine is going to be very pleased.'

Glen smiled, this time with a conspiratorial glint. With judging finalised, protocols relaxed.

Excitement buzzed in the room. Annabel raised her hand for attention.

'I know you'll not all be attending the awards dinner tomorrow evening for the official thank yous, so I'm taking this opportunity to thank the stewarding team now.' Annabel looked at the faces around the room. 'You wear blue lab coats, but deserve black ninja robes for your stealth and efficiency. Glen, under your leadership, this seamlessly run show is a favourite of those I have the pleasure to judge.' The judges clapped spontaneously. Annabel looked directly at Glen. 'I know you're coming to the dinner, but I truly hope you'll be on board again next year.'

Glen smiled, raising his eyebrows as he moved to clear glasses from the judging table. Through his dark, handsome features, she detected the hint of a blush.

With formalities over, Annabel retired to freshen up for the dinner to mark the end of judging. Reflecting on the last couple of days, logistics had run smoothly, allowing the judges to focus totally on the wines, which from year to year were more polished and exciting.

She checked her phone and smiled, noting a missed call from Freddie. A quick shower and she'd call back.

Stepping under the water, she wished she could call Lewis

too, knowing it would be completely unethical. She'd have to put her excitement on hold until the awards dinner the following night.

Lewis and Annabel went way back. She had been a science academic; a little lost and bored when meeting Lewis inspired her transition into the world of wine. It was a fond memory. She'd been dragged by a friend to a winemaker's dinner where she witnessed him speak with intelligence and passion. After dinner, Lewis visited every table personally. At least that was the plan, until he met Annabel—the plan combusted in the spark between them. Lewis and Annabel spoke together for nearly an hour, to the annoyance of some of the other guests. Event organisers eventually intervened ushering him on, but not before a frantic exchange of numbers. The following morning they met for coffee. Within two years Annabel completed a post-grad in oenology, working in the industry on some research projects. Currently, she lectured and judged on the international circuit, one foot loosely earthed in Sydney.

Annabel and Lewis's friendship deepened at every step, never once spilling into romance, to become a relationship neither recognised a name for; not lovers or friends, an intimacy beyond one yet lacking the physicality of the other. Trust and respectful restraint set it apart from anything familiar. In the depth of their bond they could be siblings, but while the relationship was platonic, they perceived attraction in the other's eyes, around drying lips and acute awareness of their bodies in close proximity. It defied the laws of nature, humble gravity grounding them amid the superior force of magnetic pull and they cherished its unconventionality.

An insatiable theorist, Annabel found Lewis refreshingly forthcoming in conversation. It was a rare quality in a male, one she presumed only possible with great intelligence and self-awareness. She savoured him as a precious resource, taking pleasure in exploring the complex nuances of his mind.

Annabel imagined she challenged Lewis beyond the usual parameters established with a woman who wasn't his wife, understanding she often unsettled him pondering lateral ideas of love and life he may contemplate but rarely discuss.

Minds broad, together they stretched integral platforms exploring ideals and philosophies. They spoke of wine, politics and religion, current food trends, ageing parents and growing children.

One night, the conversation led in another direction entirely. Previously he'd kept one leg firmly earthed during their exchanges, but this evening, she kicked at his shin, sending him spinning wildly into orbit.

It was the final night of the Wine Industry Technical Conference hosted in Melbourne. Usually well-attended, the convention provided opportunity to catch up professionally and socially with industry peers from across Australia. The closing event was reasonably subdued, many participants nursing hangovers from dinner the previous evening, which ended in the early hours at a local club.

Lewis and Annabel crossed paths, circling the room, deciding a quiet martini would be a more enjoyable finale. One or two hopefuls always trailed Annabel's wake, so she was relieved when Lewis took her arm and steered her determinedly to the door.

Lee's Wine Bar had them guessing.

'So is the owner named Lee or are they talking about wine lees?' Annabel queried.

'Can't tell you anything about this place, except it's bloody dark.'

The bar occupied a subterranean space in the CBD, moodily lit and decorated in a warehouse theme. Windows had been painted along the entire length of one wall depicting the night sky complete with neighbouring high-rise buildings to mind-boggling effect. They had just descended a long flight of stairs to feel they were alighting on the tenth floor.

'Seriously cool,' remarked Annabel absorbing the surroundings.

Lewis grimaced. 'You know I don't like heights.'

They were shown to a table in a corner of the room where they relaxed, taking in the whole effect.

Annabel perused the menu. 'A martini could keep me awake. Glass of red?'

'Your beauty is again overshadowed by your uncanny ability to be sensible.'

'Ha. You'll thank me tomorrow.'

'No doubt. Do you have a red in mind?'

'Cabernet. Something fine and delicious.'

'Margaret River,' Lewis said with a hint of a smile.

'Naturally,' she passed the list. 'You can decide which.'

His eye snagged on a newer producer releasing some smart wines. He chose a single vineyard Cabernet which he knew contained a small percentage of Malbec.

When the wine arrived they did the obligatory assessment, listening attentively to the other's observations. Annabel wasn't familiar with the producer and Lewis captivated her attention with insight into their production methods.

'It's good,' they agreed.

Annabel laughed softly. 'You know it's actually better than good. If I came across this wine in a show anywhere in the world I'd point it a gold.'

'Do you think we take it for granted what we're producing in Margs?'

'Abso-bloody-lutley!' Annabel exclaimed. 'We just expect that a Cabernet from Margaret River is going to deliver and consistently it does. You're blessed you know, making wines there.'

'Sshhh!' Lewis raised his finger to his lips. 'We know. We just don't want the rest of the world to catch on.'

'Well you know that can't last. It's only a matter of time until your secrets out.' There was the briefest pause before she added. 'Who are we kidding? The game's already up. You've won too many international trophies to think you're still undiscovered. Time to man-up and get used to the idea. Margaret River is up there with the best Cabernets of the world,' Annabel raised her voice and her glass with the declaration.

Lewis clinked his glass with hers. 'So, favourite thing about the tech conference?'

She clapped, eyes wide with excitement. 'Cross-modal correspondence.'

'I shoulda guessed,' Lewis nodded. 'That's about the relationship between taste and sound?'

Annabel's head bobbed. 'Exploration of the interaction between our taste and sound receptors. They've started mapping neurological pathways, measuring and recording correlations.

'God! We've been relying on the interaction between our senses since we swapped our gills for cave space. The human race wouldn't exist without it. Are they really trying to make it sound like something new?'

'No! Of course not. But the truth is, our reliance on aspects of our senses has become less acute over time as we rely on them less for survival.'

Lewis shrugged. 'I'm less enamoured with the concept.'

'Seriously?' Annabel tilted her head and rolled her eyes. 'I wasn't getting that.' Suddenly she leant forward cradling her glass. 'The science behind it is amazing. Every minute discovery in the field of brain function is advancement for our species.'

'Okay.' Lewis laughed, raising his hands. 'I agree. But that's not why I brought you here, to agree on something. I'm ready for your next curve ball.'

Annabel shuffled on her stool. 'Okay, here's one for you. Something I've been meaning to raise for a while.'

He waited, watching her intently.

Annabel held his eyes. 'I love you.'

Lewis couldn't hold her gaze. 'Christ Annabel. I ask for a curve ball and you slam me with a bouncer.' He ran his fingers through his hair. 'I'm married to Mae. I love Mae.'

'What a strange reply to my disclosure,' she answered casually. 'And yet I know you're not a stupid man. Why are you telling me these things? Was I not at your wedding, witnessing your nuptials? Bloody glad to hear you love Mae,' she sniffed.

'So what do you mean? You love me as a friend?'

'I'm not going to quantify it. I love you. It's a fairly simple notion I would have thought. When did people get so afraid of that little word?'

'Maybe small in letter count but conceptually it's one of the big guns.'

'Wanna hear my theory?'

Lewis wiped a hand across his brow. 'Maybe.'

Annabel laughed. 'I'd like to journey back in time, visit the scene of the first 'I love you' ever uttered.'

'We could Google it.'

She smacked his arm. 'Seriously. I doubt it involved sex or marriage, any commitment sought or offered. I'm sure there was a time when the phrase simply translated feeling into language.'

'Love thy neighbour,' Lewis offered.

'Exactly! The purity in that. It didn't mean jump the fence for a bonk or suggest the sentiment should come echoing back. When did we start attaching all this other stuff, complicating something so simple?'

Lewis shook his head. 'You're complicated.'

'No, I'm complex. So are you, along with every other human. It's our birthright.' She carried on. 'You know we talk about it abstractly. I love him, he's awesome. We sign birthday cards with lots of love or all our love, my love, whatever. Why do we falter saying it to someone's face?'

'Maybe it's fear. Once said, you can't retract it.'

'They're words Lewis.'

'Possibly the three most meaningful in life. You don't just want to bandy them around haphazardly.'

'No. But you don't want to be mean with them either.' Annabel drifted.

Lewis watched her intently.

Her eyes flashed. 'I'm fine. You know I just love teasing out these threads.'

Lewis smiled, taking her hand. 'God I know it.'

They fell quiet, sipping at their wine.

'Any reason love's topical right now?'

Annabel moaned. 'Not so much an open book as audio podcast. You don't have to turn a page to know my story.'

He smiled, leaning back. 'It's only fair. You already know mine.'

Annabel finished her wine. 'Maybe. But it's early days, baby-steps. I'm not saying anything to jinx it.'

Lewis nodded. 'We both have early flights. Let's call it a night?'

As they rose from their stools, Annabel leaned into him and spoke quietly. 'It's like nothing I've ever experienced Lewis. You can have a name. Freddie.'

'Interesting,' Lewis mused. 'Pet name. Not Frederick, Fred. Rick, Ricky,' he teased.

Apprehension gripped, compressing her ribs. 'Freddie. Short for Frederique.'

Annabel's eyes fixed on his face. He could never hide or disguise himself under her scrutiny. His eyes told her everything. In this moment they were dark, liquid pools of warmth, softening the tightness in her chest.

'We'll look forward to meeting her.'

Chapter 7

D ifferent!
   Looking in the mirror of the brightly lit Perth hotel
bathroom, Maddie felt okay about what looked back. Better
than okay. Her hair looked sleek, bordering sophisticated,
and she loved the dress.

On receiving the invitation to the awards night, Maddie's first
thoughts were wine and food related. However, initial pre-
occupation with all things gastronomic eventually turned to
what she should wear. Knowing there was nothing appropri-
ate in her largely work/exercise/casual wardrobe she made a
mental note to pick up a fashion magazine on the way home
and do a little research.

   A couple of magazines, glasses of wine and hours of

internet trolling later, she seriously contemplated cutting up some uniforms and piecing them together with cable ties, making a statement. Not really formal though. Tough cotton work-wear and plastic cable ties just didn't cut it against credit cards and safety pins. *Bloody Liz! Setting the bar so high.* Head awash with Picasso snapshots of runway couture, surely never worn anywhere but the runway, she sensed trouble before finally conceding her level of expertise in this area—nada.

In hindsight she should have galvanised and leapt on reading the invitation. Under dress-code, the fine print clearly stated: 'Maddie, you better get shopping.' But no, here she was a couple of days from the big event, desperation escalating panic-ward—outfitless.

Bussell Highway, the heart of Margaret River's shopping precinct was not Avenue des Champs Elysées, or even Chapel Street, however there were a couple of trendy boutiques surely worth a try.

She stepped into a neat little 'L' shaped boutique, immediately aware of the immaculate assistant looking her over with that sealing-your-fate-on-sight kind of intensity. Maddie turned her back to close the door and made her own assessment.

Straight from the winery on her lunch break; steel caps, woolly socks (striped, not matching), unflattering shorts, work shirt, cap, hair in a messy ponytail. In her favour, mostly clean apart from some crumbs clinging to her shirt, remnants from stuffing lunch down on the drive into town. This wasn't going to be good.

Breathe Maddie, breathe.

'Hi.' A cultured voice sang out.

Maddie cringed and turned to face her fate.

'Welcome.' The assistant studied the logo on Maddie's shirt. 'I'm a huge fan of Kite's wines.'

Maddie swiped blindly at the crumbs. The assistant was smiling, not telling her to step away from the merchandise. Unhinged, she blurted: 'My friend tells me I may know a lot about grapes, but I wouldn't know a pashmina from a poncho if it tried to strangle me. Does that mean anything to you?'

The assistant's brow lifted and she sucked in her top lip. 'Well, my name's Angie and accessories know better than to mess with me.' Raising a hand to her chest she looked Maddie up and down.

Maddie froze, holding her breath.

Finally, Angie gave a little nod and sashayed toward the racks blithely stating. 'Emerald, your eyes are screaming for it.'

Maddie exhaled, knowing she was in good hands.

Now, with her hair and makeup done, she was bewitched as the mirror confirmed the grape-leaf green number was a good fit. It was a layered affair with a fitted satin slip sitting at a still, but only just, respectable height above her knees, revealing a good flash of cleavage at the other end. Respectfully tit-elating. She bent forward heightening the effect, making a mental note to be more adventurous, putting her *breast* foot forward more often.

'Maddie, you should be in stand-up,' she quipped, raising eyebrows at her reflection.

Unable to remember the name of the outer shell that floated on top of the slip, sheath maybe, or even the name of the material, being a sensory person, she knew it was the most ethereal fabric that had ever graced her body; alluring and overwhelmingly feminine.

Excitement building, she fished from her bag the box containing her new heels and bag. 'Sorry Angie—clutch.' She smiled, running her hand over the textural purse. They were matching black suede with satin detail; the heels two storeys higher than anything previously attempted.

She checked the time on her phone. The dinner was being hosted by a restaurant within the hotel complex, a five-minute walk from her room. Maddie was in the mood.

One last fiddle with her hair, a smear of gloss over her lipstick and, her big indulgence of the evening, a fine mist of perfume. Maddie loved fragrance, rarely getting to wear it as most wine-related events were fragrance-free zones. Perfumes, oils, even heavily fragranced deodorants had the ability to overpower the subtle scents of wine. However, tonight was a social occasion, an opportunity to smell lovelier than something in a glass. The perfume was intoxicating. One light spray left her feeling edgy and mysterious, a regular female Bourne. Stepping her feet apart she aimed the atomiser at her reflection in the mirror. *Without assassin tendencies.*

She dropped her mobile and gloss into her clutch and left the room.

A couple were making their way down the corridor towards her. As she stowed the room card in her clutch, she could feel the woman studying her feet. Maddie was pleased—shoe envy.

'Sorry honey, but they're just not working with that gorgeous dress,' the woman said with a smile over her shoulder as they swept past.

Maddie, momentarily off-balance, looked down. 'Damn!'

She fished out the room card. She was still wearing the hotel's complimentary scuffs.

Shoes. Clutch. Head. She performed a mental check walking as quickly as she dared, adjusting to the new stratosphere. Feeling a little faint, she wondered if a couple of inches would really make a difference to the oxygen levels before remembering she hadn't eaten since breakfast. Her mouth watered at the thought of bubbles and canapés.

The dated hotel corridor with uninspiring framed prints and woeful floor covering was a stagnant tunnel to wonderland. Maddie's stiletto touching the luxurious carpet-pile of the restaurant was the trigger that sent her reeling through the vortex. She absorbed it all in a breath, happily removing a glass of sparkling from a tray appearing before her.

The venue was sophisticated, cream and dark earth tones, lush textures and elegant lines. Soft lighting from oversized black pendant shades hanging from the rouched ceiling which absorbed the higher pitched noises in the room, leaving a convivial hum of conversation interspersed with tinkling glasses and a moody, pulsing beat.

Standard lamps illuminated shadowy corners fitted with brushed suede couches, fur and hide cushions and throws. Running the length of one wall, the dark panelled bar. Golden light reflected from the array of bottles standing and stacked, and the slick beer taps. Tables glinted softly—polished glasses, metallic cutlery, gleaming china, crisp linen—and in the smoky, dark-glass panels that lined the length of the other side of the room, the lights of the city sparkled across the wide, inky Swan River.

Adjusting to the darkened room, she glanced around

for familiar faces. Lewis and Mae were standing a few groups away.

Maddie was on her way towards them, when someone touched her arm.

'Carmel,' they exchanged a two-cheeked kiss. 'I didn't know you were coming.' Maddie ducked her head. 'Who are you here with?'

'Brendan actually,' Carmel tried for smug, but was too obviously happy to pull it off.

Maddie, eyes wide, shook her head. 'And? So?'

'I'm his date,' she broke into a broad-mouthed cartoon grin.

They threw their spare arms around each other in a loose hug, balancing champagne flutes and clutches.

'That's great news.'

'I still can't really believe it,' Carmel whispered.

'Quick. Where are you staying? Here? Together?'

Carmel nodded, eyebrows rising, smile growing with every response.

'Oh my God,' Maddie cried. 'Is tonight the night?'

Carmel smacked her arm. 'Sshhh!' she laughed. 'Not everyone in the room knows yet.'

'Sorry,' Maddie laughed, lowering her voice to a whisper. 'I mean, sorry.'

'And, no, is the answer to your question,' Carmel said, finally managing smug.

Maddie's eyebrows shot up.

Carmel took a slow, measured sip of bubbles. 'I have to tell you,' she said leaning in.

'Yes. Tell away.'

'This Tassie sparkling is really rather good.'

Maddie looked injured. 'You're just teasing me now.'

'Yes,' Carmel conceded. 'Yes, I am.'

'Well, we don't have time for that. Details, quick.'

Carmel laughed. 'Well, I was at work when Brendan wandered in, looking lost.'

Carmel worked as a nurse at the Margaret River Hospital.

'He walked up to the doors twice, returning to his car each time. The first time I thought he must have forgotten something. I had no idea what was going on at the second attempt. Anyway, I was too busy trying to phoof my hair and slap on some lip balm.'

'When he eventually managed to cross the threshold, he looked a little dazed. My immediate thought was he may have been in an accident and was concussed,' Carmel giggled. 'I met him in the foyer, steered him over to a chair and asked what I could do for him. Just when I'm thinking he's about to black out and I should call for a doctor, he blurts that he'd come in looking for me and asked if I would consider accompanying him to the Fine Young Cabernet Awards dinner in Perth.'

Carmel shook her head. 'It was such a shock, I had to sit down. Finally, I managed to answer, I'd love to. So there we were, sitting stunned like two idiots in the emergency waiting room.'

'Then Brendan said—so dryly, 'I could use a little oxygen'.

'It was so absurd, I started to giggle, then Brendan giggled and we both just lost it. One of us snorted and that was the end, we were gone.'

'It was one of those surreal, and I think rare, moments in life when your expectations are spectacularly exceeded.' Carmel looked reflective.

'Oh, that's so cool. Bethany is going to love that story.'

'Anyway, we met at Morries for drinks two nights later.

I walked in to find him sitting at a table by the bar, martini waiting.' Carmel looked intensely at Maddie. 'When a reasonable amount of time has passed, we will marry and live happily ever after.'

Maddie slapped her arm. 'I'm so happy for you.'

'God, I'm happy for me too.'

They chinked flutes.

'I always thought the pizza on the door was an invitation to good things.'

Carmel nodded. 'I've had lovely people in my home, now I've got a lovely man in my life.' She winked. 'Must have been a Supreme with the lot.'

They did the one-arm hug again, both tearing up.

'Can't be crying,' Maddie announced. 'Too much time and effort applying make-up to have it all water affected. Where is Brendan anyway?'

The room was filling quickly. They looked around and spotted Brendan talking with Lewis and Mae.

As they neared the group, Maddie's gaze snagged on Roley's back as he turned to take a beer from a passing waiter.

Lewis greeted her with a kiss on the cheek. 'Hi Maddie. You look lovely. Maybe our uniforms should be green.'

Mae leaned in for a hug. 'You look gorgeous Maddie. Your dress is divine.'

'Thanks Lewis. Thanks Mae. You both look fabulous too. Everyone looks so chic out of uniform.' She was about to ask what they had done with the kids for the night, when Roley turned back to the group.

Their eyes locked.

Maddie's brain emptied. The sight of Roley looking damn fine caused her to inhale, the exhalation temporarily on hold. She'd always thought him good looking, but man, what a well-fitting suit could do for a body. She felt she should do something—breathe perhaps—but Roley was looking at her with, God knows what in his eyes.

'Hi Maddie,' he leaned close to kiss her cheek.

The sudden movement sparked her clumsy exhale, close to his ear. Roley pulled away, looking at her questioningly.

'Sorry. Hi Roley,' Maddie coughed, wishing herself invisible.

'I was going to tell you how beautiful you looked, but then you blew in my ear and I completely lost my train of thought.'

Maddie felt herself blush. 'I…I…' she stammered before realising Roley was maximising his amusement at her expense. She straightened. 'I was choking. Bubbles went down the wrong way. Where's Vieve?'

Roley's features hardened. 'Not coming tonight.'

'Oh, everything okay?'

'Vieve's fine. She never was coming tonight Maddie.'

His tone signified the conversation was done. Curiosity burning, she moved on.

'Suit suits you,' she said casually with a smile.

'Feels like a wetsuit with lapels,' Roley shrugged his body inside the suit trying to make some room.

'Well, lucky it's not your work uniform, terribly distracting for the vineyard girls.'

'Yeah, I can see them laughing hysterically as the bird-netting snags on all these buttons, dragging me screaming into the NetWizz.' He tilted his head and looked over his beer. 'Actually, it's Westy I worry about.'

'Really?' Maddie asked wide-eyed enjoying their banter. 'How so?'

'Well,' Roley paused. 'He's often lurking around in the

morning when I get changed for work. I'll just have a towel around me and suddenly he'll be there just metres away.'

Maddie laughed. 'What, you mean he's there in the car-park too after a surf? Getting changed too—along with ten other blokes? Oh Roley, lookout. Sounds like trouble.'

'It's always the quiet ones,' he nodded solemnly. 'You, on the other hand, should totally never look like that at work.'

Maddie raised her eyebrows.

'I don't have enough excuses to visit the winery and those heels could get trapped in the catwalk mesh. You could be stranded for days before being rescued.'

Roley said the first bit quickly, in a barely audible whisper, but she heard and savoured every word.

'Here, let me show you something amazing.' Maddie leaned close, putting her hand on his upper-arm for balance as she slipped one foot easily from her shoe. 'Secret ejector switch, I wouldn't be stuck for long.'

Roley laughed. 'Mmm that's why women's shoes are so expensive. All the cutting edge design features.'

Maddie loved the flirty exchange. There was no need to keep her hand on Roley's arm, but she was desperately reluctant to remove it. Motivation arrived as a waitperson offering a tray of tiny dill blinis topped with smoked salmon appeared before them. The connection temporarily broken, they turned back to the group.

Carmel and Brendan were on her left. Brendan worked at the agricultural supply shop in the little town of Cowaramup. He had helped a couple of times when she ordered winery supplies. Maddie didn't know him well but he seemed quiet, completely affable and—Maddie couldn't help herself—a cracking match for Carmel.

They chatted easily as plates of delicious nibbles were

presented. Carmel and Maddie exchanged sparkling flutes for glasses of Pinot Gris from the Great Southern.

'Strong vintage for Margaret River Cabernets,' Brendan stated evenly. 'You must be in with a chance?'

Lewis was understated. 'We've got a couple in the running, one from Jupiter Rising.' He gave a sideways nod. 'Either could possibly pick up the trophy, but I haven't seen what's happening around the rest of the state.'

Roley nodded. 'It was a solid vintage for lots of regions.'

Brendan smiled. 'Modesty aside, I'm backing Margaret River. I'd love to see it go to Kite.'

'Thanks mate. A trophy's always welcome.'

Within the room the slightly stiff, formal atmosphere of first appearances morphed into an energised hum. Wine writers casually circulated through the crowd. Well known to most, they were usually interesting or quirky individuals, ready to fire off amusing anecdotes.

Competition was open to all West Australian producers and the state's wine regions were well represented. Lewis and Mae, knowing many of the guests, were busy cheek-kissing, hand-shaking, hugging and waving. Their group splintered as they migrated in different directions greeting familiar faces. Maddie was pleasantly surprised how many people she recognised considering her short length of time in the state.

Time slipped quickly by, wait-staff began moving through the crowd armed with empty trays inviting guests to return their glasses and move to the seated area for the next part of the evening.

The crowd, enjoying the opportunity to mingle and catch-up, were slow to make their way to the dining area. People loitered in front of the seating chart, locating their tables, matching names that eluded them to the faces they had seen, or just having a good sticky before moving on.

Maddie was waiting to check the plan when Roley moved up close behind. He placed his hand low on her back and began steering her slowly through the crowd. His body leant into hers as he spoke.

'We're sitting with Lewis and Mae on a table by the windows.'

They stopped abruptly in the glut of bodies filing through to take their seats.

'You smell good.'

He was literally at her back. Maddie felt herself against him, realising for the first time the sensitivity of her spine. A moment longer she would have melted into him.

Roley's hand stayed on the small of her back until they reached their table. Removing it, he pulled out her chair.

A couple Maddie didn't know arrived at the table at the same time. They introduced themselves, shaking hands before taking their seats. As she sat, Maddie was aware the couple mistook her and Roley for a couple too, but neither acted to correct the impression. Josh wasn't an issue. That chapter was dusted and done. But Maddie couldn't help wonder what was going on in Roley's mind. What was happening with Vieve? She focused on the strange sensation affecting her lower back; indelible energy pulsed an imprint of his hand.

Lewis and Mae arrived in a flurry taking their seats on Maddie's left. Mae looked flushed and happy. She leant across Lewis, putting a hand to her chest. 'I love these events. It's the only time I get to play with adults.'

Lewis kissed her cheek. 'My poor house-bound wife. You look far too sexy without your apron for me to let you out.'

Mae's eyes opened wide in mock indignation. She slapped

his arm before settling back on her seat, greeting others at the table.

The dining arrangement was tables of ten. Lewis, Mae, Roley and Maddie were the only four from Beneath The Kite. The couple they had already met owned a small family winery out of Denmark. The remaining four were two couples from neighbouring properties in the Ferguson Valley.

Introductions over, Lewis turned to Maddie. 'Do you know many people?'

'I recognise more faces than I anticipated, really only the Margaret River producers though. You must know practically everybody in the room?'

Lewis laughed. 'Not even close. The industry has grown quickly and I'm not a big player. I recognise more than I personally know. I think a lot of the people, especially from the big companies, are marketing and admin staff.'

Their exchange was interrupted, Maddie suddenly distracted by a glamorous woman moving through the room. Half listening to Lewis, she fixated on the vision that seemed headed their way.

The woman wore an ankle length, gold slip dress with a choker collar, revealing exquisite shoulders. Silky long hair pulled up in a high ponytail. Shiny, shimmery, breath-taking elegance, holding half the room captivated.

Lewis must have sensed he had lost her attention. He made to turn, to locate the source of distraction, when the woman signalled, putting a finger to her lips.

'Can you pass the water please?' Maddie blurted.

It gave the woman enough time to step between Lewis and Mae undetected. She put her hands to their shoulders.

Synchronised they turned and exclaimed in unison. 'Annabel.'

'Hello, you two.'

Lewis and Mae jumped to their feet and hugged her with gusto.

Maddie sat dumbstruck, unable to avert her eyes from the spectacle. Annabel was even more beautiful close up.

She must have felt her staring. As the excitement of the reunion relaxed, Annabel turned to Maddie.

'Hi. I'm Annabel.'

'Sorry,' Lewis jumped in. 'Annabel this is Madison, vintage winemaker at Kite. And you know Roley?'

Roley stood taking Annabel's hand as she leaned across to kiss his cheek. 'Good to see you Roley.'

Maddie smarted as Roley basked in Annabel's glowing attention.

'Thanks for distracting him,' she addressed Maddie. 'It's never easy to sneak up on these two. They seem to have a sixth sense when I'm around.'

'It's because we love you,' Mae beamed.

Lewis took Mae's hand. He began introducing Annabel to the rest of the table when the master of ceremonies commandeered the microphone, asking the room to be seated.

Annabel smiled, nodding to the people opposite before leaning forward. 'I'll catch up with you two later.'

Even the compère seemed dumb for words until Annabel was seated. Taking a sip of water, he cleared his throat and began.

Maddie took a long drink of water too. So, that was the legendary Annabel Estelle. Maddie had always thought the hype surrounding her must comprise a degree of urban myth. She was floored, the goddess everybody worshiped lived, breathed and walked among them, worthy of the adulation.

She felt Roley lean across to refill her glass, detected the heat of his proximity before he whispered: 'She has that effect on people. This industry seems to attract smart, beautiful women.'

Maddie didn't dare turn to look, feeling a warm blush rising. She knew Roley had sat back in his chair, the charge leaving the air to suddenly cool around her.

Taking a sip of wine she looked past the lights reflected in the windows to the lights of the city beyond. Less than two hours into the evening, Maddie was having the night of her life.

'Good evening and welcome to the celebration of Western Australia's fourth Fine Young Cabernet Awards.' The compère looked confident addressing the room. 'A celebration of the noble Cabernet grape, its history, success, and indeed, promising future in the wine regions of Western Australia.'

The compère possessed the winning combination of formality, exuberance and wit, each skilfully nipping at the heels of the other keeping all in check, allowing the audience to relax and be entertained. He outlined the evening's order of proceedings, the crescendo leading to the climax—the presentation of the Fine Young Cabernet Trophy.

Maddie felt the first flutter of anticipation. Lewis was modest in his appraisal, Kite's Cabernet was exceptional. When he'd announced entering the wine or in his words 'giving it a crack', there had been no exclamations of surprise. All recognised its potential for success.

The volume in the room had risen making it difficult to converse as a table. They turned and chatted with neighbours instead.

Destabilised by the poltergeist possessing Roley's normally mild mannered self, Maddie wasn't in the mood to dwell. There would be time for dwelling later. For now, she intended to stay in the moment, revelling in his flattery and attention. But right now, he was busy chatting with the couple on his right. Maddie hoped they didn't have a lot to talk about.

She turned left, unsure how to ask Lewis about his relationship with Annabel. It was personal territory, therefore none of her business, but her curiosity nagged regardless.

Fortuitously, Lewis broached the subject.

'Have you heard of Annabel?'

'Of course,' Maddie gushed. 'She's a legend. I've been hearing about her for years, although I've only ever seen photos of her wearing a lab coat with a wineglass pressed to her nose. What a stunning woman.'

'Don't be rushing to compliment her on her looks. Annabel's not the least bit interested in appearances.'

Maddie raised her eyebrows, lips hinting at a smile. 'She must be a little interested. You don't just find a dress like that in your mother's wardrobe.'

Lewis laughed. 'That is a really valid point Miss Anderson.' He narrowed his eyes. 'You remind me a little of Annabel.'

'In my dreams.'

'Seriously.' Lewis was undeterred. 'You're both smart and incredibly driven. Passionate about wine,' he hesitated, thoughtful, 'and your place in the industry. You don't just want to make great wine, you want to make a contribution. You believe in what the Australian wine industry has to offer. More than that, you want to see it deliver. Will work to see that it does.'

Maddie didn't know how to respond. 'I must be a real pain-in-the-arse employee?'

Lewis looked at his wineglass, both hands tracing round

the stem. 'I'm so pleased to have you working at Kite at this stage of your career. In a few years you'll have outgrown the challenges and opportunities I can offer.'

Maddie rolled her eyes up to a corner of the room.

'Trust me,' Lewis said seriously. 'A few years from now people will clamour for your services, luring you with obscene sums of money Kite could never afford.'

'I don't know that money will be a big motivator for me,' Maddie stated evenly. 'Who knows?'

With Lewis in a philosophical mood, she stole her chance. 'So how do you know Annabel?'

He paused, thoughtful. 'I know her…very well.'

Lewis was having a Bond moment. Man of mystery, charmer.

'I meant, how did you meet?'

'One question was all you were permitted on that subject. Sadly Miss Anderson, you'll have to find a new topic,' Lewis teased.

Maddie put her hand to his arm. 'I'll just ask Mae.'

Lewis laughed and nodded, 'Yep. Mae will tell you everything. Do you remember me saying, you were smart?'

Mae leant across Lewis. 'Did I hear my name?'

Entrée was placed before them. Despite the trays of nibbles consumed, beverages evaporated just as quickly, leaving everyone incredibly hungry. The whole room hushed as they attacked the food on mass.

Maddie centred the cutlery on her empty plate. She turned to Roley pulling down the corners of her mouth. 'Bold flavour combination…I really enjoyed that.'

Roley was spreading butter thickly on his second bread roll. 'Flavour was the only bold thing about it. I could have eaten two.'

Maddie smiled and passed a tiny bowl of olives. Her

phone pinged from inside her clutch, announcing a message. 'Forgot to turn my phone off.' Maddie reached to retrieve it.

News?

Maddie texted a long reply before turning the phone to silent and replacing it in her clutch.

'Josh?' Roley asked offhandedly.

'Bethany. Looking for news.'

Roley looked quizzical. 'That was a long message to say…' moving his thumbs he mimed a long text. 'No.'

Maddie laughed. 'Roley, Roley, Roley. The announcement? Do you really think that's the news Bethany is waiting for?'

Roley shrugged. 'What else?'

'Carmel and Brendan. Annabel.' You, here solo, driving me slightly wild. Maddie kept the last bit to herself.

'Thank the Lord for mobile devices, eh. An application for all manner of emergencies.'

'Ha! Wouldn't you text Genevieve in the event of interesting news?'

The question sounded innocent enough, an extension of the conversation. For Maddie, it was a subtle attempt to connect the dots. Work out exactly what was going on.

Roley acquiesced, turning to look at her fully. 'You know Vieve isn't interested in wine like you are Maddie.'

Maddie responded cautiously. 'Sure, but she's interested in you. And, being the Manager of Viticulture at Kite is a big part of who you are.'

Roley dropped his eyes. 'It's just…complicated.'

It was the most Roley had offered about his relationship with Vieve. She felt more anxious about what would come from his lips than any trophy announcement. She held her silence, hoping he'd continue.

'I met Vieve through my viticultural appointment before

126

Kite. She was, is, the daughter of the owners. Not being arrogant or anything, but the owners love me. They had just purchased the vineyard and were so passionate about their new baby. We hit it off from the start and became really good friends. They embraced me like family, were overjoyed when Vieve and I started going out. Even though I left for the Kite position, I still consult for Ed and Louise.' Roley shrugged, sighing. 'It's like I'm part of the family.'

Maddie's heart sank at Roley's revelation. Love, entangled with family loyalty, equalled infinite complexity. Extrication would be painful, difficult for everyone. It would take powerful motivation to contemplate breaking bonds and deal with the fallout.

Maddie drained her Chardonnay.

She was about to ask how they felt when he applied for the position at Beneath The Kite, but already knew the answer. Encouraging. Supportive. They were the perfect parents of the perfect daughter, adopting Roley into the family, no ceremony required.

Roley studied her. 'I told you it was complicated.'

'I need to pee.'

Maddie pushed back her chair. She really needed air and possibly someone to hit her over the head and tell her to get a bloody grip. Roley wasn't just unavailable, he was ensconced on another planet light years away and someone had just clamped her rocket.

Carmel looked at her quizzically as she passed, immediately leaving her seat to follow.

'Maddie, slow down. I can't sprint in heels.'

Carmel caught her outside the bathroom, steering her to the small lounge area off to the side. She pushed her gently onto one of the couches.

'Sit. You look awful. What's happened?'

'You know where you are in love right now? Floating on that feather soft cloud feeling immortal?'

Carmel nodded.

'Well, I've just hit the concrete at a zillion kilometres an hour breaking every bone in my stupid body.'

'Oh! That's not good,' Carmel took her hand.

Maddie sighed heavily. Then her vision snagged on Annabel, walking towards the bathroom. Posture perfect, she moved like mercury. Beauty incarnate fuelled with fluid, rolling grace. Suddenly, Maddie's intuition prickled. Beneath that flawless skin a foundation of grittier attributes must fortify her structure.

Acknowledging Annabel's substance, tasered her reverie. She slapped her forehead.

'Are you alright?' Carmel asked, not sure whether to laugh or restrain her.

'No! I am weak and jelly-like.'

Carmel's eyes opened wider. 'You're not going into shock on me, are you?'

Maddie squeezed her hand, before releasing it. 'No. I just needed a moment. It's just hit me how much I like Roley and...' Maddie rolled her eyes. 'Although I already knew this, Roley has a girlfriend. So, not going into shock so much as careening out of denial.' Maddie hesitated then looked Carmel in the eye. 'It's just that...'

Carmel gently squeezed her arm.

'I get the feeling, he really likes me.'

Carmel looked at her. 'Roley is a man, Maddie. A good man. He'll make his own decisions.'

Maddie let the words hang. 'I wonder,' she grimaced at Carmel, drawing herself up. 'Now, I really do have to pee.'

Arm in arm they headed to the Ladies'.

Between courses, people moved and mingled around the room. Maddie made her way back to the table concentrating on walking tall; the shoes helping. Carmel was right. Roley was an adult, responsible for his choices. Little point pre-empting; might as well enjoy the moment.

Their table was empty except for Roley, cutting a forlorn figure, sipping on his wine. She smiled. 'Something you said?'

His eyes met Maddie's. 'I hope not.'

Her brain bucked at the innuendo. Maddie fussed with her clutch. 'So, catch up with anyone interesting while I was gone?'

Roley filled her water glass and they fell into easy chatter until the smell of food pervaded the room. Dinner was served. People returned to their seats. It looked delicious and more substantial than entrée. This time their table raised their voices, enjoying some fun repartee as they ate.

As guests talked and laughed, tables were cleared and glasses refilled. Activity in the room slowly shifted from the floor to the stage. The awards presentation was imminent.

'Nervous?' Maddie asked. She had never seen Roley flustered, he was the epitome of calm.

'Hopeful,' he answered calmly.

'I've got my fingers crossed. You and Lewis deserve this.'

The compère called the room to attention once more. The crowd took time to settle until he introduced Annabel. Whole tables hushed as she passed gracefully to take her place on the stage.

Annabel seduced the room. Beyond her appearance, her passion captured imaginations, validating their reasons for celebration, leaving all inspired. 'I love this gig,' Annabel announced unashamedly. 'It brings out my inner pioneer.

You represent a blip on the world wine map, producing truly beautiful wines. And you do it...' Annabel took a pause, looking slowly around the room, 'year, after year, after year.' She smiled conspiratorially. 'Not something the renowned wine regions can claim.' Annabel dazzled, the room cheered. As the crowd calmed, she honed her dialogue to the trophy announcement speaking of the strength of the wines.

Maddie shuffled subconsciously, literally to the edge of her chair.

'I believe I detected a house style in the face-off of the final two wines; exemplary concentration and balance in both.'

Lewis leant in and whispered to Mae, before turning to look at Roley and Maddie.

'However, the winning wine displayed fruit expression as pure as I've ever seen in such a balanced and complex style...'

Things were adding up. Maddie tensed as the suspense built. Roley's hand rested on her seat back, gingerly she placed hers on top. His hand rotated to enfold hers, and they exchanged an excited squeeze.

'...intense concentration of blackcurrant, I've rarely witnessed.'

Maddie noticed a tiny deflation in Lewis's posture.

Annabel introduced the sponsor to make the announcement.

Lewis looked at them with a small shrug, mouthing 'Jupiter Rising'.

Maddie recalled the barrel sample tasting session. Jupiter Rising's Cabernet certainly fitted the description; just thinking about it conjured the blackcurrant essence to her nose. They had all passed comment on the similarity in style between the two wines, but more remarkable the intensity of blackcurrant in the Jupiter Rising wine.

'Blackcurrant, has to be,' Maddie whispered to no one in particular.

The room fell silent as the sponsor adjusted the microphone.

'The winner of the Fine Young Cabernet Trophy is— Beneath The Kite.'

They sat for a beat, stunned. Then bedlam erupted.

Mae screamed, pulling Lewis close for a kiss. On their feet, Lewis extended his hand to Roley, drawing him in for a back thumping embrace. Exuberant, Maddie was caught in the middle.

'If you'd like to accept your trophy?' the sponsor beckoned. Annabel's joy illuminated the podium.

Lewis threw his arm roughly around Roley and they headed for the stage, the applause continuing long and loud. Maddie moved to claim his chair, leaning in to hug Mae.

Halfway to the podium, Lewis turned and back-tracked to the table. 'Don't keep the room waiting, Maddie.'

She looked at him blankly. 'But I had nothing to do with that wine.'

'You're part of the ecoscape,' Lewis winked, pulling her to her feet.

Lewis gave a short, humble acceptance speech, dispersing kudos generously around the Kite team before embarking on formalities; photo commitments, one-on-one chats with sponsors and event organisers and a short interview with a writer covering the feature for an international wine magazine.

By the time he finished, dessert had been cleared and the restaurant was almost empty, wait-staff covertly clearing tables, resetting for the following day.

Maddie insisted on a group selfie with the trophy, immediately forwarding the image to Bethany and Westy before Lewis, eager to bring the celebration back to the team, suggested an upstairs bar for champagne.

Industry folk already populating the bar were quick to congratulate Lewis and Roley as they entered. Lewis ordered champagne and the party atmosphere revived.

Mae and Annabel found a plush circular lounge. Annabel slipped out of her shoes and tucked one leg beneath her without losing a smidge of elegance. The easy friendship between the women felt like a cashmere wrap, Maddie relaxed on the lounge shrugging into its warmth. Time raced while they chatted until eventually the party started to thin and Roley and Lewis wandered over to join them.

'Ah, the men of the moment,' Annabel smiled as they sank onto the cushions. Lewis sat heavily, close to Mae, and Roley perched near Maddie.

'How are you holding up?' Mae stroked Lewis's arm.

'Truthfully,' Lewis shook his head, 'I'm still in shock.'

Mae stopped stroking. 'What do you mean? You must have known you were in for a chance?'

Lewis looked at Annabel. 'I was certain you were referring to the Jupiter Rising wine.' His gaze drifted to Roley. 'At the mention of that blackcurrant character…' Lewis slowly shook his head, 'I was convinced it had to be.'

Roley raised his eyebrows. 'I remember the barrel tasting session. We all remarked on it.' He shrugged. 'Maybe it looked different in the line-up at the show.'

Annabel appeared slightly pressed. 'There was definitely a house style in the final two wines. Maybe Jupiter Rising was the bridesmaid.'

Lewis shrugged, but didn't seem convinced.

Maddie had her own misgivings. That blackcurrant character had been so out of the box. As the conversation lulled, she took a breath about to voice her concerns, when Roley touched her arm.

'I'm calling it a night. Can I walk you to your room?'

Maddie's head was spinning and it wasn't the champagne. That was responsible for the furry, feathery feeling, not this heart racing, blood pumping palaver. Maddie knew full well what was driving it, but what to do?

Her arm was linked through Roley's and the feel of his jacket on her bare flesh was like some weird kind of foreplay. She could still feel the imprint of his hand, low on her back where he had guided her to the table hours earlier. See the look of, what was it—intensity, lust, longing—when their eyes had met. In moments they would be at her door.

Was this the time to succumb to desire? To fess up to Roley that this whole friends' thing was making her crazy, while unrepentant she seduced him—kissed him, undressed him, traced her hands over his body...

'Goodnight Maddie,' his voice brought her plummeting back.

Awkward. They were at her door. She stood dumbly.

'Are you okay?' he asked, looking concerned.

'Yes. No. Oh, man. I don't know. I just don't know Roley,' she stammered.

'I think I know how you feel.'

Their eyes held.

For a second, maybe two, they were unmasked and defenceless. Words would choke in their throats, next breaths unleash reality back upon them, but for the briefest beat in time, there was yielding and recognition; they were together in this.

The lift pinged from the far end of the hall. Back at her door, the view had altered.

'Madison, Margaret River suits you,' his lips brushed her ear before finding her mouth.

The kiss reorganised her entirely, her body floating above her black suede heels.

Her lips searched to find his again, but couldn't. She opened her eyes. A reflex part-sigh, part-sobbing sound came from her as she watched his frame walk down the hall.

She slept fitfully.

Madison. He had used her full name. Serious. Deliberate. He wasn't talking to Maddie his light-hearted, fun friend. He was reaching out to Madison, the one who would take his sincerity on the chest. Madison had been the one mirrored in his eyes, they both knew it; the one who dealt with repercussions and consequences.

But…Margaret River suits you. What was she supposed to do with that? His eyes told her she was special in the world, why did his words only extend to Margaret River?

She suspected it had to do with Genevieve, but she was guessing. She would never know unless they talked.

Blokes were insanely hard work.

So, not a commitment. No way. Maddie was confident in that. But was it, I need time to work this out? Like, a promise? God. Maddie knew it was a stretch; she was clutching at existential threads. But she needed to make sense of it. There was a wellspring of energy fuelling that kiss and Maddie wanted to tap it.

She rolled over, restless.

Thoughts of the kiss flooded her with sensation. Her skin tingled beneath her touch. In a dreamy half-sleep she rolled onto her side parting her legs. She trailed one hand across the breast pointing to the ceiling, her nipple already hard under the cool weight of the sheet. The fingers of her other hand found the part of her pubic mound. She slid them deftly down until she found wetness. As her fingers slid around her vulva she pictured Roley on the rock, pictured herself next to him, peeling his wetsuit down. Drawing her hand up, she moved her finger slowly back and forth over her clitoris, orgasming way before she got anywhere with the wetsuit. Rolling over, she snuggled her head into the pillow. At least now there might be sleep.

Chapter 8

Maddie woke later that morning feeling, ever so vaguely, troubled. Standing in front of the unrelenting, can't-hide-anything lights of the hotel's bathroom mirror she ran through some options, observing her reactions.

Hung-over?

No, not really. Her stomach agreed. It was looking forward to the breakfast buffet and her head wasn't fuzzy or aching, just kind of bothered.

Tired?

She hadn't slept sensationally. Replaying the scenario with Roley had taken some time but at some point, after deciding there was going to be no big ah-ha moment, she'd let herself drift off.

Excited?

Yep. No denying that. It had been a huge night full of anticipation. The announcement, a new all-time high. But it was all so totally positive. Joy mingled with little puffs of pride for the Kite team. Nothing disturbing there.

Roley?

Total, utter frustration and bewilderment. She opened her eyes wide shaking her head. *How did we get ourselves into this mess?* The whole situation was perplexing, but in a ludicrous way. It didn't make her feel troubled. This was different.

Panda eyes?

Now that was worthy of concern. She stepped into the shower; some things she could control.

Spotting Lewis and Mae in the dining room she smiled and waved.

Lewis jumped out of his chair. 'Morning Maddie. Come and join us.'

'Really? Thanks Lewis. I was going to leave you guys to it. Wouldn't be often you get to have breakfast together without the kids.'

Lewis smiled. 'We're both a little slow this morning. Just been reliving the events of last night. Don't think I'll be able to focus on much else today. How are you feeling?'

'Great. I'm so happy for you guys,' Maddie pulled out a chair. 'Hi Mae.'

'Ohhh Maddie. It's so exciting. Have you spoken with your family yet?' Mae enthused warmly.

'Just a quick text. I said I'd call later with the details.'

'You did a great job getting those wines together with such short notice. We almost didn't get there.'

Maddie felt a jolt; her liquid sensory mass solidifying for a split second before softening back to normal. It was almost painful.

'Yeah. I've decided I work well under pressure.' Maddie smiled but her trouble detector had crept up a notch. She quickly excused herself and made for the buffet.

It was a feeling she was learning to recognise. Deep seated, powerful gut instinct sending out its *uh-oh, better buckle up* tremors. Maddie wondered if it was anything like the first stages of labour, vague but stubbornly unrelenting, alerting cells they were about to be redeployed to the front line; stand-by status elevated to active duty—although going into battle was possibly a disturbing way to view delivering a child into the world. Maddie conceded total ignorance on that.

'Is there anything I can help you with?'

A waitress stood in front of her, head tilted, eyebrows raised.

Maddie was frozen, in front of the bread and pastry section…on another planet.

'No. All great thanks,' she flashed a smile. 'Just deciding.'

Absent-mindedly she reached for a croissant, stopping just in time, realising she was beyond troubled; breaking her own code for successful navigation of a buffet. Avoid anything in the bread and pastry section that looked desirably crusty, flaky or crisp. The bread and pastries were never, ever as crusty, flaky or crisp as they looked. It was one of the most basic rules of the code which, if followed correctly, could allay disappointment in the precarious matter of buffet satisfaction.

Recovering from her close call, two pieces of toast dropped from the belt of the toast conveyor to her right. The code was clear; toast conveyors were not to be trusted and avoided at all cost. But this toast looked perfectly browned, crunchy and warm. Popping both pieces on her plate, she looked with anticipation at the smiling chef, cooking to order behind the egg bar.

'Sorry lady, that's my toast.' A boy of about twelve stood in her path.

Maddie glared, menacingly.

The Rubik's Cube clutching terrorist defiantly stood his ground, fingers working nimbly to solve the puzzle without looking.

Maddie couldn't compete. Sighing, she handed over the plate.

Things were going downhill fast, breaching the buffet code and intimidating children. Maddie snatched an apple from the fruit basket and retreated.

A weak summer front hovering over the coast brought intermittent showers during the hour and a half she was on the road. It was good to be south bound but she was only half way there. Tension had built in her shoulders making her tetchy and uncomfortable. Time for a break. Coffee. She put the next service stop on her radar.

The pedestrian crossing from the carpark to the roadhouse was slick with two centimetres of water, not compatible with footwear unless you were rocking gumboots. Irritatingly, either side of the painted stripes, the road was puddle free. Maddie picked her way across, annoyance compounding with every splash.

The roadhouse was a hub of parkas and rain jackets sitting, milling and otherwise waiting for their orders from the coffee machine. A bus-load of bloody tourists. Her politically correct brain winced at the thought. Coffee, tea, hot chocolate were international comforts and anyone enclosed in a coach for any length of time was entitled to their cup.

Estimating a wait time of twenty minutes-plus—over-ruling the incompetent adolescent operating the till suggesting ten—she headed back to the car, deliberating as she sploshed. *The holiday-makers were relaxed and smiley, maybe she could tackle one, seize their coffee and run.* The thought was candy to her wicked inner child who was proving good company this trip.

But it was serious now. While one side of her brain dealt with manoeuvring the car back onto the highway, another part was unrelenting—coffee, now. She remembered a drink coaster with an amusing quip about the wasted hours between coffee and wine. She was there, in that desolate landscape, without the caffeine.

The weather intensified as she drove further south. Rounding the corner of the bay above her home, the sea and clouds smudged into one misshapen grey mass; an abandoned papier-mâché piñata carcass, bashed to pulp, pillaged of treats.

Parking in her driveway she looked back up the road. All she wanted was a fucking coffee—and to stretch. Zipping up her jacket, pulling the hood low, she marched towards the shop.

Living in a small town, avoiding people was tricky. Stomping up the street, she noticed Stubbsy sitting on his front veranda, newspaper spilling over the small table. He was an all-weather, sitting on the front veranda, watching the world go by kind of man with a million-dollar view from his balcony seat. Maddie often joined him, but not today. Today she raised her arm in greeting and kept her head down, in no mood to talk.

The local shop was empty of customers, manned by a

backpacker who got a gig there every once in a while. Maddie sighed ungraciously, dubious of his coffee making skills.

When she stepped outside, the rain had eased to a persistent light drizzle. Heartened by the steam rising from the cup she clasped with both hands, she set off for the point overlooking the main surf break.

It felt good to move. The coffee was better than anticipated and she felt relieved to be home. Her crankiness slowly lifted along with the weather. But still a light fog of malaise persisted. She stopped at the low limestone wall that marked the most western point before stairs led down to the beach, and stared across the steely Indian Ocean.

She loved this ocean of many moods; vast and powerful—swallowing the sun every evening for the Pacific to spit out in a new dawn. Not romantic, the crude analogy pleased her today. Thinking about the way time moved—so unaffected by humans—was something Maddie usually relied on to ground her. Its consistency, literally casting light, drawing shadows, offered perspective.

She needed some now. She should be feeling large, enjoying the moment, calling family and friends. Yet she stood staring at the slippery, grey sea with something niggling her brain; flummoxed, irritable, annoyed.

Coffee gone, weariness and damp discomfort set in. She ditched her cup in the bin and walked home.

Maddie's usual Sunday afternoon routine involved sculpting a little domestic order for another work week. She began with unpacking the car. Running her hand over the luscious fabric of her dress, she left it hanging on the hook in the back seat. The tag said 'dry clean only'. Maddie knew from experience that didn't have a double meaning. Once she had interpreted 'dry-clean only' as 'well if you promise to be very careful, you could give it a go'. The only piece of the garment remaining intact, was in fact, the tag. She would drop the dress off at the dry-cleaning agent in town.

Later that evening, emptying her cosmetic bag back into the bathroom cabinet, she wistfully sprayed her neck with perfume and was transported back to the awards ceremony. She visualised them all at the table, dark tailored jackets and shimmery, draping dresses. Hair styled, nails polished, clean shaven jaw-lines and smoky, made-up eyes; everyone so happy. Light positively glinted off their dazzling, pearly teeth as they talked, smiled and laughed. The spectacle was blinding. A veritable toothpaste commercial. Maddie shook the vision away. Closing the bathroom cabinet, the mirror framed her sullen face. It was all very weird. Maddie snapped off the light and brushed her teeth in the dark.

Chapter 9

The shadowy, haunting thing pounced while she slept. Maddie woke with a start.

The samples!

Her stomach churned and an overwhelming sense of foreboding confirmed her assumption. Twenty-four hours of apprehension had distilled to six unmarked bottles. She channelled her energy, forcing synapses to fire, trying to think.

Crap!

She tried to visualise the labelling station but the barrel room wavered in a haze on the periphery. The harder she tried to focus, the further the picture retreated, blurring in the feeling of dread descending with every beat of her heart.

Shit!

Her brain was shorting, overloaded. She jumped out of bed.

She had to retrace her steps. Sick with the thought of harming Kite's reputation, she grabbed at clothes, and headed to the loo. As she caught sight of her dark shape in the bathroom mirror Maddie froze. What have I done?

It was just after 3a.m. when she hit the road, eyes scratchy, nerves raw. It was apocalyptic quiet. The huge gums lining the road's edge, beacons of life force in the daylight hours, were dark guardians of malcontent in the moonlit night. She flinched as her headlights caught the shape of a huge kangaroo off the verge to the left. It turned its head towards the lights before pushing off with its tail, moving deeper into the bush.

A little comfort arrived in the crunch of tyres on gravel as she turned into Kite. She loved this place. Whatever transpired, it didn't involve malice or intent—the only certainty in the ominous fog.

The back of the winery came into view, alien and inhospitable. A chilling lunar diorama with moonlight reflecting off the concrete surface, silver catwalk entrails linking lofty, fermenting tank organs. She parked close and kept her eyes on the ground.

Maddie used her key to let herself through the rear door, flicking the switch for the cellar lights. A slow buzz followed by a quick double flick and the industrial bulbs illuminated the room.

To the right was the workstation where they kept sampling hoses, bottles and sticky labels used for collecting and marking samples.

She stood at the bench trying desperately to recall her movements.

The white square labels sat haphazardly where she'd left them. They were different from the ones they used in-house.

Automatically, she placed them in the pigeon hole where they belonged. She was a systematic worker who believed clean-up formed part of the job. It wasn't like her to leave them lying around.

Suddenly a face appeared around the door.

Maddie jumped at the memory, putting a hand to her chest as it all came flooding back. She was organising the samples when John arrived with the tanker, calling her away, followed by the whole unsettling debacle with the courier. Maddie felt sick.

Preferring not to dwell on that morning, she hadn't given the samples another thought. Lewis had mentioned them a day or two later, confirming their arrival and the news infused her body with relief. It seemed a small miracle in the course of the day's events.

But now, remembering her rush to get stickers on the samples, she wondered if she could have mixed them up? In the chaotic circumstances, it wasn't only possible she'd stuffed up, but almost inconceivable that she hadn't.

Two barrels, three samples from each, six bottles, six labels, her head started to spin.

'Focus, Maddie. Focus.' Her voice sounded small in the cavernous cellar.

Retracing her steps, she walked to the barrels. Nothing in the cellar had been rearranged and she identified them without hesitation. There was no doubt she had taken three samples from each of the barrels. She remembered the hose over her shoulder, balancing the bottles in one arm while she removed the bung stoppering the barrel, filling the bottles, replacing the bung and carrying them back to the bench.

Maddie was always touched by the innocence of cleanskins. She could picture the six naked bottles huddling together on the bench, vulnerable without artwork or words.

She'd placed them methodically, knowing exactly which samples were which but that was where it ended. A big, bloody, uncertain 'but'.

Had she written the labels correctly was the first question she couldn't answer, and from that point any further questions were like tumbleweeds rolling through the desert, no clues to catch them. Even if she had written the labels correctly, her desperation to get them on the bottles had been pure mayhem.

Maddie pulled up a stool and, crossing her arms on the bench, laid down her head.

That's how Lewis found her in the morning. If he was surprised, there was no trace of it in his greeting, but when she didn't return his smile his face changed—resolved. He pulled up the stepladder, raising his eyebrows while wiping at the corners of his mouth, suggesting she do the same, before sitting down to listen.

Maddie dealt with her drool and began.

Chapter 10

Everybody makes mistakes. It was one of the oldest clichés on the planet.

Queen Heterpheres surely used it while soaking in a milk bath to placate her husband Pharaoh Snefru while he ranted about the incompetence of his architects. Little did they know, the pyramid he commissioned—'Snefru is Shining in the South'—would one day be known as 'The Bent Pyramid'.

Everybody makes mistakes.

It would definitely feature in the top one hundred most frequently used clichés of all time, maybe even secure a top-ten rating, and it may well be the cliché most used and heard by humans under the age of twelve.

All Maddie knew was if one well-intentioned person moved their lips in that direction she would scream. Perhaps put her fingers in her ears, throwing herself to the ground, while screaming, so those questioning her disposition would be left no doubt.

She knew it was true. One of the great truths of life. But Maddie hated—with a passion usually reserved for positive pursuits—making mistakes.

She understood she stuffed up regularly; errors of judgement, bad choice of words, taking things the wrong way. Everyday provided opportunity to miss the mark. But she prided herself on not making mistakes at work.

And there it was, pride. Her pride wasn't simply wounded—another great cliché—no, Maddie's pride was shredded, haemorrhaging, fighting for its life. A bloody, pulpy mass unlikely to survive the next twenty-four hours.

When she was younger Aunt Bling, surely solicited by her mother for the job, had broached the subject of perfection. It was the period in early high school when Maddie, under an extension program, started getting the odd result that wasn't one hundred per cent. Aunt Bling was engaged following a particular incident with Maddie's maths teacher.

Maddie's mother had been summoned to the school. She walked into the principal's office just in time to witness Maddie's teacher having some kind of frustration fuelled meltdown.

'Maths is truth. There is no basis to argue for a reasonable outcome. The answer is either correct or incorrect. You, Miss Anderson, recorded an incorrect answer and I have marked you wrong. End of story. Maths—the truth—has spoken.'

With that, Maddie's usually demure maths teacher, nodded curtly to Maddie and the principal, raising her eyebrows and shaking her head at Maddie's mother before adjourning to that mythical place that must exist in educational facilities; the stronghold for teacher sanity.

Exactly how they managed and maintained their sanity was a system understood only by teachers themselves; remaining a gobsmacking mystery to everybody else.

Following the altercation, Maddie announced her intention of hunger-striking between less than perfect results, and Aunt Bling was invited to dinner the following evening.

They got through the meal, Maddie spending most of it moving food around her plate. As soon as she reasonably could, Maddie's mother retired to clean up the kitchen refusing all offers of help, insisting Maddie and Aunt Bling spend time catching up.

Once she was out of earshot, Aunt Bling winked at Maddie. 'Ready?'

Maddie, fighting any show of weakness in the impending defence of her hunger-strike stance, looked away quickly, sucking in her lips.

Both knew the drill. Whenever Maddie's behaviour ventured into a perplexing realm, Maddie's mother called for reinforcements—well just one, Aunt Bling.

And in her eternal love for them, Aunt Bling always appeared, calm, wise and ready to listen.

'I brought cake for dessert,' Aunt Bling began. 'Black forest with cherries, fresh cream and more shavings than you'd find in a cabinet maker's workshop—only chocolate.'

'I got it Aunt Bling. Got it before you explained it actually,' Maddie retorted.

'Oh actually. Well good for you,' Aunt Bling teased. 'I remember it's your favourite because it's my favourite too,' she patted her stomach affectionately. 'One of them anyway.'

Maddie sighed, 'I know you brought my favourite cake because mum's told you I'm not eating until I score a hundred per cent in my next test or assignment.'

'Maddie you're a smart girl. I'm sure you understand what a silly idea that is. How worrying it is for your mum to hear you talk like that. Denying yourself nutrition because you're not achieving one hundred per cent is setting yourself up for a scary life of eating disorders.'

'I don't have an eating disorder. It's not like I'm anorexic. I'm just disciplining myself, taking a stance against imperfection.'

'Good grief Maddie,' Aunt Bling boomed, 'I think you'd do better with an eating disorder.'

Maddie rolled her eyes.

'Seriously. I'm sure you're aware of the meaning of unsustainable?'

Maddie gave a 'yeah whatever' almost indiscernible shrug.

'Seeking perfection in life is almost as likely to result in death as not eating.'

Maddie cocked her head.

'Well, not eating may kill you quicker but aiming for perfection is guaranteed to result in a slow, painful starvation of joy. A life without joy—sadder than death,' Aunt Bling shook her head slowly. 'Horrible.'

Maddie's teenage-self was no match for her aunt's original ideas and penchant for drama. Before realising, she'd dropped the tough campaigner facade and was wide-eyed sponge.

'But we all want to do the best we can Aunt Bling. We've been encouraged to do that all our lives. You, mum, teachers. It's a universal expectation.'

'Well, of course. Do the best you can is a world away from spit the dummy—or your food—if your best is not perfect.'

'Why is the word in the dictionary in the first place?' Maddie, indignant, wasn't caving.

'Well, perfection as a concept, does apply to some things,'

Aunt Bling pulled a face. 'Mathematics for example—that's topical. Diamonds. But it doesn't translate to people, to humans. There are just too many variables when it comes to us.'

Maddie appeared unconvinced.

'Let's look at it this way. Even if you knew all the answers you could still go into a test situation and make a mistake. You could be rushing or you could be tired and not concentrating. You could have perfect knowledge, but being human can trip you up. There's no fighting it.'

Maddie narrowed her eyes.

'Okay, you're really testing me now.' Aunt Bling looked up to the ceiling. 'I have a vague recollection that 'perfect' is a derivative from the Latin 'perfectus' which means to finish or complete. How are you going to apply that to humans? We're perfect when we're dead. How about just thinking of it as a figure of speech instead?'

'Okay, so what if I say I don't want a perfect score but I want to get everything right?'

Aunt Bling raised her arms. 'Go for it. Aim high Maddie, but don't punish yourself for falling short of the mark. Learn young what it means to be human. To be fallible and make mistakes. Enjoy the humanity of being beautifully flawed.'

Maddie looked at her with wonder. 'You're not like other adults.'

'And Maddie.'

'Yes, Aunt Bling.'

'Don't argue with your teachers.'

Maddie smiled shyly. 'She was really mad.'

'So your mother said.'

Maddie's mother appeared at the door. 'Cake anyone?'

Neither woman blinked when Maddie asked for seconds.

When Maddie finished recounting the fiasco of sending off the samples, Lewis looked her squarely in the eyes. 'What's your gut telling you?'

Maddie met his interrogating gaze. 'My gut has been trying to tell me something since the announcement on Saturday night.'

Lewis sighed. 'Mine too.'

He crossed one arm over his chest, finding the pressure points inside his eyebrows with his other hand. Seconds passed. Maddie, in another dimension, received a static shock when Lewis announced: 'I'd better make some calls.'

Later that morning, a hire car pulled up outside the winery. Maddie watched Annabel Estelle climb out, arching her back, stretching away the drive.

Lewis met her outside his office. They talked for a while on the wash-down pad before he ushered her into the barrel cellar. Thirty long minutes later, they re-emerged.

Annabel caught Maddie's eye. She waved and walked purposefully towards her.

'Hi Maddie. How are you holding up?'

Maddie rolled her eyes, not trusting herself to speak.

'Yep, that's bad,' Annabel's smile was warm and reassuring. 'You know, it's how you move forward that matters.'

Maddie swallowed. 'I've made mistakes, but I wouldn't have believed myself capable of one of this magnitude.'

'Well, the higher you rise in the chain of responsibility the harder you hit when you fall. But are you a water balloon or super ball?'

It was a cool analogy, worth a smile, but Maddie wasn't up for it. She was drained. 'I'm a super ball—stuck in the gutter.'

Annabel laughed. 'Something I try to keep in mind is a mistake is better than a bad call. Making mistakes is requisite of being human, whereas we have a degree of control over the decisions we make. Mistakes, we must accept and move on from. Bad calls, you have to live with,' she smiled. 'And sometimes the grieving goes on and on.' She placed her hand gently on Maddie's shoulder. 'This too will pass.'

Maddie was reaching her upper limit of over-whelmed-ness. How many times had Aunt Bling said the same thing? Maddie struggled to fathom the connections being made.

In an arrangement without words or, perhaps with those four, Annabel became a mentor for Maddie. Aunt Bling ruled love and life, and Annabel career and wine.

'Call me if I can ever help with anything,' Annabel straightened, looking around. 'Now, I need to find Lewis. I don't want to miss my flight.'

Lewis's door was open. Annabel tapped lightly on the frame.

He offered up a smile, ending his phone conversation and they walked in silence together to her car.

Lewis turned to face her. 'Thank you for driving down.'

'You did the right thing,' she reassured. 'Not sure how many others would have.'

Jaw set tight, he looked past her shoulder.

'They are both stunning wines, equally deserving of a tro-phy…' she let the sentence hang until he met her eyes. 'It's your integrity I'm celebrating.' She pulled him towards her for a parting kiss, a soft press of lips, light and reaffirming.

Lewis held her hand.

'Annabel, I love you.'

She scrunched her nose. 'So much pleasure in our friendship, relationship...whatever.'

He opened the door and she climbed in.

'I've got to dash. I'm meeting your lovely wife for a quick coffee, and I'm determined to make my flight.'

'She loves you too, you know?' Lewis replied, eyebrows raised.

Annabel shook her head. 'Mae and I have been sharing our feelings for years Lewis. I doubt we've ever said goodbye without an *I love you* thrown in.'

'Yeah, right,' Lewis closed the door and Annabel let down her window. 'I should know better than ever underestimating Mae.'

'One of the smartest, most together women I know.' She brought his hand to her mouth and kissed the fleshy part of his thumb before turning the key in the ignition. As Lewis stepped back, she called through the open window, 'I'll look forward to your next vintage.'

He smiled. 'I'll look forward to your unbiased, glowing reviews.'

Maddie was on autopilot in the warehouse, packing orders with the forklift when Lewis entered giving her the signal to stop. Watching him trace his finger across his throat, Maddie wondered if it was really the forklift he wanted killed. Parking it up she followed him to the smoko room.

Roley and Bethany were there. Emma was making coffee, keeping an eye out for customers. Liz had come across from the office and Westy, who'd been racking barrels, was wiping his wet hands on his shorts and eyeing the celebration cake Mae had sent with Lewis.

Normally they were a lively group, but following the stern directive to meet in the smoko room, the mood was subdued, tension tangible as Lewis entered. He held the door open for Maddie, before moving to the centre of the room. Maddie felt like throwing up.

'We're going to have to put our celebrations on hold,' Lewis gave a tight-lipped smile. 'You are all aware Beneath The Kite was awarded the Fine Young Cabernet Trophy on Saturday night. Unfortunately, it has come to light the results were incorrect.'

Maddie did a quick scan of the faces. Roley looked intently at Lewis. They would have already spoken. Liz and Emma were both open-mouthed in shock. Westy looked thoughtful as he tilted his head from one side to the other, draining water from his ears from the morning's surf.

Bethany openly studied her. Feeling tears well, Maddie quickly raised her eyes to the ceiling.

'The good news,' Lewis continued, clearing his throat. 'Is the trophy has been re-awarded to Jupiter Rising.'

Liz, Emma and Westy all looked around. 'What?' 'How did that happen?'

'I have spoken with Jeff and he's ecstatic.' Lewis looked around the faces in the room. 'Asked me to pass on his thanks to you all. When he's back, he'll drop by and thank us personally.'

Maddie searched Lewis's face for cracks but found nothing. He was an amazing leader.

'There will be talk in the press. Our stance is…while it's unfortunate for Kite, Margaret River Cabernet is still the hero. Please direct all enquiries to me personally. Any questions?'

'Yeah. What the hell happened?' Westy sounded dubious.

Emma shook her head. 'Surely they can't just award a trophy and then take it back and give it to somebody else?'

'It just seems odd. How can they be so sure?'

'Somebody fucked up.'

Maddie flinched. Roley's words silenced the room.

'Mistakes happen,' Lewis said, raising his hands. 'Fortunately in this case, the Chair of Judges and all parties involved have been able to agree unanimously that the wine from Jupiter Rising was the highest pointed, winning wine. And that's really end of story. We're taking it on the chin. Mistakes happen.'

'Still, it's disappointing,' Liz ventured looking at Lewis, her eyes eventually resting on Maddie.

Maddie nodded dumb agreement. 'It certainly is.'

Slowly, the strained scene evolved. A visitor's car pulled up and Emma hurried back to cellar door. Liz grabbed her cup and walked with her across the grass. Westy's phone sounded an incoming call and he moved outside to answer.

As the room emptied, Lewis nodded at Maddie. It was a question. Maddie grimaced giving a subtle nod back. Then he too left the room.

Maddie moved towards the kettle.

'I'll make you a cuppa,' Bethany cut her off. 'Sit down. You look like shite.'

Maddie was wrecked. She surrendered to Bethany's gentle push, sitting back on the chair.

Roley moved to sit next to her. 'Hell of a way to end the weekend.'

She sat motionless, still stinging from his earlier remark.

He leaned in close as he rose from his seat. Centimetres from her ear he spoke softly, 'Sun's gonna rise again tomorrow.'

The words hugged her.

As Bethany placed a steaming mug on the table, Roley punched Maddie lightly on the arm. 'Nice shorts,' he teased before disappearing out the door.

Maddie looked down. They were her pyjama bottoms, pink and white striped with teddy bears sitting around picnic baskets.

'I'm still in my pyjamas,' she murmured abstractly.

As tears ran down her face, Bethany massaged her shoulders. 'Lucky your Victoria's Secrets were in the wash.'

Chapter 11

The vineyards appeared reposed. Lush with whispering leaves, laden with fruit, the green rows imposed soft formality on the landscape. In late autumn they would shake off their fading multi-coloured plumage and enter a reflective phase, becoming naked, gnarled stumps for their desultory native-bush neighbours to mock. But it was summer and the responsibility of ripening fruit consumed them. Sunshine fuelled a manic cellular response—dramatic contrast to their relaxed facade.

Since last harvest, the vines had meandered through their annual cycle. Relieved of fruit, they squirreled sustenance before slipping into dormancy to harmonise and reenergise. Then, warming soil triggered yawning buds to shoot, grow and flower, luring bees and wasps. Flowers clung tight during spring storms to develop into tiny, hard berries which plumped and blushed their way through veraison. As they ripened, the grape's acid levels declined, sugar levels increased and flavours developed until they hung on the vines in luscious, voluptuous bunches ready for winemakers to make their most important decision of the year—when to pick.

Beneath The Kite celebrated the first harvest of their estate fruit with a pagan ceremony; a ritual they performed every year. In the late afternoon of the day before picking, cellar door and office employees migrated outside to join Lewis's and Roley's teams assembled in the vineyard. Once gathered, snips were passed around and everyone picked a bunch of grapes. On mass they held the grapes aloft while Lewis gave thanks for the generosity and abundance of the vine's precious gift, promising respect and sensitivity in the process of taking the grapes through to wine, evoking the essence of nature's bounty from vine to bottle.

Then, Roley began the countdown.

'Three. Two. One. Crush.'

Everyone squeezed their bunches forcing juice from the ripe, plush berries, the nectar running in sweet streams between fluffy furrows of forearms to drip from elbows back to the land.

Born from a simple concept, the connection of alchemist and raw material, people recognised sanctity in the ritual. For Lewis especially, it was grounding. Machinery and technology would be employed almost unconsciously over the next few months, it was easy to lose sight of their pure intention.

After the prescribed licking of arms and grape throwing, they opened bottles of sparkling in more typical celebration. A philosophical mood infused the crowd, everyone enthused for vintage.

Maddie mingled, knowing administrative staff sometimes felt excluded from the vineyard and winery cliques while understanding it wasn't intentional. Vineyard and winery workers were just blissfully unaware how interested others were in their day-to-day operations.

She approached the steelcap-less crowd with two brilliant ice-breakers. 'More bubbles anyone? Are you all ready for vintage?' As she poured, she was peppered with questions.

Emma held out her glass. 'Don't take this the wrong way, cos I know you're really fit. But working in the winery's pretty physical right? Do you just like, have nightmares about vintage?'

Maddie laughed. 'No way. I'm one of the crazies who sees vintage as a huge opportunity. It's our big chance to get the fruit at its best and handle it in the best way we can, to make the best wine possible. I dream of perfectly ripe tannins and cool ferments and flavours that rock. Sweet dreams.' Maddie put a finger in front of her flute in the sign of a cross. 'No nightmares allowed.'

Emma pointed at Maddie's boots. 'Getting to wear those boots would almost make the hard work worthwhile.'

They were her new purple steelcaps. 'I love them,' Maddie admitted, 'and for every pair purchased, the company donates to breast cancer research. Happy all round.'

Westy and Roley joined the group.

'On the crest where function meets fashion, those boots ride the barrel.' Westy nodded.

Maddie smiled at the metaphor. 'Surfing and winemak-ing—so connected. Barrels rule.' Forcing the smile to stay put, she turned to Roley.

In the weeks since the trophy debacle, Maddie and Roley, via unspoken agreement, assumed their pre-kiss relation-ship—somewhat unsuccessfully. The friendship had assumed a perfunctory quality which felt unnatural, unsatisfying and more than a little sad. She'd been hanging out for the start of vintage, knowing there'd be less time to think.

'Great countdown, Roley. I wouldn't have picked you as the theatrical type.'

Roley counted on his fingers, 'Four words is my limit without an auto-cue.' There was a pause while he mused. 'I like the ritual though.'

Maddie and Westy nodded.

'I remember the first year Lewis did it. He asked me about it first, told me what he had in mind.' Roley smiled, 'I didn't know what to say. Lewis was so serious and sincere and I was sure that it would be taken as a bit of a joke.'

'What happened?' Maddie ventured.

'It's hard to explain. You saw what happened today. I don't know exactly what to put it down to, passion or ambition. But that year, and every year since, there's just an atmosphere of, like…we're all in this together and care about what we're doing here.'

'Magic happens,' Westy nodded gravely.

Maddie and Roley stole a quick glance at each other.

'That could be a bumper sticker,' Roley joked.

'Seriously,' Westy continued undeterred, 'magic bloody happens. Crush is a powerful word.'

Maddie nodded emphatically. 'I agree. It's one of those brilliant multitasking words that conjures feeling and changes meaning without altering its stripes. The ruthless crush of a powerful oppressor. The start of the winemaking process—the vintage crush. And the sweet infatuation of one person for another—a romantic crush. I love words that hold their form, while switching their natures completely.'

It was Westy and Roley's turn to share a look.

'Yes,' Maddie laughed. 'I'm a bit of a word nerd. Always

have been, not changing anytime soon. More bubbles? Then I'll leave you to contemplate the state of my mental health?'

Feeling lighter than she had in a while, hopeful they could procure an easy friendship once more, Maddie was about to wander off when Lewis walked over to join them.

'I'm heading home,' he pointed his free hand towards her. 'I think you've got the last bottle there Maddie. Once that's done, we're done.'

She nodded.

'I like this to be a whetting of the palate occasion. Save our big celebration for the other end when the fruit is in the winery and ferments are through.'

'Yeah.' They collectively agreed, knowing they would be tested and challenged before all was done. The theoretically simple idea of vintage—pick grapes and ferment the juice into wine—was a fraught reality.

'Here's to a cracking vintage,' Lewis drained the little left in his glass. 'Tomorrow, we get our hands dirty.'

Home at the shack, Maddie performed her own pre-vintage ritual.

Starting in the kitchen, she cut and seasoned some vegetables and put them in the oven to roast. Then she headed for the bathroom to pluck her eyebrows and apply a face mask and hot oil hair treatment. Towel wrapped hair, yellow goo covered face, she raided the basil pot on the deck and whipped up a jar of grainy pesto. A drizzle of balsamic and a sprinkle of salt on the roasting vegies, she jumped in the shower, wielding exfoliating mitt, pumice file and shaver in dizzying succession. Drying off, she smothered moisturiser from top to toe, taking special care to tone and hydrate her face.

Back on the slick floor-tiles of the kitchen, the peppermint foot lotion added a degree of difficulty as she negotiated making couscous without sliding into the splits. Stirring the roast vegies through she portioned serves into containers, adding goat's curd and a simple lemon juice dressing to the bowl she was having for dinner. After a flurry of finishing touches, a grind of pepper, a sprinkle of herbs, pouring a frosty glass of white, she headed to the back deck. It was a stunning late summer evening, and Maddie planned to make the most of it.

She contemplated some tunes but settled on the background roll and crash of waves. Sporadic wind gusts added percussion in the flap of her beach towel hanging over the rail and the deep, hollow tones of the wooden wind chimes. Occasionally the wind delivered sounds from people at the park; kids barking orders, a tonal range of laughs and the shrill cries of birds darting low over the bush. Maddie closed her eyes.

During a recent phone call, Aunt Bling had asked what it was that made Margaret River so special?

Desperate to explain, she blurted a list of the region's natural wonders. Landmarks fell together like the edge pieces of a jigsaw, framing the picture leaving the puzzle unsolved.

'Margaret River is…I mean, it's just…well, it's like…'

Maddie had nothing. No words came. Frustration grew and she eventually gave up trying to articulate it to her aunt.

Perhaps the essence of a thing existed beyond discourse. She could feel it now, in a hazy sixth sense that teased at the edge of reasoning. Trying to grasp the wispy tails saw them scatter. It was fleeting and intuitive, fed by the other five, stoking imagination, where the truth of being lives. Maddie could tap it when she allowed herself *to be*.

It nestled in the differentiation of sounds, the vibrations

of life playing out against a blank score, holding their value, without being lost in a jumbled matrix of background noise.

Her nose twitched as the breeze delivered a waft of basil. She enjoyed the summeriness of it mingled with the salty whiff of the ocean and briny seaweed rot. Swirling amongst it, the herbaceous dryness of the native bush baked under a sundrenched day and the hint of seared meat from a neighbour's barbeque. Her mouth watered. It was all of this.

It tantalised her skin. Rays of sunshine touched her face and arms, gently warming while the cool breeze provoked hairs to rise in goose-bump clusters. The soft press of her cotton dress as her ribs moved with each breath, drawing clean air deep.

Swallowing a sip of Sauvignon Blanc her senses turned inward to the gentle prickle of acid and the vibrant burst of passionfruit. She had garnished the salad with toasted almond slivers and their nutty flavour lingered in pulped remnants between her teeth.

Settling back against the cushions enjoying the last of her wine, the sea sucked the sun from the sky and the rosy-gold light took her higher. Her brain fumbled ideas and words while her soul simply knew. Essence and experience existed cheek to cheek. The space and beauty in Margaret River enticed people to explore self. It elicited awakening and cast nutrient at potential. This place grounded, setting you free.

The wind either died or blew harder once the sun set. Tonight it was the latter and as it increased, the temperature dropped. With a shiver, Maddie collected her dishes and hustled inside to clean up. The pesto and the vegetable couscous would sustain her over the coming days. The profound feeling of peace that had snugged into her fascia would nourish her for weeks.

Vintage was winery boot camp; physical challenges combined with tests of mental dexterity, and a total reshuffle of routine. Most nights she would set her alarm for just after five in the morning, and depending what was picked and processed on the day, wouldn't finish until after five in the afternoon.

Westy had a later start time, so he could get a surf in before work. It meant he worked later, usually cleaning up and preparing for the following day. If the press needed cleaning, either Lewis or Maddie would stay back too. Some winery procedures weren't safe performed in isolation and Lewis made sure there were always two people for jobs that carried an element of risk.

Longer hours aside, vintage was physically demanding. She would jump on and off the forklift, unload bins off trucks, tipping them into the press or the crusher/destemmer. She would lug big hoses around tanks, connecting them to the press, disconnecting from the must-chiller, dragging them to pumps and the crusher.

She would wash barrels, fill barrels, move barrels. Climb up and down stairs, along catwalks from ground level to reach the top opening of huge stainless steel tanks. She would walk circuits from the press to the laboratory to analyse samples.

Climb her way under things, on top of things, into things. Use a pressure hose to blast and spray and soak things. She would walk, sometimes run when Lewis wasn't watching, as well as bend, twist, push, pull, shovel, drag, lift.

There would be days where she would hardly stop, grabbing a coffee when she could, eating between tasks as the schedule allowed; grabbing a handful of jelly snakes or some biscuits Mae sent in with Lewis as a communal sugar fix.

In between she was involved in the daisy chain of logistical decisions, one impacting upon the next. When to pick was their most critical decision followed by how much.

Maddie always enjoyed getting out into the vineyard but lately her interest had developed an edge. Roley's knowledge of the property extended to small sections within blocks. Coupled with his passion, every trip to sample or check a vineyard was a revelation. Maddie didn't know what she loved best, the information she was squirreling away or the enthusiasm Roley showed every time she asked to ride shotgun.

Depending on the character of the grapes and the desired wine styles, they would consider how to process the fruit. Tank space and barrel allocation would determine what went where. They would analyse juice samples and calculate sugar, acid, pH. They would calculate volumes and mix additions of sulphur and yeast. They would record temperatures and track ferments.

While batches of juice journeyed to wine, they would still be making decisions on when, what and how much to pick. This was the cycle until the vines had surrendered all of their fruit.

And, as is the nature of farming, there was always the possibility as they formulated a hypothetical plan, a blip would appear on a weather map. So they would sample, schedule, process with one eye trained on satellite images watching for developments that could see their virtual vintage plan fold neatly into an aeroplane to launch off the winery roof and splodge down in the murky sludge of the effluent pond. One solid front could bring disaster.

In the vineyard, vintage ended when all the grapes were harvested. In the winery, vintage ended when all of the juice had been fermented and the last red wine had been pressed off its skins. Maddie would be on the vintage treadmill for the next eight weeks at least.

Week one of vintage was a scorcher. Daytime temperatures soared, rendering the concrete processing area a desert plain of shifting grapes. Thankfully, temperatures dutifully plunged overnight so the only thing looking hot and frazzled was the crew; the fruit was faring much better. It had been so stifling that on day three Lewis made a quick trip to the hardware store, buying metres of nylon shade cloth which he erected overhead in a series of rough sails to shade the processing area.

Arriving home at the end of the day, regardless of time or energy, Maddie peeled off her sweaty, sticky clothes and struggled, clammy-skinned into her bathers.

It was mid-February, school was back and the hot spell brought families out in droves for late afternoon swims and picnic dinners spread on blankets near the dunes. There was always someone Maddie knew, an industry colleague or a neighbour with their dog, but she avoided conversation until her desire for salt water cleansing had been sated.

The first dive beneath the surface was like ground-hog day. Each time every day felt like the first time she'd ever experienced such exhilaration. When the little bay was calm she floated on her back and let the physical slick of the day drift from her skin, leaving the mental detritus to sink to the ocean floor—eyes closed she'd surrender to the cradling rock of the green embrace. With deep inhalations, her body rose high in the water and its rippling lips caressed her skin. As she exhaled, gravity hugged pulling her deeper.

Time lapsed unmeasured until she opened her eyes expecting to be miles from the beach, to find she hadn't drifted far at all. The ocean, recognising her terrestrial status, politely rebuffing her advance.

If the ocean was really calm, she beached on the rough shell grit in the shallows. Like lying in the bath while the water drains, marvelling at the heaviness of her limbs. Dogs loved the game, bounding to sniff and lick what washed up. Children enjoyed it too, although she suspected children would love anything that left adults wet and covered in sand.

Maddie recognised a group of backpackers working for a vineyard labour hire company. An eclectic mix of Asian, European and South American. They had picked at Kite and their collective attitude and energy was invigorating. They were students, doctors, engineers and teachers, enjoying the digression from their usual routines and responsibilities. They all admitted to falling in love with Australia, spell-bound by the South-West. Maddie waved and joined them. They had beers and a guitar, dreadlocks, tattoos, tiny bikini bottoms and leather and silver jewellery around ankles, wrists and toes.

Accepting a beer, she stayed with them for the sunset. As soon as the sun dipped from view, the temperature dropped and the mozzies bit, driving the group to disperse. They were picking again at Kite in the morning. Marco—swarthy, gorgeous, Italian—gave Maddie a micro-salute and the cheekiest smile before kicking a soccer ball after Juan—tall, tanned, Brazilian.

'OMG,' Maddie fanned herself with her towel, retreating from the beach in the other direction.

Her shack seemed especially dark and quiet after the energy of the travellers. It was only the start of vintage but already the house had the air of abandonment. The emptiness, usually vanishing from the room when she entered, now only seemed to duck behind the couch. Maddie lit some incense, turned on the telly and all of the kitchen and living room lights. She checked the time. It was already too late to call the east coast. Bethany? Stubbsy? They would only worry, want to run to her rescue. She didn't need rescuing. Just someone to talk to would be nice. Maybe someone to cuddle up with on the lounge. Her thoughts wandered to Roley. She let them saunter briefly before rounding them up. She didn't even feel like wine—melancholic better than alcoholic. The thought brought a smile, breaking her reverie. She filled a tumbler with water and scrambled some eggs.

Fork to her lips, there was a quiet knock at the glass door. She swung around to look. The glass acted like a mirror, reflecting the room back. Questioning herself, she turned back to her eggs. Another rap sounded. Maddie swivelled again and strained to see beyond the glass to the deck. In the darkness beyond the glass, she couldn't discern a thing. She stayed seated, staring into the black, not moving, holding her breath to listen. She was about to swing back when the tapping sounded again. Maddie's heart raced. The noise sounded low to the floor. Soundlessly, she slipped off the stool and walked towards the glass, flicking on the outside light. Maddie jumped as something charged the door.

A big, brown tank of a beetle fell backwards onto the deck. Legs swimming through air, it rotated slowly on its armoured back, bits of wings carelessly tucked, protruding from its hard panels. Suddenly, a leg snagged purchase, flipping the beetle over. It walked drunkenly in one direction to stop, turn and pursue another.

Maddie watched while her heart slowed. Its wings

began to twitch. 'Uh oh. Man, you're going to knock your-self out.' Quickly she flicked off lights, walking through the darkened house to fetch the candle from her bedroom. It flickered casting random shadows as she carried it to the bench to finish her eggs.

It was the end of a long day. Westy had the afternoon off to meet a winemaking course commitment and Lewis ducked in and out, sampling vineyards to determine picking sched-ules. Short of hands, with a hectic workload, Maddie began to tire.

Her last task was to prepare a tank of Sauvignon Blanc juice for the addition of yeast the following day. The batch was vibrant with passionfruit zing and one of her favourites so far. At every step she was required to taste it, she affirmed aloud. 'And that is why Margaret River Sauvignon Blanc, Semillon blends kick arse.' Alone in the cellar, she would point at Taxi, and paws crossed, he'd wink his tan eyebrows in considered agreement.

Maddie was nurturing the batch through its journey. She had made the call, with Lewis's blessing, on stopping the press, ensuring only the brightest, cleanest flavours made the first collection of juice. The juice had been cold settled, resulting in the pulpy sediment—lees—falling to the bottom of the tank to form a fluffy, green bed, leaving clear juice above. Then the juice was pumped into another tank, sep-arating it from the sediment altogether. However, in a juicy subplot, the yeast they added to begin the ferment didn't do well in really clear juice. They floated to a point then, with nothing to suspend them, slowly sank to the bottom of the tank and died.

So, after making the juice clear, winemakers needed to cloud it back up, just a little, for the yeast to do its thing. They did this by adding back some of the lees. More twists than a best-selling thriller.

Maddie positioned a hose in the bottom of the lees tank, pumping a small amount into the tank of juice. Then she ran up the stairs and across the catwalk to the top of the tank. Through the narrow opening she inserted a long plunger which she dragged up through the juice to mix the two together.

There was an art to plunging, a rolling action got the juice moving in a circular current around the tank. When she figured the addition sufficiently mixed, she ran back along the catwalk, down the stairs to take a sample of juice from the tank and measure its turbidity.

Maddie had just finished mixing a lees addition and was ready to test the juice when Michael Jackson's *Thriller* blasted from the speakers. The riff went straight to her feet, an ingrained reaction that didn't bear fighting. She did a slick 180° turn and moonwalked her way to the stairs. The metal grate of the catwalk required way more effort to glide than the smooth concrete of the winery floor. Focusing hard on keeping her feet moving smoothly, she heard a noise and spun round.

'Nice moonwalk, Maddie,' Roley declared, jaw straining to suppress a grin.

In the monotone silver-grey room, she felt blood rising in her cheeks, like infrared beacons.

'You may address me as Ms Jackson. And, if you're planning to appraise my moonwalk, you should announce yourself first. Seriously Roley, I could have gone over the edge in shock. Moonwalking one minute, dog-paddling through gravity the next,' she talked fast, willing the redness in her face to fade.

He looked openly amused. 'Actually, I'm about to bail. Just thought I'd see if there was anything I could help you with. Been a long day for you, yeah?'

She rubbed the back of her neck. 'Starting to feel it.' Normally she'd decline the offer. Long, physical days were standard during vintage. But, she was whacked. 'I could use a hand if you can spare fifteen?'

'Yeah, Ms Jackson. I've got fifteen minutes to *thrill*.'

Maddie groaned. Shaking her head she headed for the steps, motioning for him to follow. She began explaining the process loudly before fiddling with the MP3 player, killing Michael mid-song.

'That's better,' her voice returned to normal.

They got a sample from the tank and headed to the workstation where the turbidimeter sat.

Roley examined the device. 'It lives,' he mused.

'So what, you thought I was making it up?' Maddie asked.

'No!' Roley sounded affronted. 'I've just never come across this little piece of equipment.'

'Here, I'll show you how it works. The device runs on electricity,' she explained lifting the lid, extracting a glass vial filled with juice. 'This was my last sample. It read fifty-five.' She held the sample to the light for Roley to see. He nodded and she tipped the juice into the floor drain and filled it with a fresh sample, placing it back in the dock. She closed the lid and pushed the start button. 'Light passes through the juice measuring refraction which indicates matter present in the juice. Filtered drinking water has a turbidity of zero.'

'What do you need the juice to measure?'

'Anywhere from eighty to one hundred,' she checked the display. 'Damn. Seventy-three.'

'More lees?'

'More lees.'

'I'll pump them across and get you to go up and mix it. Then I'll take another sample. All without having to climb another billion stairs.'

Roley headed up and Maddie began the transfer.

He found the open tank and retrieved the handle. 'So just pull this up and down?'

'That's it. Try to get it going in a rolling motion.' She did a little plunging demonstration. 'Just not too rolling, there's a temperature probe at the back of the tank.'

He started working on his roll.

'And Roley…'

He stopped and looked down.

'The tank has been gassed, so don't go putting your head inside.'

He rolled his eyes.

After a few minutes, Maddie yelled, 'I'm going to take another sample.'

Roley stopped plunging. He stepped back from the tank, rubbing his arms.

Maddie gave a little whoop. 'Ninety-five,' she called from the turbidimeter. 'Perfect.' She spun around performing a mini-moonwalk.

Roley shook his head.

Then she was back at the bottom of the tank closing the valve and removing the hose, working fast and efficiently. She connected the hose to a smaller tank reserved for the lees and started pumping once more.

Roley pulled the plunger from the tank and laid it on the catwalk. Then he found the hose, and rinsed it off.

Maddie looked up at the source of the water.

'Cheers Roley.'

'Lid open or closed?' he asked.

'I'll get it. I have to check it before I leave. I will get you to bring the hose around and rinse this tank out though.'

He dragged the hose to the top of the tank Maddie had just emptied.

She cut the pump and disconnected the hose, leaving the valve open before signalling to Roley to start rinsing. Meanwhile, she flushed water through the pump and hose and packed them away.

She noted the rinse water sluicing out through the valve and looked up to observe Roley moving the hose around the sides of the tank giving it a thorough clean.

Excellent. Having helpers could be awkward if you had to redo the work. Roley was doing a great job. She left him to it, turning off and cleaning the turbidimeter and updating the ferment record of the Sauvignon Blanc.

Back at the tank, she noted the water running clear. 'Okay Roley,' she yelled the signal to stop. She waited for the water to drain before pulling out her pocket torch and shining it through the open door of the tank to check it. 'Awesome,' she yelled, smiling.

'Lid open, or closed?'

'Fully open and the hose can be rolled up back near the tap.' Maddie used her hose to quickly flush pulpy remnants off the concrete floor into the drain. Then she ran up the stairs to close the lid of the other tank.

She sidled past Roley, coiling the hose on the catwalk.

'Thanks man,' she smiled. 'You saved me an extra thirty.'

'Next?'

'Done.' She sighed with relief and they climbed down the stairs.

'Tank's not going to start fermenting?' Roley queried.

'Shouldn't. Juice is still too cold. I've turned the cooling off now though and it'll warm up naturally. Hopefully it'll be ready to inoculate tomorrow.'

'Ah, tomorrow,' Roley sighed.

'Let's get out of here.' Maddie gave the cooling control panel a cursory glance and waited for Roley to exit the winery before killing the lights and locking the door.

Outside, a chilly breeze was shooing the warmth from the day.

They walked across the wash-down pad. Rounding the press they could see Lewis through the window of his office, working at his computer. He raised his head, waving as he stood to join them outside.

'Recruiting cellar hands?'

'God, no way,' Roley rubbed his arms. 'Five minutes plunging is enough.'

Maddie smiled. 'I'm beat. Today felt as long as it was.'

Lewis nodded. 'And, another big day tomorrow.'

'Good night's sleep, I'll be right.'

'Westy's in at ten tomorrow morning. Hopefully we can knock things on the head a little earlier.'

He turned to Roley. 'Tomorrow's pick organised?'

'Nets are off, bins are out. I've told Mal to have the team here ready at five-thirty. Soon as it's light enough, they'll be into it.'

'So we should see our first fruit by six-thirty?'

Roley nodded. 'We're good for the first eight rows?'

'Yes.' Lewis confirmed. 'Start where we left off the other day. I'll come through and make the call on how far into the block we'll go. It'll be at least eight to ten rows.'

While they talked logistics, Maddie crouched and stroked Taxi's velvety ears.

'Get out of here,' Lewis exclaimed. 'All of us.'

Taxi knew the drill. He sprang to Lewis's side, almost knocking Maddie over.

Roley held out his hand and helped her to her feet. 'Big plans tonight?'

'Cheese on toast and a cuppa. If I can manage that,' Maddie felt pathetic.

'You've gotta fuel up after a day like today. How 'bout chilli prawn laksa and a beer?'

'Are you kidding me? You're really heading home to whip up a laksa? I love laksa. It's my comfort food. Beer sounds good too. I'd be asleep before you deseed the chilli,' Maddie did her thinking aloud.

'Maddie. Maddie,' Roley took her playfully by the shoulders. 'I got a text from Ben. Laksa is in the pot, ready, waiting, delicious. Beer should be in the fridge. You just have to eat, drink and run. A bowl of laksa and a beer should take around sixty minutes, including conversation, then you can drive down the hill for home. You'll be on your doorstep, eight-thirty—nine tops.'

Maddie laughed. 'Go Ben! I say yes to laksa, beer and dinner companions. Where did I leave my car?'

Roley leaned close. 'Don't look now, but it's the silver one behind us. I'm gonna follow you back to my place in case you fall asleep, or succumb to hysteria on the way.'

In her car, Maddie watched Roley walk towards his ute, before she caught sight of herself in her rear-vision mirror.

'Crap!'

She pulled the lacky from her hair and shook out her ponytail, using her fingers to comb it loose. There was the odd patch where they caught a splash of juice or pulp from the day's processing, dried hard and sticky. She grabbed the lip gloss from the console and noticed her hands were already stained and cracked, telltale signs of vintage. 'Better be washing those before dinner.'

She used the drive to go over the day's events, making a list for tomorrow. The lees tank was nearly full. Check with Lewis. Combine batches or start a new tank? Was all the Chardonnay from tomorrow's pick going into new oak, or were they using some of the barrels from last year? By the time she turned into Roley's driveway, she had cleared her mind. It would all wait for the morning.

There were clouds about the horizon screening the last of the sun's rays in thick streaks of pink.

'Nice sunset,' Maddie called as Roley walked over.

'Yeah. Wish we got to enjoy autumn a little more.'

'I know, some of the best weather of the year, and it's all about the grapes.'

They stopped at the door, removing their boots before padding inside.

'Hey Ben,' Maddie greeted Roley's housemate as he entered the kitchen from the other direction.

'Maddie,' Ben swooped towards her.

She whipped up her hand. 'Warning! Straight from a twelve hour shift. I am a sticky, stinky nightmare.'

Ben laughed, hugging her anyway. He was a winemaker at an estate further south. 'All those grape peptides moisturising your skin while you work—some people pay a fortune for that.'

'Good point. But I'd really like to wash my hands at least. Can I borrow your bathroom?'

'Course.' Ben showed her the way.

Roley headed down the passage. 'Ben, can you get Maddie a beer? I'm going for a quick shower.'

'He would never run to shower if it was just us for dinner,' Ben whispered conspiratorially.

Maddie used the loo and washed her hands, avoiding the mirror. When she returned to the kitchen, Ben opened the fridge door. 'Pale ale or pale ale?'

'Pale ale's perfect, thanks,' Maddie smiled. 'Don't think there's even that much choice in my fridge. Pretty sure I'm completely out. Will have to add beer to my list and then go shopping.'

Ben opened the beer before passing it.

'Thank you.'

They clunked bottle necks.

Maddie had only met Ben a couple of times but there was no doubt he was a gentleman and all-round lovely guy. She suspected he was a little older than her and Roley, though still only early thirties. His girlfriend, Aurelia from northern Spain, was equally gorgeous. They had been housemates before their relationship turned romantic. When that happened, Ben offered the vacant bedroom to Roley.

'Is Aurelia home?'

'Spain,' Ben answered, like he was still coming to terms with the idea. 'Her sister has just had her first baby.'

'That's exciting.'

'Yeah. Aurelia believes the baby needs to see her face and touch and smell her in the first weeks of its life to create a strong bond.' He shook his head slowly. 'Glad it's vintage, it's crazy how much I'm missing her.'

'Maybe it's just that crazy thing called love,' Maddie teased.

'You might be right,' Ben grinned.

They sipped their beers.

'How's vintage looking?'

Maddie launched. 'Awesome. I'm learning heaps. The Chardonnays look more minerally than I anticip…'

Ben nudged her. 'Sorry Maddie, but this is solely for your benefit.'

Roley had stepped quietly into the kitchen behind her on his way from the bathroom to his bedroom to grab a beer.

'Roley never walks around the house half-naked when it's just the two of us.'

Maddie laughed as Roley ducked out of the kitchen, naked except for a towel wrapped tightly around his waist.

He flipped the bird behind his back as he retreated down the passage. 'That's solely for your benefit Ben.'

Maddie tried dismissing Roley's form. She spun quickly back around. 'What were we just talking about?'

Ben laughed, picking up the thread.

Shortly, Roley joined them in the kitchen. As he walked through the door, barefoot in blue jeans and an old T-shirt with wet, tousled hair, Maddie felt a zap. Outside of work, Roley had this affect, knocking her off balance, leaving her floundering. It was unbelievably annoying. Moments ago she'd been intrigued about the experimental batch Ben was hatching. Now she could barely remember what he'd said.

'I think I need to sit down,' Maddie voiced quietly. 'Is there anything I can help with?'

'Come on chef,' Roley goaded. 'I told Maddie she could eat and run. We work hard at Kite. We don't knock off early to whip up gourmet food in the middle of vintage.'

'Yeah, yeah, yeah,' Ben muttered good-naturedly, turning off the hotplate.

Roley grabbed bowls and cutlery and led Maddie to the dining table in the open-plan living area. Floor to ceiling banks of louvres separated the room from a large wooden deck with weeping green peppermint trees beyond.

'Wind's picked up. Reckon we'll eat in.' Roley placed the bowls on the table.

'Sounds great,' Maddie replied laying out placemats.

Ben followed with the steaming pot of laksa. Maddie quickly put down another mat. He deposited the pot and headed back to the kitchen for rice noodles, condiments and serving spoons. He dished noodles into individual bowls before ladling over the laksa, finishing with a sprinkling of coriander and a generous squeeze of lime.

The heart-warming ceremony of the meal resonated with Maddie, grateful to be with friends and suddenly ravenous. 'Yum! I am in laksa heaven. Thank you.' She smiled across the table at Ben then turned to Roley. 'And thank you too for saving me from a night of tea, toast and kamikaze beetles.'

'Kamikaze beetles?' Ben's brow furrowed.

Roley gave him a little nod. 'Sometimes, I find it better not to ask.'

Ben sat back in his seat. 'Oh, like Aurelia and the finer points of bonding with newborns?'

Roley spooned another mouthful of laksa. 'Kind of—only crazier.'

'Hel-lo, I can hear you. How long is Aurelia away?'

'Just two weeks,' Ben grimaced. 'Such a long way to go, and expensive, but Aurelia wouldn't miss seeing her sister and the baby.'

Maddie nodded.

'We're planning to go together later this year and we'll stay longer. Travel around.'

Roley mused. 'That's the thing about living on an island. Takes time and money anytime you want to get off. If you and Aurelia end up together, you'll spend half your life in the air.'

Ben rolled his eyes. 'God you go on—I estimate a quarter. You're right though. Aurelia and her family are close. We'd be going backwards and forwards for the rest of our lives.'

'Yeah,' Maddie mused. 'Backwards and forwards to Spain for the term of your natural life. What a bloody nightmare,' she winked at Ben. Every spoonful of laksa softened her tired muscles, alleviating weariness.

'Good point.' He turned to Roley. 'Are you still thinking about Japan?'

'Yeah, not 'til December. Snow-boarding trip,' he explained to Maddie.

'Nice,' Maddie nodded. 'People froth over the powder there. And the food.'

'Vieve going?' Ben asked.

Roley shook his head, scooping the dregs of his bowl. 'Nah, mate's trip. Vieve's not interested in skiing, or Japan.'

Ben looked quizzical. 'Mate. She's not into wine, the beach, snowboarding or travelling. Tell me again, why are you guys together?'

Maddie watched Roley's jaw harden. He looked thought-ful, like he was working on a reply, but just as he looked about to speak, he tilted his head and took a draught from his beer instead.

'Indo is an easy trip from here, yeah?' Maddie blurted.

Ben was still staring at Roley, head cocked to the side. He turned to Maddie. 'Yeah. Getting out to the islands is sweet. Especially if you surf.'

Roley looked at Maddie and cleared his throat. 'If you're planning to stay around, it's definitely worth the trip from here.'

Exotic spices infused the broth, and the broth infused their spirits. They ate and talked of other things, bigger things than grapes and vintage. But after second helpings, the convivial lightness gained weight and weariness returned.

Maddie caught Roley's eye as she stood to gather the bowls. 'If someone can deal with the leftover laksa, I'll make a start on the dishes.'

'Uh, uh,' Roley warned. 'You can drop those in the sink on your way out.' He stood, picked up the pot and herded her towards the door.

'Can I say goodbye to Ben?' Maddie laughed, looking around Roley to Ben who was only just getting to his feet.

'Quickly,' Roley cautioned. 'No big Aussie goodbyes tonight.'

Maddie blew a kiss. 'Thanks Ben. Sensational laksa.'

'Drop in any time Maddie. Intelligent company is always welcome when you share with a simpleton farm labourer.'

Roley flipped him the bird again.

'…with a compulsive tic.'

He shepherded her all the way to the door. Maddie swooped to grab her boots, not bothering to put them on for the trip home. As she rose, she leant into Roley and kissed his cheek. 'Seriously, thank you. I really needed that today. Everything.'

Roley's hand instinctively moved to her waist. He dropped it again quickly. 'No worries. See you at sparrows.'

Maddie, halfway to her car, turned round and gave Roley a wave. The smile still etched on her face when she pulled up at home.

Chapter 12

Margaret River was enchanting, even as it softly snored. It turned in slumber every now and again, to reveal alluring gems hidden within folds of diversity. There was depth to its beauty, an ironic paradox, as beneath the exquisite skin lay resources that some craved and would indiscriminately plunder, taking advantage of its naive youth and relaxed custodians. Refusal to yield added a thin vein of integrity to its stash of treasures. Exploring the intricate composition of this place promised more reward than brutal exploitation ever would.

In the world of the wine-minded, the region was sleep-walking, dreamily meandering to its place centre stage. Its quaint humility could become a burden if left unchecked; souring, creeping, to lodge as a chip on its young shoulders. Margaret River needed to believe. Comparison to older regions was passé, documented over and time again to little end. Every facet of the region that caught the light spar-kled unique and exquisite. It was time for Margaret River to wake, rise and shine.

Max Monborough wasn't wearing an ap-ra-cot scarf but he strutted into the function like that dude in the song—so irri-tatingly vain. Maddie watched him walk through the door to strike a stilted pose. His head swivelled left, then right, until he found what he was looking for.

The journalist visiting from the United States didn't stand a chance. As she chatted with the winemaker and the CEO of Storylines Wines, Max muscled in, commandeer-ing her attention.

Susan Porter was a renowned blogger and one of the main contributors for New York's, *Heard it on the Grapevine* magazine. The Friday evening function hosted in town at the local Wine Association offices was her last engagement in the region, and Australia, before returning home. Consid-ering vintage was in full swing it attracted a good turnout.

Greg held a bottle of Storylines Cabernet which Maddie presumed they were drinking and discussing when Max joined the group. Through earlier furtive glances Maddie noted the conversation was animated, indicating the journo was enjoying the wine and the company. Maddie expected Greg was extolling the virtues of the region in his subdued, no-nonsense way. He was the best kind of ambassador, refreshingly real.

When Max arrived, the body-language of the whole group changed, becoming suddenly tense and guarded. Maddie couldn't stop staring. She had met Greg, the winemaker from Storylines, only once at a Cabernet tasting. He was a great guy, a passionate, quiet achiever, consistently making stand-out wines. Maddie felt anxious for him at the hands of Max.

Greg gestured to Max with the bottle. Max glanced cursorily at the label before presenting his own with a twisted smile on his smug face. Even from distance, Maddie knew it was a French Burgundy. She noticed the small jerk of Greg's head, registering the rebuff. If Max noticed Greg's response, he didn't seem to care. Instead he took the journo's glass, setting it on a side-table before handing her a clean one, proceeding to uncork the wine.

'Prick!'

'What's that Maddie?' Bethany followed Maddie's gaze, craning to see the cause of her blasphemy.

'Urrg! Max Mono-brow from Mardalup Crest. What a tosser! Do you know him?'

'Never had the pleasure. Should I spit my olive pit in his direction?' Bethany loaded a half-sucked olive pit between her teeth.

'Not while you're standing next to me,' Maddie smacked her arm. 'Feel free to walk past and accidently spill something on him though. Bloody dinosaur, Francophile.'

'Do you mean Dinophilus Max? What are you going on about?'

'These dinosaurs that insist French wines are superior to every other wine on the planet. Haven't you ever met one? There's Alsaceosaurus, they wallow on the plains sipping and swaying in their magnitude, bellowing long and loud to no one in particular. While Loire-Valociraptors attack and bully other wine enthusiasts to their own perverse delight. Why would he even bring that bottle, she's here to try our wines? I just don't understand the attitude.'

'Who is he anyway?'

'You know what Bethany, he's no one. He was someone once, but then he got sucked up in the vortex of his own self-importance and disappeared.'

'So is that the ghost of Max? Will there be a puddle of Burgundy on the floor where he stood when he passes through a wall and out of the room later?'

'Anything's possible.'

'So who is he?' Bethany pushed.

'He's the chief wine*wanker*, I mean wine*maker* at Mardalup Crest.'

'Maddie! It's not like you to be this ferocious. What's he done to you?'

'Nothing!' she exclaimed. 'He's done nothing to me personally, but he gives winemakers a bad name. He's arrogant and aloof.'

'They are olive pit punishable offences,' Bethany loaded up.

They broke into a fit of giggles.

'And, this'll send you spinning,' Maddie declared, indignant. 'The same letters that make *aloof* also make *a fool*.'

'Nice,' Bethany nodded, jutting out her bottom lip, nearly losing the olive she had just popped in her mouth. 'Shit, nearly lost my ammo.'

They were cracking up when Roley wandered over with a bottle of sparkling. 'Good to see you're enjoying yourselves.'

The girls held out their glasses.

'Bethany is threatening to pelt Max with olive pits…half-chewed olive pits.'

Roley tilted his head, looking solemn. 'Hope you're a good shot.'

They all laughed.

'Roley, you know Max way better than me, what do you make of him?' Maddie asked.

'He's okay,' Roley's response was measured.

'Yeah, just what I was telling Bethany. He's okay for an arrogant, condescending prick.'

'Don't hold back,' Roley spluttered. 'Tell us what you really think.'

'He's responsible for some decent wines though, isn't he?' Bethany questioned.

'Certainly, Mardalup Crest puts out some really solid wines. But I don't know how much Max personally has to do with them. I think he spends a lot of his time out of the winery—travelling, marketing, schmoozing…you know.'

'Yeah. It's probably Laurie who's doing the really great work. Laurie is the winemaker under Max,' Maddie explained.

'Yeah. Bit like you and Lewis,' Roley teased, eyebrows raised.

'Not!' Maddie cried. 'I love that Lewis is so hands on. He really wants to be there, the wines are an expression of him. If everyone was that dedicated…'

'Maybe Max isn't that great a winemaker? Maybe it's a good thing he leaves it to Laurie,' Roley ventured.

'Yeah. Maybe his strength is in marketing—an ambassador for Margaret River.'

Maddie nearly choked. 'God help the good things being done here,' she said rolling her eyes.

Bethany popped another olive into her mouth. 'Sorry guys, gotta chew. I've got a clear shot.'

Roley offered more sparkling.

'Not me,' Maddie put a hand over her glass. 'Driving.'

'I'm driving. I can drop you home?' Roley offered.

Maddie whipped her hand away. 'Awesome. Why not? I've got a day off tomorrow.'

Roley raised his eyebrows. 'Just tomorrow? We're not picking again 'til Monday.'

'I'll go in for an hour or two on Sunday to check ferments, make sure the cooling is okay,' she smiled. 'It won't be a big session compared to what we've been doing.'

'Got to love living in town,' Bethany grinned, offering up her glass. 'I'm on foot.'

Someone called to Roley from across the room. He finished topping her glass. 'Catch you later,' he promised, moving off.

Maddie noticed Bethany watching him intently. 'Don't even think about it girlfriend,' she raised her eyebrows and the glass to her lips in one smooth action.

'Is that because he has a girlfriend, or because he has a girlfriend and a waiting list?'

'I'm exercising my constitutional rights and not answering that question.' Maddie locked her lips with an invisible key, alluding to drop it in her champagne flute.

'Well that may mean something in the good ol' USA but here in Margaret River your constitution is really going to be screwed if you swallow that key.'

'Touché!' Maddie spoke out of the corner of her mouth.

They cracked up again. Regaining composure was taking longer each time, proportional to sparkling consumption.

With Max in her sights Maddie suddenly announced. 'Wait here. I'm going to teach that man a lesson.'

'You're being very immature,' Bethany scolded, taking her glass.

Maddie, with no plan, marched towards Max who still held the journalist hostage.

As it happened, Max assumed the lead. As she approached he flicked a hand at her. 'We need a clean glass here.'

No—excuse me. No—please. Maddie was stunned. Then it slowly dawned. Max didn't recognise her. In her black leggings and white blouse he thought she was a waitress. Where was an olive pit when you needed one? She looked at her blouse. Silky, bamboo cotton with gorgeous glass buttons and double stitching detail. *Friggin' Neanderthal! No woman in her right mind would waitress in this.*

She remembered the day she had shopped with Jacquie, her stylish Melbournian friend who never had a fashion faux pas in her life. Jacquie insisted Maddie needed 'pieces' that would work, no matter how hard she tried to butcher the look. Jacquie was under no false illusions of Maddie's dress sense. Over coffee, to develop the agenda, Jacquie had explained that a white blouse was an item every woman should possess along with a LBSD (little black sexy dress) and a serious pair of boots. Maddie was soon to learn, in Jacquie speak, 'serious' meant paying nothing less than half your monthly salary.

Jacquie cried with delight when she found the blouse. Apparently it was 'perrrfect'. She could dress it up or dress it down. Tuck it in or wear it out. Wear a lacy bra underneath or a coloured camisole. Funky pendant or a string of pearls. Scarf, jacket, belt. God, it was more functional than a forklift. Maddie wondered how she'd successfully traversed life without one.

'Clean glass,' Max raised his voice, opening his mouth wide, enunciating the words.

Christ! Maddie startled. He thinks English is my second language. He deserved punishment, no question.

Maddie nodded curtly and Max dismissed her, turning back to the journalist. Quickly she whisked a tray from the side-table, collecting a couple of bottles and some glasses before turning on her heels.

'He thinks I'm a waitress,' she moaned, setting down the tray.

Bethany appeared mortified. 'Well, picking up a tray and collecting the empties is really showing him, isn't it?'

Maddie picked up a bottle and filled two glasses with French Burgundy, satisfaction spreading across her face. 'I think I really did.'

Bethany's mouth dropped open.

'Cheers,' Maddie snorted.

Minutes later, a disturbance erupted across the room. Max looked bewildered. His head swivelled comically left to right.

Maddie spoke slowly in a modulated voice, 'not only has that foreign waitress failed to supply a clean glass but my precious Burgundy has vanished.'

Bethany and Maddie giggled uncontrollably causing a few people to turn and look. Maddie moved to hide behind Bethany, out of Max's line of sight.

'God Maddie, I need to pee.'

Heads down, backs to Max, clutching glasses and the bottle, they smothered their giggles and headed for the Ladies', bursting with laughter as the door closed behind them.

Tasting fine wine while frequenting the loos was not a usual combination of activities, even in Margaret River. However, Maddie suspected it was typical of what could be expected when she and Bethany got together, especially when bubbles were involved. Whatever—it proved popular as women hurrying into the loos hurried out just as quickly to retrieve a glass and return.

The women were delighted to try something unfamiliar in the melamine, tiled space usually reserved for perfunctory tasks. The bottle was probably empty before Max had calmed himself and the girls were thrilled with their public relations success.

It was so well received they considered heisting another interesting bottle and carrying on the new tradition, when the door opened and Maddie caught sight of Roley as he walked into the Men's room opposite.

The sight of him caused the usual unnerving reaction, literally a shock to her system. Disturbingly, it seemed to be happening more often. In an effort to counter it, Maddie had adopted an affirmation—acknowledge and let go. But this latest jab, direct to her thorax, instilled a different response— acknowledge and pursue.

'Are you alright?' Bethany asked. 'Confrontation time?'

'Bethany. How you know the capitulations of my mind before I do, I don't know. Do you have special powers I should know about?'

'We're both women. It isn't rocket science.' A queer expression took over Bethany's face. 'Is Vieve even still on the scene? You know he hardly mentions her lately and I haven't seen her for ages. Maybe it's time you put yourself out there. See what happens.'

'God, do you think?'

'I do. Just…crap, I'm sorry to say this, but just be pre- pared it may not go the way you want.'

'I know. Believe me. But I'm thinking that at least if I know where he really stands then I can just deal with it. I'll have to.'

'What if Vieve is still in the picture?' Bethany asked gently.

'I don't know. Surely he'd say. It's just I'm getting this vibe. I need to know if it's based in reality or wishful think- ing. Meanwhile I'm going crazy. I keep trying to analyse every conversation looking for signs. I'm worried I'll end up a paranoid wreck.'

'You might have missed the boat on that one.'

'What can I say? I'm sure delusional has levels. I'm playing hopscotch on the edge of the crazy-town abyss.'

'Time to jump? Let's quit the loos at least.'

'Bethany Grylls, I love your spirit. Break free from the toilet block and take on the world.'

The girls moved back into the room scanning warily.

In a strange turn of fate Maddie and Max's eyes momentarily locked. Maddie registered recognition creep into his expression but in 'kangaroo in the headlights' fashion she couldn't break contact.

'There's Roley,' Bethany yanked her arm, leading her away.

'Hey guys. I've been looking for you. Thought you might've left?'

Maddie and Bethany looked at him dumbly. 'We were just hanging out in the loos.'

'O–kay. Anyway, I'm ready to shoot.' He turned to Maddie. 'Still chasing a lift?'

What the…? What was that supposed to mean? Of course she still wanted a lift. She hadn't chased it, he had offered. He'd sounded keen to take her home.

'Yes, I'm still interested in your *offer*. Especially now I've had another glass or two.' Over Roley's shoulder, Maddie glimpsed Max moving through the crowd toward them.

'Crap. Let's go!' She took Roley and Bethany's arms and made for the exit.

The humidity took them by surprise as they left the air-conditioned building, heavy air pressed on their skin taking their breaths.

'That's come in quick. They forecast a storm but not until

early morning,' Roley cleared his throat. 'Can we give you a lift?'

'I'm good, thanks.' Bethany smiled. 'The walk home will be perfect.'

'What are you up to?' Maddie asked.

'I've got a little left over curry from last night's dinner, a good glass of red left in a bottle on the bench, if Rick hasn't drunk it already, and the end of a movie that I fell asleep watching on the couch. So I guess I'm doing the other half of what I started last night.' Bethany laughed. 'Should I be out getting a life or something?'

'Sounds perfect,' Maddie leaned in for a hug.

'Go hard or go home,' Bethany whispered, punching her arm.

'Night Roley.' She blew a kiss, then turned and did a little skip.

Roley and Maddie walked to his ute in silence.

Dusk approached bathing the town in light limbo; the in-between light where electric bulbs radiated insignificant against the fading light of day. By the time they'd driven out of town and rounded the corner above the bay, lights twinkled softly against a moody darkening sky.

Maddie felt uncomfortable on the trip home. The splinter Roley lodged under her skin, starting to throb. Confinement in his car amplified her annoyance leaving her on edge.

'I never get tired of this view,' Roley said turning his head to look at her.

What the...? She wasn't letting her head loose on that one.

'Me neither,' her eyes drilled back.

The car pulled into the drive. It had barely stopped when Maddie flung open her door and jumped out. Without looking back she slammed the door and charged towards the house.

'Beer?' she practically shouted the word and kept charging, not waiting for Roley or a response.

Roley remained seated. Seconds passed before he undid his seatbelt and opened the door. His right foot hovered above the ground. Suddenly he pulled it back, closing the door, reaching for the keys in the ignition. His hand rested there, fingers slowly tapping the dashboard. Turning, he glanced at the rear-vision mirror. He sat gazing into it for a while eventually breaking contact to slump forward and rest his forehead on the steering wheel, hands gripping the sides.

Chapter 13

The moon and stars gained brilliance in the sky. Beneath them, wispy veils of cloud sped towards the horizon where they melded together in a burgeoning mass, a storm front forming over the sea. On the ground, the evening was warm and still, the air thick and charged.

An opened beer waited on the counter. Roley picked it up, and walked out onto the deck.

Maddie sat tall on the cushions of the day bed, softly pressing a glass of white wine to her forehead. Roley moved past, standing with his back to her, looking out at the ocean. He took a swig from his beer, one arm balanced on the railing when the first flash of lightning ricocheted across the sky.

Watching his silhouette intently, Maddie let out a small gasp of surprise as a deep rumble echoed around them. Soundwaves chasing cheetah-fast slivers of light.

'Sky show,' Roley turned to face her.

Maddie studied him. He didn't flinch. She softened her gaze.

Any other time, this attentive scrutiny in close proximity, would send them scurrying to opposite poles. But this night, heavy with flux, a switch flicked and they jumped track.

'You're mad at me, aren't you?'

'Ya think?' Maddie rolled her eyes.

'This will probably make you crosser, but would you mind telling me why?'

'This is where you should feel fortunate I insist on good quality glasses. Makes me less inclined to throw them.'

'Ha!' Roley couldn't suppress his amusement.

'You *offered* me a lift,' the words were an accusation.

'I did,' Roley agreed.

Silence.

'That's important because…sorry, I'm waiting for the twist?'

'Because, there is a world of difference between 'being offered' and 'chasing'.'

'Ah.'

'I'm not *chasing* anything,' Maddie's look embossed every word.

'Okay,' Roley raised his hands. 'I get it.'

Maddie wondered if he really did or if he was just waving the white flag. Either way she'd made her point. She relaxed into the cushions.

He turned his back once more, staring up into the sky. 'The Coalsack Nebula is clear tonight—between the clouds anyway.'

The reference to the Southern Cross was an attempt to appease. Maddie raised an eyebrow. 'The Incan God who put it there must have been a woman.'

'What?'

'It's an old South American legend, Stubbsy told me. Today we know the Coalsack within the Southern Cross is just a silhouette. A dark patch of interstellar dust which hides the light of the background Milky Way stars. However, years ago, the Incans believed that one of their Gods, in a fit of rage, had kicked at that section of the sky causing a patch of stars—like a clod of earth—to land in another part of the galaxy leaving the dark patch in its place.'

'Closer to home…isn't it the Emu's head?'

'Mm, hmm,' Maddie acquiesced.

'Can I join you for the view?'

Maddie barely registered the words, comprehending only the energy emanating from him as he turned.

She shifted on the day bed, suddenly aware of her legs. Toes in a soft point, toned muscles stretching long and lithe. As she lifted her backside an intense concentration of sensations gripped her pelvis. Her body was off and running. Instinct told her that fight or flight were only two options in this scenario, the third was sex. Her body had made its decision. She reached to place her glass on the floor.

Roley sat and the points where they touched became live, completing a circuit. Maddie extended her body down the length of his side.

'Are you still mad at me?'

The question went unanswered. Centuries of evolving language and words remained ridiculously superfluous in the presence of touch. Neither uttered another.

Roley assumed the lead, bending his elbow, levering onto his side. The knuckles of his free hand traced the side of her face. When they reached her neck his fingers raked up through her hair, gently pulling her face to his.

Their lips met tentatively, barely touching before parting to meet again, creating a series of reverberations with every coupling. Lips softly parted opened wider as the force behind them intensified. Tension built quickly in their bodies, turning muscle hard and nerves ultra-sensitive. Too quickly it was unclear where they ended and the outside world began. A roll of thunder fused with the wave of their momentum.

Maddie became aware of her breasts pushing hard into Roley's chest, seeking skin. She was beginning to pant with her desire for it, frustrated with unyielding layers of cotton and lace.

Suddenly, she broke their embrace and pulling her legs beneath her, sat up. Her shins rested on Roley's upper thigh. Methodically she undid the beautiful, square glass buttons of her shirt. Roley's hands came to rest on the outside of her thighs, his eyes fixed on her hands.

She opened the last button and shrugged her shoulders, dislodging the shirt—a cool, cotton breeze sliding down her back. She undid the buttons on the cuffs, one after the other, slowly, aware of Roley's eyes. Once free of the shirt, she leant forward to unclasp her bra. The clasp gave easily and with another gentle shrug of each shoulder the straps slipped down her arms. She threw the bra after her blouse. Sitting tall, Maddie was as keenly aware of her breasts as Roley. They felt fabulous freed from restraint, firm, nipples puckered, ready for skin. Roley read her mind.

He leaned in close and wove a shaft of her hair between the fingers of one hand while two fingers of the other traced lines the length of a breast, either side of the nipple. Maddie arched involuntarily. He repeated the delicate finger tracing on her other breast before gently tugging on the coil of hair drawing her towards him.

When she was close enough, Roley let the hair unspool and moved his hands to firmly grip her shoulder blades. Holding her so, he kissed her mouth before dropping his head and tracing his tongue, encircling her hardened nipples.

God! She might have spoken it aloud. Her head dropped back and she arched, pushing into him. She hoped the word fizzled in the static of the storm. This felt divine, no intervention wanted.

As she lifted her head, Roley moved his hands to cup her breasts. Maddie was mesmerised by the look in his eyes as he watched her nipples, gently tracing his thumbs across them.

Maddie's pelvis pulsed. Beneath her skin a web of tissue and cells worked an operatic interplay sending and receiving messages, deciphering and responding; trigger, release, engorge, contract—manic activity, preparing for pleasure.

She roused from Roley's nipple teasing and with determined concentration started work on his shirt buttons. Her desire for skin was becoming vexatious toward clothing. Shirts, bras, jeans, undies, belts—God damn it—so many clothes.

Roley's mouth was set to lips parted, pleasure mode but his eyes smiled at her growing frustration. As she undid the last button, he rose to his knees, dropping his shirt shoulder by shoulder. Maddie took in his hard surfer's physique, before Roley pulled her up on her knees drawing their bodies together.

Arms wrapped around each other, maximising skin contact, their lips met in a long, hard kiss. Neither wanted to break the embrace, but momentum swept them on. Maddie could feel Roley's penis hard through his jeans, pulsing against her hip.

'God damn these clothes!'

Roley smiled broadly. He broke the embrace to release

his belt buckle. Maddie wasted no time pushing her thumbs into the waistband of her leggings, plunging them down. She took her knickers with them and once freed from her feet, threw them with exalted vigour onto the growing pile of garments, pooled submissively on the deck.

Clothes on the floor emit an engaging subtext; litter of the distracted, lazy or impassioned discard of better things to do. Their power lost, removed from the energy source. Status neutralised, reduced to fibres and fasteners. Designer dress and faded black denim, out of sync side-by-side on the street, become a harmless, eclectic tangle on a rug.

Naked now, she turned her attention back to Roley. Sitting back high on her knees, the area between her legs felt so good to be free. She could feel the night air, knew she was wet, ready for him.

Roley, belt undone, had stalled to watch her.

Maddie pushed him gently back on the bed and straddled his hips, the movement parting her lower lips. Roley groaned softly as Maddie lowered herself onto the hardness in his jeans. She ducked her head and traced her breasts forward along the length of his bare chest, raising her head to meet his mouth again.

While they kissed, Maddie traced her fingers down his abdomen and started undoing the button and zip of his jeans. Her hand slid inside, over his hard penis.

Roley groaned again at her touch.

She felt the head of his penis, trawled her fingers around it.

Suddenly Roley turned onto his side.

Maddie thought he was rising to take off his jeans. Instead, using his legs, he rolled her onto her back. It was a slick move leaving Roley levered on his side, lips level with her breasts.

He paused, rising up, taking her body in. He pulled some cushions from the side of the day bed and placed them carefully under her head, then he took a smaller one and lifting her with one arm, placed it beneath her backside, raising her hips.

If Roley had practised this move, if it was something he did with every girl he ever made love to, there was nothing in his manner to suggest it. His eyes and his touch never left her. Any energy that flowed from him was hers. Whatever had been in the past, whatever the future held, in this moment there was only her. The intensity of their coupling morphed into an electrifying now.

Maddie was lost in the haze of sensation that was ebbing over and around her body. She literally sucked in air when Roley, with one hand, parted the lips of her vulva at the mound where it began. Physically so vulnerable, she felt overwhelmingly safe with this man. She gave herself to his touch.

Roley began tracing his finger along the side of her vulva, drawing a line between the inner and outer labia lips. She heard him exhale deeply as his finger slid; slippery pleasure in finding her wet.

When his finger traced along one side he followed the 'u' around the top and feathered down the other side, then reversed the action.

Maddie could hardly breathe. Her breath had slowed to long, deep inhales, followed by shallower exhales and whispered sighs. There was a pause in the middle, where breath stalled, everything silenced by the touch of Roley's finger as it slid around the wet, swollen rim of her.

Teasing pleasure built slowly becoming an unbearable desire to be sated. Maddie wanted Roley's penis inside her.

She tried levering herself up, to formulate words but she was dumb with aching pleasure. Roley looked at her intensely.

'Patience Madison,' he whispered hoarsely. The elbow of the hand he was using to part her vulva was resting on her stomach. He applied just enough pressure to let Maddie know he wouldn't yield. She wasn't going anywhere.

Maddie surrendered. Roley's finger stayed on course. Up, across, down. Up, across, down. With each sweep her vagina ached to be filled.

Maddie reached her threshold. Supine, elegantly aroused on the outside, on the inside she was a frenzied mess. She was about to forcibly protest when suddenly—Roley stopped.

She started to move, his penis her motivation, when he pressed two fingers to her clitoris. He applied the lightest pressure, a two-fingered fairy clap and her body spasmed into oblivion.

'Oh! Oh Godddd!' Maddie didn't come quietly.

Roley didn't move until she was spent.

Her desire turned instinctively from Roley's penis to his mouth. She tugged at his shoulders pulling him up.

Roley sidled up, stopping to kiss a nipple on the way.

As their lips met, a welling of emotion passed between them—heat, tenderness, respect. They kissed it out, reaching a new understanding. There was to be nothing static in their evolvement. The altered state of their friendship was a thing of energy, growth and change. Breaking the kiss, it felt extraordinary.

'How it is you are still wearing your jeans is one of life's great mysteries that I am totally about to solve.'

Roley didn't resist as she pushed him back. Maddie got to her feet and taking a good hold of the waistband of his jeans, peeled them down. Roley lifted his hips as she pulled.

She took his jocks with them, not wasting time on theatrics.

Roley's penis stood up in appreciation—a fine decision.

The stormy soundtrack started counting in percussion. Fat drops of rain hit the tin roof.

Maddie dropped a cushion to the floor, exchanging a look with Roley before taking his penis in one hand, steering it towards her mouth. Roley closed his eyes. She loved the intimacy of this act. When instinct gave the all clear, it filled her with desire, and desire to please.

Roley's penis was a gorgeous extension of the man; sensitive and strong. Maddie moved her mouth up and down its length, stopping to circle her tongue around its tip before closing her mouth around it fully, gently sucking as her tongue worked around the head.

When Roley's breathing changed, Maddie figured she was on borrowed time. Her pleasure didn't include gagging on body fluids. She moved up to straddle him, suddenly remembering the basics. 'Condom?' as she asked, she thought of her toiletries case. She kissed his mouth and ran to the bathroom. She returned, tearing into a packet with her teeth. She gave Roley another look, sweet and intense, before lowering herself again. She kissed the tip of his penis, fondling subtly with her tongue and lips before sliding the condom over. Then she straddled him bending forward to kiss his mouth. Straightening, she used one hand to guide him into her, lowering herself the length of his shaft.

Having him inside her felt insanely good. Maddie could see the struggle in Roley's eyes. He wanted it to last but Maddie was impatient for him to share her pleasure. She smiled, rising, sliding her body up his length, to pause and slowly lower.

This feeling of one inside the other was sublime. Physical pleasure was the central theme, but deftly threaded through the weave, was the physiological desire to take each other beyond known bounds.

With each rise and lowering of her hips, Roley moved closer to the edge and when she was certain he was about to tip she reached down and cupped his balls.

The muscles of Roley's face tightened into the twisted shape of release. Maddie plunged down taking him deep inside, holding tight, his spasms etching her core.

Roley's breath gradually slowed. Any sounds he had made were absorbed by the rain thrumming on the roof. As he opened his eyes, running a hand through his hair, Maddie pulled herself up, releasing him. They lay together, entwining arms and legs, and kissed.

Maddie shivered. The rain had cleansed and cooled all that it touched. Roley rose, retreating inside the house to return with her doona. They rearranged themselves around each other, nerves still sensitive, taking in each other's smell, unable to resist stroking, the feel of the other's skin.

Neither wanted words in this space. Nothing said could have meaning here. Silly sounds dribbled from lips implying intelligence of sorts. Better holding tight, meditatively bound, focusing on the energy enveloping them, cocooning rhythm of heartbeat and breath.

The elements misted and blew, light flashed and thunder drummed. An epic scene from a classic drama played out before them, totally lost on them. Their bodies, layered, formed an intimate galaxy, impenetrable and bigger than belief.

They drifted for a time before rousing again, kissing and fondling. Roley rose on two strong arms, and sorted a condom before pushing into her once more, slowly sliding back. Her pelvis tilted and her hips lifted to meet his thrusts, the hard fullness, the sticky mustiness, the slight hold as he could drive no further before the slow, withdrawing slide.

He raised his head, looking into her eyes. Maddie smiled softly up at him before closing her eyes, lost to the pleasure of his rhythmic thrusts.

Dropping his mouth to her nipple, deftly working it with his tongue and lips, she wrapped her legs around him. With the sounds of impending climax, Roley made one last drive into her and let go.

Burying her face in his neck, he kissed her shoulder until their muscles eased. They lay like that while time did its own thing. Time, like words, had no business here.

They must have drifted again. The next time Maddie woke it was quiet and still. Roley stood close, wearing his jeans, shirt thrown over his shoulder.

Her mind ticked but drew blank. He bent and sat beside her. Maddie felt sick. He was going to speak. She braced. His words would be inadequate. His words were going to hurt.

He leant in to kiss her lips and ran his hand down the side of her face.

He hadn't intended to speak—her feelings for him overwhelmed her. It was Maddie who naively initiated the slaughter. 'Are you around later?'

An eternity passed. 'Perth.' He searched her face.

The blow rocked her. From the fallout inside her head she pulled the biggest, fattest, most complex lie she had ever told.

'I understand.'

'I understand?'

Maddie was too late pulling her mobile away from her

ear. Bethany almost yelled the words, her voice louder, higher with each syllable.

'I know. I know,' Maddie lamented.

'Damn straight. And that's exactly the reply you could have given. You could have said 'I know' with some indignation in your voice or posed it as a question even. But... 'I understand'.'

There was a pause while Bethany drew breath. Maddie knew she hadn't finished, her shoulders drooped apathetically.

'You've just given him the most perfect out at the very moment you could have sought some confirmation of in.'

Maddie couldn't summon a reply. Bethany was right. In her current mind-set anything she said would sound submissive or defensive.

'I'm just mortified for you. Where do you go from here?'

'That is a really good question. The six million dollar question of the moment. I have no idea.' Maddie shook her head.

'I feel for you, Maddie, I really do. After everything you've told me, it's just so...disappointing.'

Maddie didn't want to talk anymore. It was an effort to find words and when some did find their way to her brain, they seemed wrong. It was exhausting. 'I've gotta go B.'

'I'm working today but I'm free later. I'll text you.'

'I'm fine B, really. I'll see you Monday.'

As they disconnected, Maddie smiled wryly. *Compulsive liar—that's new.*

The storm front had passed, leaving a grey morning of chilly showers in its wake.

On the rope that served as a makeshift clothesline, her

sodden beach towel hung low and heavy dragging in the shell grit. The tendril straps of her bikini top snaked around the line in a twisted mess, the bottoms lying in a soggy scrunch in the dirt beyond.

Was it only yesterday morning she had swum, revelling in the warmth that preceded the front? It felt so long ago. Something strange had happened to time and her place in it. Last night didn't feel real. If it was real, where was Roley now? They should be heading to the markets for croissants. Sitting together watching umbrellas clash in the drip and run of the rain. Pastry flakes clinging to their hoodies, buttery fingers clasping coffee cups. Bodies close, sharing warm breaths and sticky kisses.

There was a glitch. Something deeply flawed. If last night was real, Roley would be with her now. Her brain could not conceive an alternative. Other possibilities seemed irrational. On one level she knew Roley was in Perth with Vieve but the idea of it was too alien to entertain. She knew her brain would process events in due course, but for now the image of her and Roley last night and the thought of Roley and Vieve together did not compute. Too ludicrous for words.

With her head threatening to implode, Maddie sought the solace of a hot shower. She moved to rise and her pelvis twinged, stiff from a night of sex. It hit Maddie like a rockfall. Last night was real. Roley was with Vieve. Her thoughts stampeded, shorting synapses, spinning the cogs of her brain, pushing her down once more.

Sometime later she summoned the energy to try again. Once on her feet she resolved to keep moving, no dwelling. The water of the shower warmed and soothed. As she made her way down the back steps to rescue her beach gear, the soggy disarray of it brought overwhelming sadness. She turned on her heels and raced back to the shack. Ten minutes of extreme vacuuming later, she smiled at the thought of being rattled by bathers and a towel.

She rode the roller coaster of disturbed, okay, fragile into the afternoon. When she wanted to rest, she couldn't face being alone. As she headed up the hill, the sight of Stubbsy on his front veranda brought instant calm. On seeing her, Stubbsy raised his hand and waved her up. If he was taken off guard by her heartfelt embrace when she reached his balcony, he didn't let on.

'Kettle's just boiled. We'll start there, eh? We can always go north for something stronger,' Stubbsy winked.

It was a reference to the gin on top of his fridge. Maddie pulled up a chair. Stubbsy had to have thirty-odd years on her. He wasn't quite a father figure but he knew things and he loved to talk. Maddie accepted a steaming mug of green tea and curled up in the chair, ready to bathe in his conversation that she knew could take them anywhere.

'I've heard it's not long 'til we see the first set of traffic lights in Margies, eh. Me mate works for the Dunsborough Shire and he overheard one of the planners there talking about it. Somethin' about the intersection of Wallcliffe and Forrest not being wide enough for a roundabout…for the trucks, you know. It's a good thing too 'cos nobody on the bloody road knows what to do on a roundabout, eh. They indicate when they're going straight ahead. Then the buggers who are taking a left or right exit don't bother indicating at all. No bloody idea.

'The ones I love the best, are the ones that sit there. Stop and sit there, just giving bloody way. Have a little cup of tea and a blueberry muffin. Check the footy scores or somethin'. And there's bloody nothin' on the roundabout to give way to.

'I was driving the other day along Railway Terrace, almost at the roundabout, when the car in front just stops. After a few minutes I got out and asked the driver what they were waiting for. Was there a comet racing towards our atmosphere on course for five metres ahead or did they just hear a car turn off Caves Road and thought they better play it safe and wait just in case it was heading this way?'

Maddie laughed. Caves Road was three kilometres from that intersection.

'You're a tough audience today Maddie,' Stubbsy looked at her, sitting back in his chair.

Maddie smiled and sipped her tea.

'You know the roundabouts are bad enough but I'm really worried about the effect the new parking bays in town are gonna have on future generations. They've built all these new shops and buildings, commercial premises, in the centre of town. Forgot about the bloody cars though, didn't they. So they've decided to let them park all the way up the road to the corners.'

'What about the underground parking?'

'Oh, you mean the car dungeon? Maddie, Margaret River and car dungeons, I dunno, a thousand tonnes of cold, dark concrete closing in around our heads.'

'Handy when it's raining.'

'Hmmm, our backyard is an adventure playground. I'd rather park on the roof and abseil down.'

Maddie smiled, shaking her head.

'Around the Post Office now you want to see if the road is clear, nothing speeding down the hill to clean you up, and you have to get out of your car and walk halfway 'cross the intersection to get a clear view.

'Well now, you know I'm exaggerating. You have to crane

your neck like that Go Go Gadget fella. I'm beginning to understand how the town can sustain so many physios. They're all busy massaging our dislocated necks from trying to see around cars parked on corners. Future generations of Margaret Riverites are gonna start to resemble the Karen tribe in Thailand. We'll all have these elongated necks from years of craning to see if an intersection's clear.'

Maddie was laughing softly. Stubbsy therapy. She hadn't thought of Roley for at least five minutes.

'Oh but Maddie, I've been saving my favourite 'til last. Don't you love the two off-kilter intersections on the main street? The one at the hotel and the one at the tourist bureau? Poor bloody tourists who drive into town thinking they've got the road rules sussed, hitting those intersections.

'People stop in the middle of the road to turn right and they stop too far back from the turn so other people turn in front of them. People going from east to west don't know whether to treat it as an intersection or a T-junction. Do I give way? You go. No I'll go. No you go. Bamm!'

Stubbsy gesticulated wildly. 'Good for mosaic artists I s'pose, all those smashed mirrors and lights.'

'And talking about the tourist bureau what do you make of the bloody wombats?'

'The megafauna?' Maddie smiled, knowing full well Stubbsy knew what they were. The megafauna were ancient animals, related to present day wombats. Skeletal remains had been found in the network of limestone caves that existed beneath pockets of land between the two capes.

'First time I saw 'em, I wondered what the hell they were thinking putting bloody polar bears on display. Wrong bloody colour! Wrong bloody pole! They would have been better off putting hi-vis vests on 'em and planting 'em in the middle of the intersection. Serve the community as traffic control.'

'Oh, Stubbsy,' Maddie laughed.

'Good to see another cafe on the main strip nearly ready to open, eh. We must be the biggest users of coffee beans in the free world. I don't know who's drinking all this coffee but you'd think with sixteen coffee shops on the main drag people wouldn't be sitting at roundabouts waiting for cars to come by. They should be racing about escorting coffee bean delivery trucks or somethin'.'

Maddie laughed, lost in the world of Stubbsy. It was welcome reprieve from her encumbered thoughts. He had barely taken breath mocking local idiosyncrasies. Somewhere in his storytelling he'd made her a G&T. She hadn't noticed the fading light and was well into her gin when Stubbsy drew her attention to the car moving slowly down the street. It pulled into her driveway. Not one she recognised. Maddie drained her glass.

'Stubbsy, you're funny. I'll never look at a roundabout the same way again—ever. Thank you.'

'Maddie girl. My balcony is a better place for you having graced it. Now, go and see who your visitor is, and if you need anything, you just holla,' he tilted his head.

Maddie nodded and set off. Maybe not father figure, but Stubbsy was looking out for her.

Maybe Bethany had borrowed someone's car? But it didn't belong to any of her housemates.

As the distance increased from the cocoon of Stubbsy's balcony, lethargy settled into her step. She wasn't up for visitors. With a gin under her belt, all she wanted was to curl up on the couch, watch telly, drink tea and let her brain be mush.

The car's occupant was nowhere to be seen. Maddie walked through the front door.

'Hey Beth, I've just been up to Stub...' Holy fuck! Her stomach lurched and her feet fixed to the spot.

Genevieve stood holding the rail of the back deck, looking seaward. The exact position Roley assumed the previous night—before they had unbelievably great sex.

She watched dumbly, as Vieve brushed the back of her hand against her cheek. Christ, was she crying? Her heart kicked up a beat. Maddie quickly looked around, a guilty search for evidence. Vieve hadn't noticed her yet, maybe she could slip back out, make a run for Stubbsy's. Fight or flight? Fight or flight? No third options in this scenario. Maddie put her hand to her chest. Vieve turned. Their eyes locked.

Vieve's mouth twisted into a tortured smile. Maddie raised her hand feeling the corners of her mouth involuntarily lift in response. She moved towards the back deck, nausea shadowing every step, her vocabulary of original responses evacuating the scene.

'Genevieve. This is a surprise.'

'Hi Maddie,' Genevieve looked like she was trying hard to hold it together. She hurried on. 'I'm so sorry to just turn up like this, but...' her words faded. She took a deep breath. 'But...'

Maddie jumped as Vieve re-fortified.

'I'm worried about Roley. I don't know where else to turn. Can we talk?'

Maddie's brain worked frenetically. She was being called to account. Behaving badly in and around relationships had consequences. And right now, they were staring her in the face. In the chaos, another synapse campaigned for distraction, registering how lovely Vieve looked. Her face rendered tight with emotion lost none of its attractiveness. Under duress, her speech remained measured and cool. A little thing like despair unable to alter her appeal—if anything, she became more interesting.

Maddie realised Vieve had stopped talking. 'Oh,' she replied lamely. 'Sure.'

Still, Maddie's brain tried fervently to distort the situation, procuring a visual image of how she would look if the situation was reversed. Red, watery eyes, runny nose, puffed and splotchy face. Everything she said, punctuated with miserable sniffs. People would see her coming, hunched and morbid, kilometres away and sprint in the opposite direction.

Maddie blinked the image away and tried to concentrate. She knew Vieve was still on the scene when Roley left last night, but did she know it before? She was rooted in Vieve's distress, yet part of her wanted to reach out and offer comfort. A micro-rocket of anger fired, heat seeking Roley. What about his responsibility in this?

Vieve's strained blue eyes bored into her.

'Tea? Wine?'

Vieve relaxed with the offer. She smiled weakly. 'A glass of wine would be great, if I'm not imposing.'

'Please, sit. I'll be right back and we'll talk.' Maddie walked to the kitchen and rested her head against the fridge. She removed a bottle of white and put it on the bench to fetch two glasses. The initial shock was dissipating, but the situation remained surreal. Vieve looked sad; young and sad. Maddie could barely piece one thought to another but understood she had a responsibility to meet. She warned herself, whatever unfolds, whatever direction the conversation takes, be real.

Vieve perched on the edge of the day bed.

As Maddie handed her a glass of wine an image of her and Roley occupying the space less than twenty-four hours earlier screened in her head, followed by a flash of pain between her temples.

Maddie thought carefully before she spoke. 'I didn't know you were coming down this weekend. I thought Roley was heading to Perth?'

'That was the plan. There was some function on last night, something for a wine writer from the States. Did you go?'

'Yes, with Bethany. It was one of those 'industry only' events, partners not invited.' Maddie winced, aware of sounding defensive.

'I know. Roley knows I don't love those things,' Vieve paused, taking a sip of wine. 'He'd said he wasn't going to be drinking, that he'd play things by ear. Thought he might drive up after the function depending how he felt.'

Maddie felt Vieve's scrutiny. This conversation was a minefield. She swallowed, trying to ease the tension in her throat. 'He seemed fine when I saw him. He brought over some bubbles for me and Bethany but I got the impression he wasn't drinking much himself.'

'Anyway, he told me he'd text later in the evening and let me know what was happening.'

Maddie nodded. 'And?'

'I never heard from him.' Genevieve raised her hands in the air like it was an epic mystery.

'Maybe he had too much to drink and didn't want to drive. Or caught up with some mates.'

While both suggestions were within the realm of possibility, they were also smoke and mirrors masquerading a game-changing truth. Maddie put down her glass. The wine tasted acrid in her mouth.

'I understand that. It's just, he didn't call or text and that's not like him. I tried calling but his phone went straight to voicemail.'

Maddie was torn. 'You know that's not unusual in Margaret River. Signal drops in and out.'

Vieve looked perplexed. 'I know Maddie. I sound paranoid. It's not just that he didn't contact me last night...that happens, not usually with Roley but I can understand that happens. It's just that when I eventually spoke with him early this morning to see if he was still coming up he was really strange. Kind of evasive. Not himself at all.'

'Maybe you woke him? What time did you call?' As the questions left her mouth she felt herself sink, invisible weights dragging her down.

'I waited until after seven. I knew if he was driving up this morning he'd want an early start. Anyway, he was apologetic but didn't think he could make it. Said he wasn't feeling well and wanted the morning in bed.' Vieve took another sip of wine. 'To cut a long story short, when he said he wasn't coming up, I decided to drive down and surprise him. Thought I could cook a nice dinner, do a little shopping for him. Tidy up. You know.'

Maddie's thoughts raced. Thank God Vieve hadn't driven down last night. More curiously, why hadn't Roley driven to Perth as planned? 'So, what happened?'

'Well, I arrived at the house just before lunch.' Vieve paused, looking off to the ocean.

'And?' Maddie was desperate to bring her back.

'Well, he's just been strange. Really quiet and distracted.'

There was a tiny surge of relief. There would be no

confrontation. Still Vieve sat passively waiting for answers. Maddie studied her face. Not answers, reassurance. Maddie had no business offering either. This was between Vieve and Roley. She tried to focus, looking beyond the deck, situation impossible.

Looking back at Vieve, she quietly counted a list off her fingers. 'He could be tired. He could be hung-over. He could be tired and hung-over.'

Vieve closed her eyes and sniffed.

'Maybe all of the above.'

Minute quantities of life force were snuffed out with every word Maddie spoke. She had to end this.

Vieve smiled and scrunched her nose. 'I am being paranoid, aren't I?'

In her periphery Maddie caught sight of the brown beetle supine on the deck. A trail of ants suggesting things hadn't ended well.

'No, actually.' A wave of heat swept through her body and her pulse raced. 'You're not being paranoid. You're worried. Your instincts are telling you something's not right.' Maddie swallowed. 'I think you should talk with Roley.' Her heart pounded. She had to end this meeting.

Vieve's phone signalled a message. She picked it up and Maddie registered her tangible lift as she read. 'It's the tired, hung-over man.'

Maddie smiled weakly.

Vieve stood, picking up their glasses. 'I'd better go. Roley doesn't know I'm here.'

Maddie's brain absorbed the blow.

'Thanks for the wine.'

This was beyond awkward. They reached the front door.

'…and for listening to my rant.'

Maddie couldn't speak if she tried. Keeping it *real*, being *real*—she had just had fabulous sex with this woman's boyfriend, and her feelings for him went way beyond physical. She held the door open.

Vieve leaned in and kissed her cheek. 'I can't tell you how happy I am with your options. When I first saw Roley today, I could only come up with one—he isn't happy to see me.'

The words jabbed at Maddie's ears, her knuckles turned white around the doorhandle. Vieve walked down the steps to her car. Maddie closed the door not waiting to wave goodbye.

Chapter 14

Maddie pulled up in front of the turreted stone castle dominating Ravenshead Domain. The winery assumed an even grander air in the fading evening light, free of the visitors that swarmed during opening hours. Shadows highlighted the imposing crenellated tops of the perimeter walls and soft golden light spilled out the main entrance; a huge wooden drawbridge permanently lowered over a water-filled moat.

Maddie knew its design had caused controversy over its young years. It was ostentatious. It didn't suit the landscape. It was un-Australian. No historical connection to wine. A disproportionate display of wealth in what had been a poor farming district.

Despite, or perhaps intrigued by the controversy, visitors flocked to it in droves. They would all pass judgement, joining the debate but they wouldn't miss visiting Ravenshead. It was a Margaret River icon sitting high on the itinerary along with watching sunset at the main surf break.

Maddie thought it was kind of cool, a real-time anthropological disco ball calling people to the floor to contemplate values and ideals. She loved anything coaxing would-be fence-sitters to rise and put a foot forward—the direction they actually stepped of little significance. When people asked why, Maddie felt inclined to ask why not—a trait her mother dismissed as argumentative, Aunt Bling labelled questioning and Maddie understood was just her way.

Sitting in the car, her thoughts rose above the click and ping of the engine's metal parts as they cooled. Could she really be bothered being social? The alternative, a night on the couch watching a movie, drinking wine, eating chocolate, didn't sound so bad. Except it would be the sixth in a row.

Maddie sighed heavily. Perfect bubbles of life floated around her, taunting with wondrous iridescence. When she reached to claim one, they popped, leaving her fingers slimy.

'Bloody drama queen,' she rebuked her reflection in the rear-view mirror.

It was Friday night, but during vintage that didn't mean a lot, she was working tomorrow. But it was time for company other than Hugh, Colin, Ryan and Jude. They were great company but, it pained her to admit, becoming a little predictable as she watched them over and over again.

Men outside the big screen certainly weren't predictable—or available to play. One in particular seemed to have forgotten she existed. If she hadn't been there when they spectacularly got it on together, she would never have believed it happened.

Earlier in the week, they landed together at the same time

in the smoko room. There ensued a farcical demonstration of social anxiety disorder as they stalked carefully round the other, focusing on their boots. When Maddie did raise her head it was to catch Bethany eye rolling, Lewis frowning and Westy grinning, rotating his fist in a *shaka* sign. It felt like the joke was on her.

The following day, they accidently met outside Lewis's office. It was an awkward, mumbled exchange of 'how are you', neither offering nor waiting for a response.

Enough!

Maddie got out of her car and crossed the drawbridge into the castle's inner sanctum, a large rectangle of immaculate grass bordered on all sides by wide stone steps leading up to large glass-panelled walls. The panels in front of the long wine tasting counter served as doors. They were drawn open and a small group sat on cushions on the steps in front.

Bethany raised her arm in greeting as she walked across the grass. Maddie scanned the faces. Most were familiar. She smiled, spotting Bethany's friend Donna, who worked behind the tasting counter at Ravenshead. The sound level and laughter indicated they were having a good time.

Bethany had an empty glass waiting. As Maddie sat, she slung an arm around her. 'I'm so glad you came.'

Maddie shrugged, 'I'm developing couch sores.'

Bethany offered a bottle of Ravenshead sparkling.

Maddie tipped her glass. The group smiled and nodded when she joined them, but conversation continued unabated. Another laugh erupted. Maddie chinked her glass with Bethany. 'What's going on?'

Bethany swallowed a sip. 'Cellar door stories,' she whispered. 'Bloody hilarious.'

Donna was animated.

'I had this really pretentious guy in the other day. From the moment he walked up to the counter I knew he was going to be a handful, so smug. Anyway, I hardly had a chance to say hello when he starts telling me what a good friend of the owners he is.' Donna rolled her eyes. 'He leant across the counter like we were co-conspirators, very close actually. Yes, Derek and I go back to university days. He always was an entrepreneur, even as a student. Our families holidayed together. Rebecca is such a stunning girl. The perfect couple. I always knew they'd make their mark. Are they in residence at the moment?'

'I didn't know what to say. Up until that point I had been able to smile and nod, knowing if I opened my mouth I would lose it big time.' Donna shook her head, a smile breaking over her face. 'God, what I would have given to have said what I was thinking.'

'Yes! I've heard that *David* and Rebecca were a perfect couple right up to the point Rebecca found out about the affair he was having with Bella, now his second wife. And sorry, you've missed the opportunity to meet her. She's currently enjoying a sabbatical in the States after filing for divorce while David is holidaying in Europe with his latest mistress, timed possibly to avoid the tax evasion rumours. What a shame you've missed them. Always such a pleasure when really good, close friends drop in.'

The group broke up in stitches.

Sam, worked at a neighbouring cellar door.

'I had a similar situation. A guy dropped in talking about the owners. Their children went to school together and their family came camping out on the vineyard in the early days to help pick and prune. He went on for ages until finally he mentioned that their daughters were still best friends. At that point I felt obliged to tell him that the owners only had sons. I remember he looked at me like I was hallucinating until, taking a step back, he looked around the room and, finally checking the label on a bottle declared he was at the wrong winery.' Sam laughed. 'Pissed myself when he left. I wonder if his friend ever realised he'd done all that work for his neighbour.'

Donna jumped in again.

'Not long after starting here, this really sweet lady commented on what a lovely touch it was to drape the vines with tulle, asking if a lot of couples got married here. I had no idea what she was talking about. Thankfully, Joyce overheard.' Donna smiled at Joyce. 'She came over and explained that no, we didn't host weddings at Ravenshead. The tulle was actually netting to keep the birds from the grapes. You handled that so well,' Donna tipped her glass towards Joyce.

'She was lovely. Let's face it, most people who come to cellar door are either interested in wine or they're keen to learn. Sometimes it's a fine line giving people information without embarrassing them. That lady was so genuine, I wanted to explain without making her feel stupid.' Joyce shrugged. 'When you look out over the valley the netting does look soft and draped, too pretty for something so practical.'

'I've learnt a lot from listening to you. You're so patient with people. Remember the group that asked where we get the passionfruit from? Did we grow it on the estate?'

Joyce nodded.

'I was standing back trying to figure out what the hell they were talking about, and you calmly asked, do you mean the passionfruit in the Sauvignon Blanc, Semillon blend?' Donna laughed, shaking her head. 'I was gobsmacked, people actually think we add vanilla pods, blackberries, lemon zest...'

'And butterscotch lollies. Don't forget those. A family once asked if we kept extras at cellar door for the kids?'

'So how are you?' Bethany murmured, leaning into Maddie's shoulder.

Maddie's head dropped, her reply barely audible. 'When I think of Vieve, I feel really bad. When I think of Roley,' Maddie lifted her head and looked Bethany in the eyes, 'I feel very angry.' She took a sip from her glass and looked into the distance. 'When I think of Roley and I...I just feel super sad.' Maddie bumped her shoulder against Bethany's. 'Sorry, no simple answer to that question.'

Bethany nodded slowly.

'What about the wine wankers who know more about wine than anybody else in the room, which quite often means they know just enough to make everybody within earshot cringe,' Sam announced, clearly unimpressed.

Donna pulled a face. 'Oh yeah. Joyce. Remember that condescending dude, telling those young girls that wine was an acquired taste and one of life's true pleasures. I felt sorry for his wife. She looked so embarrassed.'

'They asked if we had any sweeter styles because they didn't like dry wines and *Mr Big Ears* piped up, 'Girls, keep trying the dry wines, your palates will mature eventually".

'That way of thinking is so old school. Soon as *Big Ears* was out of range, I told them that sweeter wine styles were just as legitimate as drier styles and to keep drinking whatever they enjoyed.'

'I love it when people surprise you,' Eddie drawled.

Eddie was a Margaret River cellar door veteran who worked a couple of shifts at Ravenshead to complement his creative pursuits. He was a fine wood craftsman by trade who enjoyed chatting with people about wine and life; his personal repose from the solitary meditation of designing and crafting original furniture pieces. His reputation for both was legendary.

'One of the most valuable lessons I learnt when starting out was not to judge people, simple and straight.'

There was a murmur of agreement from the group.

Bethany nudged Maddie, 'Eddie has the best stories. It doesn't matter how many times you hear them. They're addictive.'

'I remember years back, the early days working at Las Gammas,' Eddie began. He talked slow and sure with a mellow voice. 'Even in those days their wines were exclusive and would set you back a serious chunk of your pay packet. Not many people just dropped by. It was usually by appointment. Anyway, I used to do all manner of things there. On this particular day, I was pruning the roses in the half barrels lining the entry road to the winery. It used to take me a week just to prune those bloody roses, but the owner's missus insisted you couldn't conduct a wine business without them. Never saw her when she wasn't smiling. She smiled when she talked and every time she opened her mouth, you just didn't know what was going to be coming your way. It was like a circus for your ears, and working there gave me a ringside seat.

'Serve beef without Cabernet in my country and you will be sent out of the cocina to scratch dirt with the chickens. Vino and rosas are the same. Scratch dirt in the barrels around the roses and then you don't have to scratch with the chickens. But then you have to add the pooh. No one thinks of this, eh?

'Her metaphors didn't always translate but she was a

funny lady. She would cackle with laughter at her own wit. So, lots and lots of rosas.

'Anyway, I was pruning my way through them when this old Kombi van starts backfiring its way past me up the drive. It was the coolest, crappiest old Kombi I'd ever seen. It had this faded red paint job embellished with big flowers and peace signs. There were surfboards and fishing rods tied onto the top, plastic leis hanging from the aerial.'

'I remember following it up the driveway, wondering if they were lost. I expected a...what's the collective noun for a group of hippies? A sway? A folk festival?'

'A Woodstock?'

'An incense cloud?'

'A love-in?' piped Sam, receiving a welcome cheer from the group.

'Okay, so I expected a love-in of hippies to come tumbling out. But there's just this one guy. Barefoot, tattered old boardies and lots of long, wiry hair and a beard that would put the young guys trying to reinvent that look to shame. Tanned and skinny, he looked like he'd been camping for weeks.'

'When he saw me walking up he grabbed a T-shirt from the Kombi and walked down to meet me calling out, 'Hey man, is this Las Gammas?''

'So he had meant to find us. I was on the back foot from the start.'

'So then he asks me about the roses, so I start thinking that's what his visit is about. So we talked about the roses for a while and then he just sort of stood there until he actually had to ask me who does he see about wine?'

'I remember feeling embarrassed. I started my spiel about not really being open for tasting, offering to point him in the direction of some other cellar doors.'

'He just kind of looked at me pityingly. He knew I had pegged him wrong. He wasn't smug and he didn't get angry, he just smiled and acknowledged that he didn't fit the mould of a serious wine collector but he was keen to buy some just the same.

Even at that stage as I led him into the winery I was expecting a meagre sale, maybe a bottle or two. So I hand him the price list. At the time, Las Gammas was making a Semillon, Chardonnay, Cabernet and a Cabernet blend. There was a bottle of the Cabernet open and so I offered him a taste.'

'Nah, thanks mate. I know these wines. I'll take two of each of the whites and three each of the reds.'

'I don't know what surprised me most. The fact that he knew the wines—they were pretty exclusive at the time—or the fact that he was almost ordering a case.'

'I started fumbling around for an empty carton and he politely interrupts. 'Sorry mate. Probably didn't make it clear—cases not bottles. And I'll take them with me, I'm heading for home.'

'In those days, people just didn't buy wine in those quantities and they were expensive, the Cabernet was around thirty dollars a bottle.'

'I was pretty flustered knowing I looked like the biggest jerk in history, yet I was still ready to tell him we didn't accept personal cheques.'

'He just smiled and handed over his platinum American Express card. We both knew I had handled things badly. There was no going back or making up ground. By the time I had got him to sign and had phoned through for authorisation—everything was manual in those days—I'd made a decision. As we loaded the wine into the Kombi, I put my ego aside and told him I had learnt something valuable that day.'

Eddie shook his head, 'I'll never forget it—he grabbed my hand and thumped me on the back saying that was really cool. He said people usually asked if he wanted to use the telephone or if he was out of fuel, so I shouldn't feel too bad. As he backfired his way back down the driveway, smoke and dust clouding behind, I made a resolution; leave your judgements at the door. It was a good early lesson.'

'Oh Eddie, I love your stories,' Joyce cried. 'You know these young girls probably haven't heard the one about Mr Gammas.'

'Ah yes. Margaret River's celebrated customer service ambassador, Mr Gammas.' Eddie grinned, adjusting his position. 'Possibly his finest moment that I was privileged to witness was at the wine festival.'

Joyce smiled, nodding.

Bethany whispered to Maddie. 'How are you going? Do you want to make tracks?'

Maddie smiled. 'One more story.'

'It dates back to the days when there used to be an annual wine festival held on the town oval. It was a one-day event and anyone who was a member of the Wine Association was invited to set up a stall and showcase their wines. It was a fairly new concept for the region and many producers had never participated in anything like it before. I suppose for the Gammas', who didn't really even offer cellar door tastings, it would have been a total shock to the system.'

'Anyway, the day was going really well. The crowd was larger than anticipated and everyone was in the mood to party. It was the days before 'responsible service of alcohol' training was mandatory too.'

'Ha!' Joyce chipped in. 'Irresponsible service of alcohol

was the order of the day. People expected it.'

'Yaah,' agreed Eddie. 'Which brings us to Mr Gammas. Now, Mrs Gammas was her usual self behind the counter— laughing, smiling, embracing whoever graced their counter with her affable nature. Losing more people than ever with her English-Spanish conversation, her accent heightened, running parallel with her excitement. Anyway, later in the day one of her friends called by and insisted that Mrs Gammas get out from behind her station and tour around the festival with her. I was caught up with a couple chatting about distributors or some such thing, when this guy walks up to the counter and calls out to Mr Gammas, who is hovering in the background, that he'd like to try the reds.

'Now, Mr Gammas was a behind-the-scenes kind of guy. He made sure we had ice to keep the whites cold, checked stock, filled water jugs, that kind of thing. Dealing with Joe Public wasn't his forte, and Mrs Gammas usually made sure he was never alone with the customers. She had a special phrase for him, *el espantapájaros para la gente agradable*, which I always thought was some Spanish term of endearment.'

Eddie smiled at the faces round the group. 'This job certainly has its moments. It wasn't 'til years later I was pouring wine for a very pretty Spanish girl and I hit her with that line in my best accent and discovered what it meant. Soon as I said it, there was a horrible silence. I started kicking myself, wondering what the hell I'd just said. She must have sensed my discomfort. She looked at me with her beautiful brown eyes and started to laugh. 'So, you are calling me a scarecrow for the nice people?'

'Ah, Mrs Gammas…' Eddie leaned back, straightening his legs, crossing one over the other, 'entertaining the masses with her original turn of phrase.

'But back to Mr Gammas, a man of old fashioned sensibilities. I knew for a start, he wouldn't have appreciated being called out to.

'So while I'm serving my customers, I'm keeping one ear and one eye trained on this other exchange. You didn't need a degree in psychology to recognise the man at the counter was an obnoxious boor. He was off-hand with Mr Gammas, sculling samples as soon as they were poured, didn't seem interested in any information about the wines…or anything Mr Gammas had to say. He was, what we used to call, a tyre-kicker—a tyre-kicker with a bad attitude.

'Mr Gammas poured him a taste of the Cabernet. He explained it was their prized wine, winning gold in several agricultural shows. I remember thinking Mrs Gammas would have been proud. Then the guy interrupts. He looks at his glass and says, 'There's hardly enough to see what colour it is let alone taste it'.

'With this, something inside Mr Gammas snapped. You would have had to know the man to recognise it. Without another word he slowly trickled a little more into the glass. The man rested the glass on the counter holding onto the stem while Mr Gammas poured.

'That's more like it, the man commented, looking smug. Still Mr Gammas continued to pour, not taking his eyes off the glass.

'Woah, that's looking good. Now you're talking. The man couldn't help but open his mouth. Mr Gammas continued to pour. We used little XL5 tasting glasses and the level was rising—fast. I wondered just how this was going to play out with ten millimetres to go to the top of the glass. I saw a flicker of hesitation in Mr Gammas.

'Then the idiot opened his mouth again. 'Now that's more in keeping with your *I-talian* heritage'.

'That was it. Hesitation turned into resolve and as the man held the glass on the counter, Mr Gammas continued to pour. I think the guy was too stunned to take his hand away. They both watched as the wine ran down the glass over his hand, pooling in a dark lake on the counter, eventually tumbling over the edge of the table in a red cascade to the grass below.

'Mr Gammas continued to pour until the bottle was empty then he slowly set it upright and turned from the counter to place it with the empties. He didn't flinch or miss a beat.

'I handed the man a cloth. Finally, too late, he had stopped talking. His mouth was open but nothing was coming out. He wiped his hand abstractly with the cloth before picking up the glass and just kind of being reabsorbed into the crowd—Las Gammas jetsam, to wash up wine-logged on the festival's fringe.

'A few people had been surreptitiously watching the drama unfold. When it was over, the details buzzed through the crowd and by the end of the day everyone knew the story of Mr Gammas and the man who dared ask for a little more. From that point on, Mr Gammas was affectionately referred to as Charles Dickens of Margaret River.'

Donna clapped. 'Best story ever.'

Sam shook his head. 'Mr Gammas had cred, eh?' He lowered his voice. 'I'd love to do that to some of the tossers we get through. Shame to waste a good bottle of Cab though.'

Joyce laughed. 'Eddie, you've seen it all over the years?'

Eddie started to rise, 'I've certainly been around long enough to know I should drive home before having another wine. Goodnight, good people.'

Joyce and a couple of others rose with him, picking up glasses, cushions and bottles.

Bethany turned to Maddie. 'My place?'

'Awesome, a change of couch.'

Bethany tilted her head and looked at her.

Maddie smiled. 'Want to grab take-away from the Korean Barbeque on the way?'

'Yum. Yes.'

Joyce, within earshot, handed Bethany an opened bottle of Rosé. 'Here girls, this has your name on it.'

'Thank you,' Bethany cooed.

Joyce smiled and turned to Maddie. 'How's life at Kite?'

Maddie's eyes sprung wide. 'Loving it. Such a great crew.'

Joyce laughed. 'Everybody says that about Kite. I think Lewis must be one of the nicest bosses to work for. I know Mae really well, the loveliest family. And Roley...'

Maddie's heart leapt.

'...lucky girl who wins his heart. If I was twenty years younger...,' Joyce looked dreamily up to the sky.

Bethany rested her hand on Maddie's arm as they followed Joyce inside.

It was playful banter, but in her raw, vulnerable state any reference to him conjured emotion to surface. She felt protective and defensive; emotions that didn't even make sense. As far as she knew there was no link between sex and insanity but damn, it was worthy of research.

Bethany whizzed around enthusiastically gifting hugs, thankyous and goodbyes before returning to Maddie. 'Let's go.'

Chapter 15

The calendar ticked to Saturday; Carmel's annual, mid-vintage party.

Maddie looked up into the rear-vision mirror pulling her lips wide to examine her teeth. They were sensitive. It had been another long week of tasting grapes with sugar and acid attacking her tooth enamel. She wasn't seeing grapes in her sleep yet, but she was getting over tasting them—fast. A beer would be good.

Carmel always made her smile, she was quirky and upbeat and the most sympathetic supporter of the wine community, without having a hand or foot directly invested. Maddie had been out to her place once, not long after she first arrived. On that occasion, Carmel hosted a combined blind-tasting and pizza night. It had been a wild night in the end, most people actually getting blind during the tasting, not making it to pizza. But it was crazy fun and a great introduction to the area.

Walking down the driveway, Maddie remembered back. It was Roley who extended the invite. They'd made a great team, bantering and laughing loudly while drinking some fabulous Italian wines. Fortunately, they made the pizza course, which was tasty, and certainly a blessing regards the next day. No one could remember how one piece of pizza came to be nailed to the front door, but Carmel left it there for weeks, only removing it for her quarterly rental inspection.

'Hi Carmel,' Maddie greeted her warmly. 'Hardly recognise your place without the pizza out front. Brendan here?'

'Hiya Maddie,' Carmel swooped for a two-cheeked kiss. 'Sadly, the pizza was evicted but the madness remains,' she smiled. 'As long as I'm living here anyway. Brendan's working, but he'll be here later. How's vintage?'

Maddie was forming a reply when she noticed Carmel looking past her. Roley and Vieve were making their way down the driveway. Maddie's stomach lurched.

Carmel put a hand to Maddie's arm. 'Hello, hello,' she sang out to the new arrivals, moving round Maddie to land more kisses. 'Roley, great you could make it. Hi Genevieve. Welcome.'

Roley placed his arm around Genevieve's waist. 'Hi Carmel. This is the most fun we have all vintage.' His smile looked measured.

Carmel laughed. 'You lot would have fun inside a paper bag.' Spinning around she pointed towards the house. 'Make yourselves at home. Food and eskies round the back. Lots of crew here already.' Carmel was already making eye contact and waving at another group walking in. Turning back quickly, she just caught Maddie's attention, raising her eyebrows.

Maddie shrugged. 'Hi guys,' she greeted Roley and Vieve. The three of them turned and walked towards the house.

'Hi Madison,' Genevieve smiled. 'I'm glad you're here, I still hardly know any of Roley's wine friends.'

Maddie grimaced internally. *Here we go again. Could the local authority of awkward situations please come to the stage? Maybe I should write a friggin' book.* 'How are you Genevieve? Roley tells me you've been snowed under with work and study. Good to see you enjoying a weekend off.' Small talk, until she could escape.

In truth, Roley and Maddie had hardly spoken a word since the night of the wine function. It had been an extraordinarily long, uncomfortable two weeks. Roley deferred everything to Lewis, avoiding her where possible. The atmosphere tense and strained when they were forced to confer. Now he'd adopted an 'I'm with my girlfriend' texture. It felt unnecessary, and it stung.

Vieve nudged Roley's arm.

'Sorry. Hi Maddie,' he leant across Vieve to deliver a perfunctory kiss on her cheek.

His reticence was tangible. Maddie shrank. His clean shaven cheek felt soft and smooth and smelt good—earth and violets; mental tasting notes on his aftershave to distract her bubbling emotions. He wore tight fitting jeans and a navy tank top under his unbuttoned shirt. Looking urban cowboy hot, behaving unpleasantly cold.

'Drink?' he asked.

'God yes!'

Genevieve and Roley both turned to look at her.

'Thirsty,' she flashed a smile, wondering how long until she could politely leave them.

'I'm sure you've earned it,' Genevieve smiled. 'You guys work so hard this time of year.'

Maddie studied her. Genevieve looked amazing. She

always looked some version of fabulous. No bad hair days there and so sweet and perky. Roley wouldn't be with anyone less than wonderful, it only made sense.

There was a sign above the esky, a bunch of grapes in a red circle with a severe red slash drawn through the fruit. Maddie laughed.

Roley handed her a beer. 'There's Bethany.' He tipped his beer coolly in Bethany's direction before pointing Vieve towards a group of his mates. Vieve giggled, reaching her beer back to clunk bottle necks with Maddie before allowing him to whisk her away.

Maddie rolled her eyes at their backs.

She leaned against a veranda post, studying the couple as they interacted in the group. Roley hadn't looked at her once. He was right. They should have talked.

The intensity of the night of the function and Vieve's visit the following day had left Maddie shattered. She could hardly relate herself to the circumstances. Maddie didn't cheat. She didn't do lying or subterfuge—whichever way she inclined her perception. Roley had thrown her off balance or, if she was totally honest, they had both teetered and fallen together.

Maddie had worked on the Sunday of that weekend, feeling rattled all day. That evening Roley called by her house. Maddie heard his ute pull up and loped silently to her bedroom, ducking down alongside the bed. Not something she'd done since adolescence. He knocked loudly a couple of times at the front door. Holding her breath, she watched his form pass her bedroom window to access the back deck. She felt giddy. The back door was wide open. Roley knocked again, loudly.

'Maddie. Please. We need to talk.'

Maddie curled into a ball by the bed. How could she talk? She could barely think.

Then everything went quiet. Eventually, Maddie crawled across the floor and spied down the passage. Roley stood motionless, one arm bent against the door jamb, resting his head. His other arm hung heavily by his side.

Maddie nearly caved. Nearly ran to him. But becoming a human door jamb didn't seem like the answer, hadn't she complicated things enough? Roley needed to sort things with Vieve. For himself. Didn't he? Maddie's mind swirled. Her heart ached.

Eventually, he pushed off the frame and walked slowly back to his car.

He sent a text the following day. 'Please. Can we talk?'

When Maddie read it, she visualised him at her back door. The complexities raw, overwhelming. She must withdraw from the mix. She never sent a reply.

Watching him now from the vantage of hindsight—it was the wrong decision. A lump rose in her throat.

In her periphery, Maddie noticed Bethany waving for attention. Maddie lifted an arm, gulping the last of her beer. She went to join her, grabbing another on the way. It was going to be a long night.

'So Bethany—my BBFF—best Bethany friend forever...' Maddie threw her head back laughing. 'What is it about Carmel's that makes people drink too much and do naughty things?'

Bethany put her arm around Maddie's shoulder. 'Mmmm.' She looked up at the kitchen ceiling before bursting into laughter. 'Dunno.'

'Here's one for you two,' Carmel walked in putting an

arm around them both, forming a huddle. 'What is it about drinking too much and doing naughty things that makes people blame poor, innocent Carmel?'

Maddie and Bethany erupted.

Suddenly Maddie stopped laughing. 'I have a hot date waiting. Why are we in the kitchen?' She looked around.

Bethany giggled. 'You wanted a drink of water—like that's going to help.'

Carmel found a clean glass and filled it from the tap. As she handed it to Maddie she looked her in the eyes. 'Are you sure this is a good idea?' She found another glass, filled it and handed it to Bethany. 'Here, may not help but you'll thank me tomorrow.'

Maddie and Bethany chinked water glasses. 'Here's to Carmel the mostest, hostest—eva.'

Carmel shook her head. 'Maddie?'

'Maybe not the greatest idea I've ever made, but he's hot,' Maddie nodded like she'd made a point of great importance. '…and he doesn't have a gorgeous, blonde girlfriend fetching his drinks, staring into his lovely brown eyes.' Maddie drew her face close up to Bethany's.

Bethany pushed her away. 'My eyes are green. A ruly, truly BFBF oops, BFFF…BF would know that.' Bethany took a drink of water and pulled a face. 'This tastes watery.'

Carmel ignored her. 'Maddie?'

Maddie sucked in her top lip to keep herself from laughing. 'Carmel, I know it's not going to end in a marriage proposal, although he lives near Barolo in Italy and that's really cool, I really want to go there.'

Carmel raised her eyebrows.

'I'll be careful. He's a nice guy, Carmel.' She took a big gulp of water. 'Don't worry mum.'

Bethany giggled.

'He knows I exist—that's nice.'

'Maddie,' Carmel pleaded. 'Give Roley time to work things through.'

Maddie rolled her eyes.

'I've been watching him tonight. He's been constantly looking around—and it's not for the girl by his side.'

Bethany laid her head on Maddie's shoulder. 'Sshees right. You're the one that he wants, ooh, ooh, ooh, honey.'

Maddie and Bethany stumbled forward, cracking up, breaking into song and dance numbers from *Grease*.

Carmel smacked Bethany's arm. 'I'm off to check on my other guests. You girls are trouble.'

Marco was waiting. Every possibility suggested if Maddie left with him now it would lead to sex. He sat half-twisted in the driver's seat of his station wagon, one leg out of the car, one hand on the wheel with the warmest, widest smile.

'Let me take you home, bella,' he called as she walked down the steps from the house.

'I think that is a very reasonable suggestion,' Maddie giggled. 'And so I say, si Marco por favour.' Her words tumbled in a silly foreign accent. With equal eloquence she opened the passenger door and fell in. 'That wasn't even Italian was it?' Maddie giggled, closing the door.

Neither of them noticed Roley, standing in the shadows of the veranda, hands on hips, staring hard.

Marco's digs were beachside, a kilometre or so from her shack. Waking in the early hours, she pieced together her ensemble as best she could in the dark, and walked home. She slipped off her shoes on the deck and subconsciously exhaled deeply as she crossed the threshold, padding into her darkened room. Without undressing, she slipped between the sheets and slept.

Sunday promised contemplative chaos. Thank God she had the day off. Waking early, she thought a drink of water and a swim might be a good start. Sitting up ready for action, her brain sloshed in her skull, making her nauseous. She lay back on the pillow. Movement perhaps not an option just yet. *Bloody Carmel.*

It was after nine o'clock the next time she stirred. With happiness and relief, she decided surviving the day may be possible, after some headache tablets. The thought of tea or toast wasn't working for her so she sipped at some water before wrestling into her bathers, sunnies and the biggest straw hat she owned and making her way to the beach.

Normally her greatest comfort, the beach seemed excessively harsh and glary, the waves were unpleasantly loud and all the sand, plain bloody annoying. She found a possie close to the dunes and haphazardly spread her towel before proceeding to sleep some more.

An hour later she woke. Drugs doing their thing, she was able to sit and contemplate the last twenty-four hours. Marco topped the list. What was that about? But Marco, the gorgeous Italian God, was a rare gem. She couldn't regret having sex with him. He was lovely, she had really enjoyed—oh, she needed to lie down. Was this what it means to swoon? Was she swooning or just horribly hung-over? She was certainly getting hot and bothered thinking about Marco. Hmmm. Not regretting much of anything there.

Except for the disturbing possibility it might indicate she

was a low-down, two-timing slut. Maddie cringed, two different men in as many weeks. Worst of all, it felt like she'd cheated on Roley. How did that even work?

It was official, she'd gone mad. Her wanton behaviour with Roley was bad enough, but sleeping with a hot Italian dude? Images of the night filled her mind as she re-lived Marco's hands on her. She wished the sand would bury her. The warm sand pressed against her body and his hot, naked body was all she could see. Cooling down was required—quickly. She struggled to her feet and, void of grace, stumbled into the waves.

She wished Aunt Bling was here. Aunt Bling so named because she was full of life, a little left of centre, bright. She loved shiny things. Mainly, she had a different outlook to other people of her generation, especially her mother. Hard to believe they were sisters really. Her mother would be suitably horrified with her behaviour. But Aunt Bling would get it and even if she didn't, she would be generous, not judgemental. She would tell her that mindless gratification or indulgence wasn't always a bad thing. As you got older, you don't moralise so much about the brush strokes that worked your canvas, you just enjoy the colour.

Years ago in high school, Maddie had tried smoking pot at a party. It hadn't been a fabulous experience, resulting in a headache, leaving her sleepy. Somehow her mother got hold of it and had gone on and on about the evils of drugs, telling Maddie she should have said no. It went on for days and rather than turn her off drugs it made her wish she had some, anything, to ease the pain of that nagging.

Aunt Bling, the next time she visited, just quietly asked Maddie about it. She had laughed when Maddie told her she hadn't enjoyed it, offering with obvious amusement that her reaction wasn't unusual. She'd teased her about being the life of the party, suggesting she stick to bad dance moves instead.

But she also told Maddie that it was okay to be curious and to try things. Life was not compartmentalised into dos and don'ts, and that living well probably meant experiencing a bit of both. Aunt Bling was a big advocate of instincts, and the consequences of choices.

She'd told her once: 'We make choices based on information available at the time. If we consult our instincts, then despite the outcome there can be no regret, just moving forward with greater self-awareness.' Aunt Bling predicted, since Maddie was an incredibly intelligent young woman, that had been lectured about right and wrong over the years by a well-meaning mother, Maddie would be fine. She would love life and life would love her in return.

She also told her, she should never disclose any of their conversation to her mother and Maddie certainly got that.

When she emerged from the sea, thoughts of Marco had retreated to a pleasant tingling.

For some people, fizzing vitamin water was the answer to a night of over-indulgence, for others, a green smoothie. For Maddie there was only one solution—greasy, salty, hot chips. And not oven baked. They had to be straight from the fryer. She walked along the beach to the café. Morsel after tasty shoestring morsel washed down with cola—the only time she drank it and she almost felt human.

Ambling back along the beach, she was ready to confront what was really bothering her. Her thoughts drifted back to Annabel's words the day she'd driven down to sort out the show judging debacle. Annabel had spoken about the grieving process around a bad call. She was right. Maddie had moved on from her sample labelling mistake, but this bad-call business was relentless.

Extrication from the messy little triangle seemed like the decent response at the time. But, it hadn't fixed anything. Getting together with Roley didn't feel like a mistake, so how could leaving him to it, be a solution. When Roley sought her out, she didn't have to talk but she could have listened. He was hurting and she was a part of that. At least she could have listened to what he had to say.

She pictured herself walking from her bedroom, to sit with Roley on the back deck and the image resonated deep. Then she pictured herself hiding and spying and the memory made her cringe. *Idiot!* She had to fix it. Tomorrow she would organise a meeting. They needed to talk.

She returned home from the beach feeling better. Making her way onto the deck, she noticed a shopping bag by the back door. Unable to guess who had called, she looked inside.

Her undies!

Her headache returned with vengeance.

Chapter 16

If Cirque du Soleil created a production titled 'Winery', Lewis (in tights) would play the lead. Maddie watched as he approached the new barrels, tipping them effortlessly head to head to move them from the loading bay.

During her last tipping attempt, almost losing one down the hill to the dam, had left her cautious. Maddie settled for circling them on one end. It was a momentum thing; in movement their weight was negligible, but when rhythm was lost, they clonked hard on the ground asserting an awkward, fifty kilograms.

Maddie was monitoring the press. The juice that flowed at the beginning of its cycle was fruity and bright, as pressing continued, more tannin was extracted from the skins and seeds, and flavours become broader. That wasn't bad, they relied on all of the components for structure in the finished wine, but at this stage, they kept the juice in separate batches to give them greater control. Noting an increase in phenolics, characters that came from the skins and the seeds, Maddie decided it was time to change tanks. She took a sample to Lewis for the final call.

Lewis was writing identifying marks on the new barrels in permanent marker. Maddie still got a naughty thrill using these pens to draw on brand spanking new oak barrels that cost something like twelve hundred dollars each.

Lewis took the glass and tasted. 'Another five should do it.'

Maddie nodded. She had ripped the plastic packaging from one of the barrels while she waited. She fumbled a cardboard disk protecting the head of the barrel as Lewis handed back the glass.

'Do you know what we do with these?' he asked, picking up a discarded disk from the ground.

'Recycling skip?'

'Watch and learn.' Lewis pulled his arm back frisbee style and sent the disk soaring at an acute angle skyward. The disk bulleted high into the air before stalling and hurtling with alarming speed back towards them.

Maddie squealed, taking cover.

Meanwhile, the wind caught the disk, shooting it off towards the red fermenting tanks, before steering it over the grass for a smooth landing.

They both laughed.

'Right, I used to be pretty good with a frisbee,' Maddie exclaimed. She pulled her arm back ready to fire. Unfortunately, Maddie's past experience with frisbees was limited to exercising the dog. She watched with horror as the cardboard disk left her hand and sailed at head height in the direction of cellar door.

'Oh shit!' her hands flew to her mouth.

Lewis's eyes widened in mock horror as the disk flew on a decapitating flight path before hitting the cellar door window.

'Better run, Maddie,' he laughed.

They were standing in the middle of the winery pad marvelling at the fun to be had with packaging products, when Bethany, not taking long to pinpoint the trouble-makers, started making towards them.

'You two,' she admonished shaking the disk. 'Lucky we didn't have anyone admiring the garden. You could have lopped someone's head off.'

'Sorry Bethany,' Maddie purred. 'I'm a lousy shot. Did we give anyone a heart attack?'

'Lucky for you, and you,' she motioned to Lewis, 'we're not open yet. Lucky for me too, because I can have a go.'

Bethany turned to face the winery and prepared to fire. Just as she pulled her arm back, the press made its whooshing noise.

'The press!' Maddie screamed, remembering her task. She charged off to begin the process of changing tanks.

The disk left Bethany's hand in a terrible misfire, hitting the forklift parked less than ten metres away.

'Lame,' Maddie yelled over the noise as she positioned herself to stop the pump.

'Incredibly lame,' echoed Lewis. 'You need to practise if you're planning to try out for the squad.' He headed for his office, shaking his head solemnly.

'Bloody winemakers,' muttered Bethany loudly, knowing they could both still hear. 'Closing ranks, bullying the slightly less-athletic cellar door babe.' She raised her voice and yelled. 'Let's make the next challenge 'balancing the till at the end of the day', see how you go with that.'

Lewis turned back, throwing her a smile before disappearing. Maddie laughed, running to the bank of tanks in the opposite direction.

With a break in her schedule, Maddie sought coffee. Checking her phone, she held the smoko room door open for Holly and Bec, two of the vineyard vintage casuals, heading back to work.

'Hi Maddie. How was your weekend? Full of sex and debauchery?' Holly teased.

'Wedding bells in the air for you too?' Bec added, jokingly.

Maddie pulled a face. 'An interesting weekend with a few clangers—but they weren't wedding bells. Have I missed something?'

'Bec and I feel like the ones missing out,' Holly feigned despair. 'Our 'hot' leader has selfishly taken himself off the market. We're devo.'

'Lewis?'

'Do you still have bells ringing in your ears?' Holly laughed. 'Honey, Lewis is already married.'

'Bastard. Hope he hasn't been lying, trying to get into your pants,' teased Bec. 'Roley, vineyard boss of our dreams. He obviously had a mind-altering weekend of sex and debauchery. He's gone and asked the girlfriend from Perth to marry him.'

'What?' Maddie asked, stunned.

'Oh man. Maddie, read my lips. Roley and Vieve got engaged.'

Her vital functions began to fail, muscles seized and her brain stopped transmitting. Her heart pumped colour straight to her face.

'Crap!'

'Yeah, that's what we reckon. He's totally denying us our ménage à trois fantasy.'

The door was the only thing keeping her upright. She managed a nod and a grim smile as Holly and Bec walked through.

'No confined space activity for you, until the coffee kicks in,' one of them yelled as they giggled away.

When the girls had reached a reasonable distance, Maddie closed the door and backed away. She needed time to let the splinters settle, to make sense of it all. She rounded the corner of the winery and headed down the perimeter road to the dam.

What had happened? Her brain seemed unable or unwilling to digest the information.

'You idiot! Stupid, fucking idiot! How did you get this so wrong?' She didn't wait for herself to answer. She had no answers, she had nothing.

Suddenly, Roley's ute turned out of the vineyard onto the road ahead.

She had sent him a text first thing. 'Sorry. You were right. We need to talk.' She hadn't received a reply.

Dread summoned her only plausible response, she turned and fled. There was no facing Roley like this. Feeling speck small, if he saw her now, she would fade completely. She ducked behind the pump shed. There was no alternative. Face to face, her fortitude imploding to dust would be disturbing for them both.

'Stupid, stupid girl!' She shook her head, incredulous. Her breath caught as she heard the ute slow before finally driving on. Hands shaking, chest aching, she slumped to the weedy gravel, taking a place among the ants.

Tears flowed in a warm trickle. Years pared away to running Ring a Ring o' Roses, falling breathless and giddy to the ground, threads of thoughts whirling too quickly to grasp. She drew in her knees, hugging tight with her arms, waiting for the world to slow. She rested her head and watched the ants.

Where to from here?

It was Monday morning. It was vintage. Go home, phone Lewis, make excuses and face it all again tomorrow. Or just, bloody toughen-up princess. Stuff Roley. Maybe he should be confronted with this—these consequences. Despair turning nasty, fat, fresh tears rolled from her eyes.

Just get through the day. Don't think. Trust yourself to deal with it.

She sat until her body calmed. Eventually, she got to her feet, imagining the ants cheering for the giant simpleton. Topping barrels in the depths of the cool, dark cellar would be perfect—therapy for the emotionally retarded.

Wiping her eyes and slapping her cheeks she set off for the cellar and managed to make it without encounter. She checked the whiteboard; item three, topping the Chardonnay—perfect.

An hour or so later she heard someone moving through the cellar. She held her breath.

'Maddie?'

Lewis. 'At the Chardonnay,' she answered.

'Hi. All good?' Lewis stood hands on hips, studying her. 'We missed you at smoko.'

'Yeah, just lost track. I'm nearly done with the Chardy,' Maddie couldn't meet his eyes, even in the half-light of the cellar.

'Right,' Lewis turned to leave. He half-turned back, not

looking at her directly. 'If you're enjoying the cellar today, the Sauvignon Blanc could use topping too.'

'Thanks Lewis. I'll get onto it,' Maddie grabbed the lifeline with both hands.

She worked through lunch. It was mid-afternoon when she emerged from the cellar.

Lewis was talking on his mobile near the empty fruit bins. He paused when he saw her.

'Hey Maddie, nothing else happening this arvo. Westy's got this. We'll see you in the morning.' He turned and continued his conversation.

It was done. Lewis was amazing. Maddie wasted no time getting to her car.

Bethany walked straight round the house to the back deck.

Maddie sat on the top step. She couldn't see the ocean but her countenance suggested otherwise as she rocked in a slow ebb and flow.

Bethany sat alongside, putting her arm around her shoulder.

'I'm okay,' said Maddie with a degree of conviction. 'I've had my meltdown, exhausted my tear quota—in record time. Think I'm almost rational.'

Bethany pulled Maddie in. 'Holy fuck! Who are you and what have you done with my friend?'

Maddie laughed and cried at the same time. She dabbed at the tears. 'Well thanks for bloody nothing.'

'Tea? G&T?' Bethany asked.

Maddie plucked up a little resolve. 'You know what? I've turned into a needy, dysfunctional sad-arse. Seems you're always making me tea these days, damn it.'

Bethany smiled.

'Let me make you a gin. Twenty-something women drink gin. And don't encourage my hopelessness. You know it's all self-inflicted.'

Maddie rose and headed for the kitchen.

'It's okay to spin out. I have no idea what's in that boy's head, but announcing his engagement two weeks after you guys get it on, I'd spin out too,' Bethany paused. 'What is in that boy's head exactly?'

Maddie eye-rolled so long and hard, she almost lost her balance. 'Oh, I dunno. Sawdust, testosterone, a build-up of sea water. But I have arrived at one conclusion.'

Bethany braced.

'It's none of my bloody business.'

'You guys didn't just have sex Maddie,' Bethany countered. 'It's obvious to everyone. You guys had…have something together.'

'I don't know about that. We've never talked about our feelings. There's been no discussion around 'us'.'

Maddie handed Bethany a gin and tonic. 'There've been no plans made, no promises on either side.'

They sat again, side-by-side on the steps.

'I could imagine all sorts of things if I let myself.'

Bethany sipped her gin. 'Go on.'

'If I let myself, my favourite scenario is that Roley got wind of me leaving with Marco the other night. His proposal a classic rebound.'

Bethany raised her eyebrows, like it could be in the realm of possibility.

'On the other hand, Roley could truly love Vieve and want to spend the rest of his life with her. I may simply have been a blip.'

Bethany didn't make any moves to judge that one.

'But, it really doesn't matter either way, because I could think up a hundred scenarios or view this from a thousand different perspectives. But unless Roley talks to me, I'll never really know.'

'So, what are you thinking?' Bethany asked quietly.

'Truthfully?' she looked at Bethany. 'I am so fucking mad, if he walked round the corner, he'd be wearing this G&T, glass and all.'

Bethany looked nervous.

'But, I am a sensible woman, and I don't have time or energy for this crap. After a good night's sleep, I'm sure my desire to run him down with the forklift will have passed, and when I see Roley tomorrow, I will extend my congratulations, heartfelt or not, and get on with…oh sorry, what is it that I'm in the middle of right now?' Maddie drummed her fingers on her chin. 'Oh, vintage. That's what I'm meant to be concentrating on right now.'

Bethany narrowed her eyes. 'You talk the talk, but I'd love to be a fly on the wall at that meeting.'

'The way Roley's been avoiding me, I may not see him before the wedding. Maybe I'll text him a little bride and groom emoticon with happy faces.'

'Happy faeces! I haven't seen that one.'

The ice cube Maddie was sucking, torpedoed spontaneously from her mouth as she choked with laughter.

Bethany erupted, thumping her back.

'What would that even look like?' Maddie wheezed.

Their laughter calmed to start afresh.

If Bethany had called first, Maddie would have told her not to come. Now, sitting shoulder to shoulder, laughing 'til her stomach ached, she was grateful Bethany knew her better.

Chapter 17

Two days later, she emerged damp and dishevelled from the press. White grapes done and dusted, it was all hands in preparation for the reds. Maddie was ready for a change of colour, it was symbolic of progression, like the vintage halfway mark. She felt her phone vibrate in her pocket and checked the screen before swiping to answer.

'Hi mum, you just caught…' Maddie started. 'Oh, Aunt Bling. Hi. What's up? Everything okay with mum?'

'Hi Maddie. Mum's fine, she's driving. We wondered if you were up for a little impromptu sleepover tonight?'

'What?' Excitement kicked instantly. 'Where are you?'

Aunt Bling laughed. 'We're nearly at Busselton? You better say it's okay, because I think we've come too far to turn around.'

Maddie threw her head back and closed her eyes. 'Timing! I can't believe it.'

Aunt Bling got on the back foot. 'We know it's vintage. We

won't get in your way. We've bought supplies and we'll cook and do some tidying…'

Maddie laughed. 'No…I mean your timing has never been better. I can't wait to see you.'

'Whew. I thought we were in trouble.'

Maddie heard her aunt talking to her mother. 'No. She's excited to see us.'

'Now Maddie, mum has the address but do we need a key? We won't disturb you at work unless we have to.'

Maddie shook her head. 'I'm not performing brain surgery. You could call by and no one would be harmed.' Aunt Bling and her mum were always conscious of disturbing her at work —typical of their generation. Maddie always made light of it but the underlying respect was kind of sweet too. 'I don't lock the doors, just let yourselves in.'

'No. No. I'll find it. I'm glad you're taking your security seriously. That's important.'

Maddie smiled as her aunt rephrased for her mum. 'Uh, huh. I didn't get a chance to clean up last night's condoms or cocaine either.'

'Behave yourself, Madison,' Aunt Bling warned, suppressing her laughter. 'We're making a big pot of minestrone with herb croutons, the lot. So we'll see you at home.'

'I'll be home as soon as I can,' Maddie squealed. 'This is the best surprise ever.'

Maddie had never been happier to see her aunt.

Their hug conjured her ten-year-old self. Aunt Bling had always been the pivotal point of her compass and Maddie desperately needed to find her way, to centre and ground. Suddenly, she didn't want to let her go.

'It's great to see you too,' Aunt Bling gave a final squeeze before breaking the embrace. 'So, what's got you Maddie?'

Maddie loved this about her aunt. She was straight in there, no hesitation, no fear. The small talk would wait.

'I don't even know where to start,' Maddie's voice was already an octave higher. 'Now you're here, I feel even more like a dithering child, failing the basics of Life 101.'

'Nobody does self-deprecation quite like you. Truly, it's a special skill,' Aunt Bling rolled her eyes. 'You've always been too hard on yourself.'

'You think? I don't know. I have expectations, but only because I know I'm capable of being more in control than this. I've turned into some kind of moronic, fixated adolescent over a boy. I can hardly believe myself. I don't know what's going on with me.'

'So you haven't lost your job? Been kicked out of your house? You've not gambled all your savings or injected them away? Here, let me see your arms.'

Maddie waved her aunt's hands away.

'Give me a break. I've lost focus. I find myself thinking about this guy. I'm infatuated one moment, heart-broken the next. So not where or what I want to be; some emotionally vulnerable try-hard. I'm wearing lip gloss in the winery for God's sake.'

'Oh, Maddie. We're going to have to keep that from your mother,' Aunt Bling teased.

'AB, I'm serious.' Frustration strangled her voice into a shriek.

Aunt Bling reined herself in. 'Sorry my love, but I'm having trouble getting my head around what you're saying. I'm trying to understand why you're so upset. Is it Josh? I thought you two were done?'

'Yes, we're done. This has nothing to do with Josh,' Maddie scoffed. 'It's crazy how quickly I moved on from him. Maybe there is something wrong with me.'

'I didn't mean to open the floodgates. If you've sorted things with Josh, let's move on. What's this about?'

'Roley!' Maddie took a breath. 'His name is Roley. He's the Vineyard Manager at Kite. We've just been hanging out. We're friends—and we kind of got together. He's got a girlfriend, who's now his fiancée, in Perth.'

Aunt Bling tilted her head. 'It has been a busy vintage.'

Maddie smiled despite herself. 'I don't know how he feels about me. The fact he's just proposed to his girlfriend strongly suggests it may be a one-way thing.' Maddie's head drooped, speaking the words delivering a hefty dose of reality. 'But that's just part of the picture.'

'Mmmm?' Aunt Bling waited.

'I can't really put my finger on it. Don't know how to explain it really.' Maddie shook her head, struggling to turn the inner turmoil into words. 'I feel like I'm letting myself down.'

Aunt Bling cocked her head, trying to grasp what Maddie couldn't. 'In what way? If not to do with the relationship, then what?'

'I'm well into my twenties. I'm smart. I'm independent, capable. I'm achieving my goals,' Maddie counted off on her fingers. 'My career is moving in the direction I want. It just doesn't gel with lip gloss and immature infatuation.'

Aunt Bling was struggling. 'So what, you're having trouble reconciling professional life with being a woman?'

'I think so,' Maddie cried. 'I'm allowing all this emotional flux to distract me. Where's the strength in that? I'm throwing hard-won liberation out the window, to the wind. I'm letting myself and women down everywhere.'

'I see so much of myself in you. You could really be my daughter, not my niece.'

'Please! No closet skeletons Aunt Bling. It would tip me over the edge.'

'No, we'll save that for another time,' she joked. 'But I'm still trying to understand. You feel that being a woman is somehow interfering with being a career girl?'

Maddie smiled inwardly at her aunt's turn of phrase. 'Yeah. It just seems wrong that I can be strong and focused and have these responsibilities at work, only to see a boy in the distance and turn to mush.'

'You don't think you can be both?'

Maddie raised her eyebrows. 'Both what—smart and mushy?'

'Woman and winemaker? You know you don't have a choice in one? Unless you're androgynous, and really, if you were androgynous you would be both man and woman and it sounds like you'd rather be neither.'

'Oh, please, you're making my brain hurt,' Maddie cradled her head in her hands.

'Well you, trying to deny your womanhood, could practically break my heart. And listen to what you're really saying… that being a professional and a woman is not possible?'

Maddie pulled a face. 'You know that's not what I mean.'

'Sorry girlfriend, but that's what you're saying. And I'm mortified. My generation played a little part in trying to move gender equality in a more positive direction. I hope you're not telling me that all of our work, our hard-won battles were in vain?'

Maddie let out a sigh. 'The whole thing confuses me. Aren't I dragging women's rights back to the dark ages by swooning over a colleague? Not just swooning but flailing about hysterically when I find out he's engaged…so emotional.'

'No.' Aunt Bling was thoughtful. 'Women's rights—God, I don't think anyone's used that terminology for years.'

Maddie sighed.

'Equality is not about denying the essence of womanhood. It's about finding a platform where we can be amazing, where we achieve and contribute on an equal footing because we are women and we have these incredible attributes; patience, multitasking, the ability to see things in front of our faces, being intelligent in a common-sense way, nurturing, compassionate. Of course, these are big generalisations. Not all women are all these things, just as many men are.'

Maddie concentrated hard, trying to follow.

'Who are some of your heroines?'

'Olivia, my first yoga teacher was awesome.'

'Was she married, engaged, in a relationship?'

'I don't know AB, she instructed me in downward dog.'

'Did she wear lipstick, designer tights, nail polish?'

'Okay,' Maddie raised her hands. 'What's your point?'

'You tell me. What was so awesome about her? I remember you singing her praises.'

'She was fabulous. She embraced her students equally, never judging lifestyle choices. And, she knew her stuff. She knew exactly where our bodies and minds were at. She listened when we had issues. God AB, do you want descriptors? She was intuitive, knowledgeable, passionate.'

'Passionate about poses? Doesn't that make her, kind of lightweight?'

'AB, you're starting to rile me. For a start, they call them asanas, not poses. And why does it matter what she was teaching, she was all over it. She lived her passion. I have nothing but admiration for her.'

'Regardless whether she had a manicure or not?'

'What the…? I couldn't have cared less what she looked like, including the state of her nails. She was impressive. Ethical precepts were at the heart of her teaching. None of that posing on the beach in a bikini bullshit.'

'That's my point,' Aunt Bling laid her palms flat on her thighs, looking satisfied.

Maddie was yet to arrange it in her head. 'Please elaborate?'

'It's about those bigger things, knowledge, passion, integrity. Those are the things we want to put forward into our lives, into our work. Whether we shave our legs, wear a push-up bra, or fall head over heels for a workmate really shouldn't be what we're judged on. Answer me this. Why the lip gloss?'

'I don't know,' Maddie was flustered 'It makes my lips feel nice, gives my face a little colour. I just feel good when I've got it on. It's my bloody choice.'

'Exactly. It is your right to choose. Does it interfere with your job, chip away at your integrity?'

'No. I wouldn't wear it when I'm tasting.'

'Then, why is it an issue for you? You've made a choice. You get to make choices whoever you are, whatever you do.'

'Do you know that female doctor who does the amazing work in stroke research?'

'Of course. She's one of my heroines, right alongside my yoga guru.'

'Have you seen her in the social pages?' Aunt Bling on a roll, didn't wait for an answer. 'She wears a diamond the size of a golf ball.'

'Your point?'

'Do you think any less of her because she wears flashy, expensive jewels?'

Maddie started to click. 'No, I wouldn't think twice about it.'

'What if she was married to a man half her age, or married to two men, or single with seventeen cats? Would it make her achievements any less awesome?'

'No. I think I'm getting it now. Of course not.'

'Maddie, celebrate being a woman in whatever way you choose. By denying your feminine self, you're trying to be something you're not. Women have fought to be liberated from constraints and ideals, to be celebrated for everything they are and what they bring to the table. For women to posture as men suggests we consider them superior. Why would we do that? Embrace being a woman, in whatever form it takes.'

'Embrace falling to pieces whenever Roley walks by?'

'This too will pass.'

Maddie chorused the line with her aunt. It was one of Aunt Bling's hallmark sayings. Four simple words encompassing a concept of epic proportion.

'Furthermore, of no comfort whatsoever, I must inform you as an old girl who knows these things, we may get better at concealing it, but that flutter of attraction doesn't fade with age. It's what I live for. Bring it on, I say.'

Maddie smiled. 'Settle down AB. I've felt so out of balance lately, a train wreck when I heard Roley, who never promised me anything, got engaged.'

Aunt Bling looked down at her hands. 'It seems out of character. Why did you get involved there?'

A film glazed over her eyes. 'It's a really good question.'

'You don't have to answer.'

'I'm not sure that I can,' Maddie picked at a fingernail. 'I really like him. There's a connection, feelings I haven't really experienced before,' she sighed. 'I hoped things had cooled with his girlfriend, but if I'm really honest, I suspected she was still on the scene,' Maddie looked at her Aunt. 'Please don't judge him on this.'

Aunt Bling's expression softened. 'I try not to judge anyone, Maddie. It's interesting, that's what you're worried about. Maybe this story hasn't ended yet.'

Maddie shook her head. 'We haven't talked about any of it.' Tears welled.

'The unsaid—biggest breaker of hearts in the world,' Aunt Bling nodded slowly.

Maddie swiped at her cheek.

'Good news,' Aunt Bling offered. 'There is an antidote.'

Maddie raised her eyebrows.

'Honesty. It's the only balm. Use it liberally when you're working back through the choices you made. Apply it morning and night to the symptoms of your hurt—confusion, guilt, humiliation.' Aunt Bling waved her hand theatrically. 'Most importantly, don't forget it going forward. Keep it close. If you and Roley do talk, slather as much of it as you can. Regardless of the outcome, it is the most important ingredient in the healing process.'

'Sounds simple enough,' Maddie shrugged.

'Simple!' Aunt Bling recoiled. 'Humans make unbelievably hard work of open, honest communication.'

'I'll try anything,' Maddie looked at her aunt. 'Once again you've earned your 'truly amazing' status. You top the list you know. Aunt Bling, stroke researcher, yoga teacher.'

'Well,' Aunt Bling sounded chuffed. 'I certainly don't mean to lecture. It's all conjectural at the end of the day, and these are big concepts. I think it's fabulous you're giving them some thought. I've always believed experience is knowledge.

And with awareness illuminating your experiences—look out world, you're already ahead of the curve.'

Maddie nodded, although she'd need time to fully digest that one. 'I've certainly done my share of head scratching lately. Is that the same as thinking?'

Aunt Bling snorted, shaking her head. 'Close enough.'

'I'm so happy to have you in my life.'

Aunt Bling squeezed Maddie's hand and the exchange settled in a quiet infusion of fondness and respect.

'Did I mention the really hot Italian guy?'

Aunt Bling smiled, circling her hands in front of her face. 'The picture's clearing. It's not squashing grapes that wears you out?'

'Mostly it's grapes,' Maddie laughed. 'You must be dying for a cuppa after your drive? Where's mum?'

Maddie looked around and saw her mother standing on the deck, arms stretching either side on the railing, head turned towards the sea. She wasn't a big woman, but her stature held its own against the expansive landscape.

As Maddie watched, she reflected. Today's scene was typical of so many others before, her mother backing away, leaving her sister to counsel her floundering offspring. A pattern so entrenched, Maddie never questioned it. Until now. Something had struck a nerve and realisation dawned. Memory could be an unreliable witness under the fickle light of perception. Her mother never fled the scene, she was always there, directing play. For the second time in her life, Maddie registered an inkling of her mother's strength.

Her mother looked skyward, following the flight of an osprey.

Maddie swallowed and walked outside to join her, feeling something shift.

Chapter 18

It was the next week before Maddie and Roley faced each other alone.

Daylight was fading. Cellar door had been closed for an hour or more and all the admin staff had left.

Maddie walked towards Lewis's office. The place felt abandoned. She hadn't seen Westy for a while but his car was there and Lewis's dual cab was gone—normally he'd find her to say goodbye. She decided to leave a note. Walking down the passage, she automatically looked in as she passed Roley's darkened office.

Maddie jumped. Roley faced his computer, his back to the door, the scrolling screen saver the only movement in the room. She tapped gently.

Roley spun around in his chair. 'Hi Maddie.'

'Hi.' The greeting was strained on both sides. Maddie leant into the doorframe. 'Any idea what's happened to Lewis and Westy?' she asked.

'Urgent business with a contract customer apparently. Didn't say which one.'

Maddie's brow furrowed. 'That's odd.'

'I thought so too,' Roley answered flatly. 'Lewis asked me to check in with you before I left. Are you leaving?'

'I was going to check something with Lewis, but it can wait. I might as well head off.' Maddie half-turned to leave. Feeling slightly ill, she turned back. 'Actually, I haven't had a chance to congratulate you on your engagement.' The words were dry and scratchy. She forced a smile.

It was wasted on Roley, his eyes were fixed on the floor. Slowly he looked up. 'Are you congratulating me now?'

'Of course. I hope you guys are happy.' The sentiment sounded hollow in the quiet room. Maddie swallowed. 'Vieve must be excited?' she asked mustering a little gusto.

Roley ignored the question.

She read raw vulnerability in his expression. Any thoughts she had of hurting him, vanished.

'It was a bit of a shock,' she ventured. 'It's taken me a while to…' Maddie hadn't realised how much courage being honest required. Each revelation felt like ripping a strip of hot-wax from her brain. 'I will be happy for you Roley. I just got ahead of myself, that's all.'

Roley ruffled. 'You've got plenty to think about with Marco and, who knows, maybe Josh still in the picture. Things should be simpler now.'

Both names were slaps but somehow, not unexpected. Her behaviour had been as confusing as his. As defensive psychobabble leached into her system, Maddie took a breath, remembering the conversation with her aunt, and ignored it.

She looked at him steadily. 'Josh and I parted ways weeks ago and Marco, was me rebelling against not getting who I really want.' Maddie felt stripped bare.

'I wasn't asking for an explanation,' Roley fired, his posture deflating.

'I'm sorry we didn't talk. I felt bad for hurting Vieve. I thought you guys needed to sort things—without me on the scene.'

'You certainly didn't waste time removing yourself.'

Maddie flinched, then bristled. 'Would you like a mirror with that? Are you even planning to tell Vieve about our—your—whatever the hell we were, before the wedding?'

Roley looked at her, his mouth opened and Maddie raised her arm. 'You know what? I don't even want to know. You're the one getting married. It's not my business.'

Roley slowly shook his head, like his thoughts couldn't stand to be still. He leant forward, resting his elbows on his thighs. 'I'm sorry,' his eyes trained on a patch of floor near her feet. 'Turns out, I'm a bit of a prick.'

The silence was excruciating. Their hearts beat and the atmosphere hummed, alive with the force of wordless space.

'You know I'm hoping to stay on after vintage. I respect you and Lewis and what you're achieving here. I hope we can find some way forward.'

It sounded formal amid the personal revelations, business-like and very grown up.

Roley's face was taut as he looked up, holding her gaze. 'We'll work it out.'

'Okay,' Maddie sighed. 'I'm heading off. I'll see you tomorrow.'

As she turned to leave, Roley straightened in his chair. 'We will work it out, Maddie. It'll be okay.'

Maddie nodded slowly. She reached and gripped the doorframe. 'I'm having some kind of internal, honesty based, catastrophic event.'

Anticipation flickered across Roley's face.

'This one's for free,' she looked down the passage. 'A real prick wouldn't care.' As soon as the words were out, head down she made for the exit.

Chapter 19

Lewis pulled up at the vineyard entrance just behind them. Maddie jumped out to spring the combination lock. She smiled, holding the gate open as the vehicles passed through. Then she climbed back into Roley's ute and they followed the gravel road down the slope. They pulled up beside the dam, rusty dust clouds billowing behind. The Malbec block ran all the way from the dam, up the slope to the top of the ridge. It looked lush in the soft, morning light.

Since the exchange in his office, Roley and Maddie had tentatively reconstructed their working relationship. In unspoken agreement they bantered about music, films, food as before, but talk of their personal lives was unequivocally off limits.

Occasionally, in a group situation, Genevieve's name cropped up. Roley's demeanour quietened and Maddie retreated to her happy place, often thinking of the 'happy faeces' emoticon, until the moment passed.

Day by day tension eased. Maddie didn't blink when Roley offered to drive her to the meeting at the Malbec block. Still, as Roley's ute stopped, they wasted no time getting out and walking over to Lewis.

They exchanged pleasantries while walking to the bottom corner of the vineyard.

Lewis stopped, scooping up the bird netting, holding it aloft while Maddie and Roley ducked under. The netting was put out a week ago as the grapes sweetened, to protect the crop from tiny silvereyes who believed vineyards were giant picnics, provided for their pleasure. The birds performed daring raids from the protection of tree-lines, diving into the vines to pierce berries with their beaks, enjoying miniscule quantities of nectar, leaving whole bunches to rot.

'It's holding up well,' Lewis remarked.

'Yeah,' Roley agreed. 'Thriving in this heat.'

'Think the leaf plucking has made a difference?'

'Definitely,' Roley replied. 'The grapes are getting a lot more direct sunlight and the Malbec really responds to that. Even with these hot days, there's no sign of sunburn and no significant shrivel.'

Walking between rows they stopped intermittently to pick individual berries from bunches. They chewed then spat the skins and seeds to the ground.

It was the most important tasting a winemaker did. Blending sessions were one thing but being able to assess flavour, tannin ripeness and acid levels in this raw state was imperative. It was a skill. One that improved with experience and the opportunity to taste grapes in their natural form then follow them through to finished wines.

Once grapes were severed from the vines there was no going back. If tannins were green or immature that is how they'd appear in the finished wine. Winemakers could tweak tannin by adding more, but they couldn't alter characteristics of the tannins already present. It worked the same for flavour. If grapes lacked intensity hanging on the vines, the resulting juice would look equally insipid. Flavour could be enhanced by the winemaking process but it couldn't be artificially put there; so much relied on the grape's natural grace.

Maddie was quiet, listening intently to the conversation between Lewis and Roley. When Lewis addressed her directly, she responded cautiously. 'I'm not familiar with Margaret River Malbec at all, so this is a huge learning curve for me. But, I'm liking the flavour and I think the acidity looks right. I'm wondering how long the acidity will hold while the flavours develop? There's still a little crispness to the skins, so I'm guessing we're a week to ten days away from picking?'

Lewis smiled, quietly nodding.

'How are the flavours looking compared to previous years?'

'Exactly where I was hoping they would be,' Lewis replied. 'Every year we've seen increasing depth, and while I agree these grapes are ten or more days out, the flavour is there and it has a brightness I haven't seen before.'

'That's exciting,' Maddie answered.

'If you think that's exciting, you're going to love the next bit.' Lewis looked quickly at Roley. 'I'm putting you in charge of the Malbec this year.'

Maddie had just popped another grape into her mouth. 'Seriously?' she spluttered, looking from Lewis to Roley and back again.

'Deadly,' confirmed Lewis with a nod. 'And we're not blending it with the Cabernet this year.'

'Straight Malbec?' Maddie's eyed opened wider.

'Dead straight,' Lewis laughed. 'You will be responsible for Beneath The Kite's first one hundred per cent pure Malbec.'

Maddie, conscious of appearing dumbstruck, punched Lewis on the arm. 'You've just made my vintage.' She didn't trust herself to say more.

'So you'll need to work with Roley on deciding the picking schedule. We'll talk about style back at the winery.'

'I already know what style I'm aiming for,' Maddie enthused.

'Good luck, Roley,' Lewis raised his eyebrows.

Roley smiled. 'Yeah, thanks mate.'

Maddie looked at them unperturbed. 'Well come on, it's got to be big, rich and juicy. I want a little complexity there, not a total fruit bomb, but really it's going to say *drink me and enjoy every mouthful*, isn't it?'

Lewis turned, walking back down the row, holding his head in his hands. 'What've I unleashed?'

Maddie thought he was mostly joking. She looked at Roley and shrugged as they followed slowly behind.

Maddie glanced sideways. 'You knew?'

Roley raised an eyebrow but wasn't giving anything away. 'Going to be a great Malbec—Beneath The Kite's best ever.'

'Beneath The Kite's *only* ever. But you're right, it's going to be fabulous. I'm sure we can achieve something exceptional together.'

Roley looked at her.

Maddie bent to fiddle with a reticulation nozzle, crossing and uncrossing her eyes. She straightened, blinking to refocus. 'So what are your thoughts?'

'It can hang for a while,' Roley stated matter of fact. 'As Lewis said, canopy's looking good. I've been through the block and there's no sign of disease. Berries are big and the bunches are getting tight but I haven't noticed any splitting or shrivelling. I thought we may have some bird damage round the tree-line further up the hill, and we did get a bit, but we've been through dropping fruit and even those sections look good now.'

Roley and Maddie reached the end of the row. Exiting from beneath the netting they caught sight of Lewis moving through the Cabernet block next door.

'We do get a bit of variation in this block. I'm thinking you'll want to do it in two picks.' Roley swept his arm towards the top of the ridge, indicating they walk further up.

As they reached the halfway mark, Maddie detected a subtle shift in leaf colour, the rich green fading.

'Around here?' she asked.

'You've got a good eye,' Roley stopped and lifted the netting.

They hunched under and walked between rows picking berries from either side, chewing and spitting.

'There's quite a difference,' Maddie exclaimed. 'I reckon we should collect a sample from this lot.'

'Good thinking,' he smiled, offering her a plastic zip-lock bag he'd already pulled from his pocket.

'Great minds,' she stated, dropping berries into the bag.

Bag in hand, Maddie took off. She ducked under vines, moving randomly along rows, working her way up the hill, tasting and collecting.

Reaching the last row at the top of the hill, Maddie popped out from under the netting. Roley and Lewis looked small, talking in a huddle by the dam. They didn't look in a hurry to leave.

Maddie held the bag of juicy berries aloft—her

Malbec—admiring the slick, purple-black spheres of joy. She drew the bag to her chest, cherishing the unexpected opportunity. She visualised it in bottle, standing on the counter at cellar door, being swirled and sniffed and showered with adulation.

When she opened her eyes she noticed Lewis and Roley were still conferring calmly. She studied them and sighed. Their passion was intense, but somehow, contained. It had longevity. Maddie thought of her own unchecked passion, it could be exhausting running unharnessed, testing her endurance. Suddenly, she was back at the pre-harvest ceremony remembering Lewis's pledge.

'Madison,' she remonstrated aloud. 'You need to put your ideas on style aside and listen to the fruit.' She lifted the bag to her ear, feeling light and silly and more like herself than she had in a while. Damn it felt good.

Roley and Lewis looked up at her. Maddie waved and mumbled through smiling lips. 'Nothing to see here, guys.'

The resident kookaburras thought she was hilarious. They pull-started their laugh boxes and the sound echoed around the valley. Maddie could feel her boots crunching gravel but with her fingers clutching the cool pouch of fruit, she was tripping across blue sky as she walked down the hill.

Chapter 20

Vintage was finished for another year. It was bittersweet for Maddie. On one hand she was ready for a break, on the other, already missing the challenges; the logistical mine-field and sensory stimulation. There was always a period of readjustment, a coming down before rejoining the world beyond the winery. It also signalled the end of her contract at Kite and the uncertainty beyond.

The vineyard crew celebrated the end of harvest a few weeks previously. Work hours no longer available to the casuals once picking was complete, the travellers packed up their vans. Many were heading north, their sights on Broome; budgets and mechanical integrity of their clapped out rides stretched to make it that far.

They marked the end of harvest with a rustic long lunch with everyone pitching in to set up. The long grass was slashed—no snakes invited—and two big wooden tables were forked in with the tractor, arranged end-to-end under the big jarrahs down near the creek line. Holly and Bec organised square hay bales, rugs and cushions to create an outdoor lounge area. Guitars, drums and anything loosely capable of percussion, spread around for an acoustic jam.

On the day before the lunch, Roley and Westy had foregone their morning surf and gone diving instead, managing to bag one jumbo and three smaller crays. Holly and Bec used them to prepare an entrée of crayfish, quinoa and mango salad.

Marco volunteered to make a fresh pasta course. He insisted on privacy while preparing the dough, citing a promise made to his nonnina to guard the family recipe. Underestimating his loyalty, one by one people helping with other things would stop to look over his shoulder until Marco's Italian started flowing in longer and louder bursts. When he started gesticulating wildly, with dough-covered hands, Juan stepped in, removing projectile-worthy utensils from Marco's reach and shooing the gallery.

Lewis was granted access to deliver Mae's pasta machine and within the hour every chair back was strewn with long strands of fettuccine, hanging out to dry.

Taxi provoked a fresh outburst when Marco caught him snatching a sample. Juan didn't understand Italian but inferred it had something to do with kelpie sauce. He led the dog back to the winery, securing him on his chain.

For the main event, Roley purchased a saddle of beef from a local grazier for grilling on the barbeque and Westy caught a good-sized dhufish which they would season and bake whole. A seasonal vegetable medley, mostly supplied from Mae's garden, completed the feast.

Lewis and Maddie raided Kite's cellar for some aged

wines and the table was set, decorated with native blossoms and red gingham napkins. Everything looked amazing.

Every Kite employee was invited and they all shuffled workloads and responsibilities to attend.

Emma and Bethany tag-teamed between customers at cellar door. Liz redirected the phone to her mobile for a few hours. Westy started early to get some winery tasks out of the way and Lewis and Roley had cleared their schedules. The Malbec was being pressed off its skins, so Maddie would work around that.

The day was a cracker, a warm, still slice of autumn. Roley had set up a volleyball net and by late morning they were digging, spiking and laughing, working up appetites and thirsts.

Maddie felt good. She was excited about the Malbec and looked forward to relaxing with good friends, food and wine on such a pretty day. Sex hadn't altered her friendship with Marco. He'd been a gentleman and a sweetheart every time they met. No awkward moments, no expectations. They sat next to each other for the pasta course.

'OMG! It's like velvet melting in my mouth,' Maddie looked wide-eyed at Marco.

'Ah, bella. My nonna would be happy to hear it,' he dropped his eyes, batting long, dark lashes. 'My nonna would like you, I think.'

'Who knows, maybe I'll get to Barolo one day. I'd love to meet her,' Maddie laughed, '…eat more of her pasta.'

Marco smiled pulling his phone from his shirt pocket. 'Please, may I have your contact and perhaps, you wish to have mine?'

Maddie picked up her phone. 'Absolutely.' They exchanged details, swiping and typing. Maddie laid down her phone and Marco asked quietly. 'May we have a photo together?'

She shuffled closer on the bench and Marco held his phone aloft. 'Fettuccine!'

Maddie laughed and they sang 'fettuccine' together.

He showed her the photo.

'Awesome. Can you forward it? Then I know you've got me.'

Marco thumbed at his phone and within seconds hers pinged, message received. He nudged her gently with his elbow. 'I don't think I have you though.'

Maddie followed the arch of Marco's eyebrows and the subtle incline of his head. Roley sat at the end of the table, watching them.

'It's not that simple,' she sighed.

'It never is bella. Still that look causes my Roman blood to run cold.'

She laughed.

'I'm not often of the one-night stand,' he held her eyes. 'It is not my personality. I hope you are feeling okay with me about this?'

Maddie put her hand to his cheek. 'I think you are a lovely man, Marco. I'm okay with you. I'm not usually of the one-night fling either. I think ours was a bit special.'

Marco leant in, lightly kissing her cheek before springing to his feet. With glass raised he shouted: 'We toast my nonnina. And so you know, Barolo is not only special about wine.'

Everyone around the table stood, arms stretched. 'Marco and his nonnina,' they chorused, clunking glasses.

While on her feet, Emma started clearing plates at one end and Roley began at the other. Lewis wandered to the barbie to check the beef. Two courses down, they all helped prepare for the next.

Maddie missed the start of main course, attending to the

press. Westy, proud of his dhufish, plated her a serve, knowing she wouldn't be long. She returned carrying as many samples of the young Malbec as she could manage, placing them randomly along the long table.

Lewis stood, seeking the attention of the table. 'This is the reason Maddie keeps disappearing today.' Maddie handed him a glass. 'A treat for the travellers who worked so hard picking these grapes and who won't be around to taste Beneath The Kite's first ever Malbec.'

Juan nodded vigorously. 'I should have known. It goes beautifully with the beef.'

'Oooh, it's like juicy black cherries. My favourite,' exclaimed Bec excitedly. 'Cheers to you girlfriend,' she raised her glass towards Maddie.

'I like it with the dhufish also,' said Marco, jutting out his bottom jaw.

'It's good Maddie,' Roley nodded. 'Blackberry, cherry and plums.' He looked at Lewis. 'What were we thinking blending it with the Cabernet?'

The praise was overwhelming, Maddie felt colour rising in her cheeks. She thrust her nose into her glass. It all confirmed her own assessment—the Malbec was bliss.

It was after three o'clock when Mae arrived with the boys in tow. The crew had adjourned to the lounge where Holly was strumming and singing with Juan beating time on the drums. The boys suddenly shy, needed a little encouragement to join in on percussion.

Mae had brought a divine looking plum crostata. Still warm from baking, she portioned it into servings with thick double cream.

Dessert distributed, Lewis pulled Mae in for a kiss and poured her a glass of sparkling. They ate and chilled before he razzed the stuffed, mellow bodies for another game of volleyball with his boys leading the charge.

The press had almost finished its cycle. It was time for Maddie to say goodbye. By the time she finished organising the wine and cleaning up, she would be sticky, wet and tired. They still had a busy week in the winery with more pressing scheduled the following day. Besides, she estimated two hours from now, the revellers would well and truly have left her behind.

She wished them happy travels, exchanging hugs and contact information before heading back to the winery to concentrate on the Malbec.

Now, it was her turn.

The vintage equipment was stripped, thoroughly cleaned and stored. The barrels were topped and racked, sitting quietly, doing their thing for a while without intervention. Data on each of the wines had been updated on computer records in preparation for invoicing contract clients and preparing budgets for the following year.

As things slowed, Westy resumed college one day a week and Lewis started planning a holiday. There were one or two weeks of work left until Maddie's position became redundant. Lewis was keen for her to join the team in a permanent role and had begun discussions with the owners about restructuring opportunities. But in the interim post-vintage period, there simply wasn't enough work to justify remuneration of casual hours.

Tonight, however, was reserved for celebration. Maddie shelved contemplative thoughts of her future which were starting to fester with complexity. They would wait another day. She'd earned some light relief and was in the mood for fun.

With the other vintage casuals gone, numbers were intimate which meant more options; fine dining, overnight accommodation, even a cultural event. However, when Lewis consulted the group, they opted for an afternoon at the beach with sunset drinks before heading to Southers with swags for barbequed marron fresh from the dam, and a bonfire.

They jagged another autumn offering of soft, still sunshine. The gentle sky wouldn't hold a kite, leaving spirits to tattoo the blue with dreams. While Westy and Roley surfed, Maddie and Bethany went for a long walk along the beach, wading in at the turning point for a swim. They weren't hot but the water looked delicious, luring them to wet their skins and float.

They walked leisurely back to base to find Lewis, esky in tow, organising a cheese plate. Mae had arrived with the boys who were amped to swim and play.

Maddie hadn't seen her since the vineyard celebration.

'Hi girls,' she greeted them with her warm smile. 'I can't believe you've chosen catching and cooking marron over going out and having someone serve them to you, already killed, cleaned and dressed.'

Maddie and Bethany looked at each other, feigning horror.

'Mae, have you not been properly introduced to Beth Grylls of 'Wacko vs. Wild' fame?' Maddie asked, gesturing to Bethany. 'Marron aren't worth eating unless you hunt them with your bare hands.'

The boys were playing with Taxi in the shallows. They stopped and looked at the adults. 'You wouldn't eat them alive would you?'

'No,' Lewis interjected quickly. 'Maddie's just pretending. We'll cook them like we always do, make sure they're sleepy first.'

'I can see two big marron ready for catching now,' Maddie teased, creeping across the sand towards them.

They squealed and ran down the beach, Taxi barking, running with them.

'It's the bonfire I'm looking forward to,' Bethany admitted. 'Nothing like the first campfire once the fire ban's been lifted. I've got the marshmallows ready to go.'

'Marshmallows?' One of the boys yelled from down the beach.

Mae shook her head. 'Sometimes I'd swear they're deaf. Obviously it's just selective hearing…from their dad I think.'

'Sorry Mae, I didn't catch that,' Lewis looked around.

Mae laughed. 'Do you mind if I open the bubbles? Think I fancy a glass before I take these two home.'

'Great idea,' Bethany rubbed her hands together. 'I'm ready for a glass.'

'I've never known a time when you weren't,' scoffed Maddie, rejoining the group.

'Well, isn't it comforting to know you always have someone ready to drink bubbles with?'

'One of my favourite things about our friendship,' Maddie smiled, accepting a glass.

When they all had a glass, they chorused a hearty 'cheers.'

Mae swallowed a sip. 'So, how many of you partying tonight?'

'Just five of us I think,' Lewis looked to the girls for confirmation. 'Are you sure you won't bring the kids out and join us for dinner?'

'I'm sure,' Mae smiled. 'The vintage circus is almost over.

When you're on holidays in a week or so, we can pitch a tent down there and take the canoes and catch marron and go spotlighting and stay for a couple of nights. The boys will want you to themselves.'

Lewis nodded, putting his arm around Mae's waist. 'My superiorly intelligent wife…that sounds wonderful.'

'A small group will be fun, and good news for the marron,' Mae grinned, turning to Maddie. 'Have you made any plans yet?'

Maddie looked at Lewis. He raised his eyebrows.

'Nothing definite yet. I will have to take some time off. Another week and there won't be enough work to justify keeping me on. I'm keen to go overseas and do a vintage in the northern hemisphere, but nothing's confirmed.'

Lewis looked at Mae. 'Remember Philippe from Cahors in southern France, Malbec country?'

Mae nodded, sipping her bubbles.

'I've sent him an email asking about vintage positions.' He looked at Maddie. 'Philippe travels a lot. If I haven't heard back within a couple of days, I'll give him a call.'

'Thanks Lewis.'

Mae put her hand on Maddie's arm. 'Philippe is a wonderful man. If you could get a position there…his family would go out of their way to look after you. Good on you for putting yourself out there. It's exciting.'

'So exciting,' Bethany enthused.

'What's exciting?' asked Roley, who had snuck up on the group with Westy after dropping their boards in the carpark.

'Maddie, going to France to do vintage,' Bethany blurted.

'Oh! I hadn't heard,' Roley stated evenly.

'There's really nothing to tell yet,' Maddie added quickly. 'Lewis has just started making enquiries. I haven't even mentioned it to my wonderful cellar-mate Westy,' she exclaimed, putting an arm around him.

'I work on a strictly need-to-know, only what I need-to-know basis,' Westy mused. 'Just let me know when you're off, so I stop making you coffee at smoko.'

The dam was on private property, so legally, they could net the marron. Lewis wouldn't hear of it, declaring snaring to be much more sporting and fun. As usual, he was right.

By torchlight, they wandered down to the dam to throw out baits, then returned to camp to nibble cheese, drink wine and pass time before meandering back to check the lures.

When they spied a marron, and there were plenty about, they would carefully position their snares behind the marron's tail, deftly easing it over and along its body before yanking the line. The weight of the marron was enough to pull the snare tight.

Often, the marron felt the snare before it got a reasonable distance over their tails. They'd flick their bodies, shooting off in a sonic burst, muddying the water for a good five minutes. It wasn't an exact science, so many things could go wrong.

Paramount was the person holding the torch. If the beam crossed in front of the marron they would flick or shy away. If the beam wasn't close enough to the back of the marron, the snarer could touch them inadvertently with the wire, initiating their escape. Sometimes, it seemed instinct alone was enough to make the marron retreat to deep water.

It was good they brought hamburgers, buns and salad, because at one point they needed sustenance, beyond cheese, to keep hunting and soak up the drinks.

They cooked and devoured hamburgers before catching

enough marron for a late night snack. Grilled on the bar-beque with butter mixed with lemon zest and garlic, the freshwater crayfish were sublime.

Maddie and Bethany had made a mojito base and insisted the cocktails be drunk with the marron. Both sure the lime and mint would match beautifully with the freshwater meat.

It was after midnight before they sat around the fire, toasting marshmallows.

Jumping on a break in the conversation, Lewis clasped his hands together. 'I think it might be time to give thanks.'

'Thanks for charcoal flavoured marshmallows?' Westy queried. 'I'm giving my thanks to the marron. They were bloody delicious.'

Bethany giggled. 'Marron and mojitos—equally delicious and deserving of thanks.'

'I'm talking gratitude for people here, people,' Lewis smiled. 'This is our end of vintage celebration and while I'm thankful for tasty marron, I didn't see them working at four in the morning supervising picking crews, or plunging tanks at nine o'clock at night because they knew it would make a better wine.'

'Of course you didn't see them in the dark,' Westy heckled. 'They're black. The unseen, unsung, ninjas of vintage. Who did you think was managing the sorting table, picking through the Cabernet?'

Roley tried not to laugh. 'Guys, Lewis is being sincere.'

'Yeah, sorry Lewis,' Maddie apologised. 'But it's not right, not to recognise the marron,' she giggled. 'I can hear their little legs making that skitter, skitter, skitter sound, cleaning out the press.'

Bethany snorted with laughter. 'Hard work with little skittery feet and no boots.'

'Next year, they can get their high-risk work licences and we'll put them on the forklift,' Westy cackled.

'Yeah, but remember the cellar is cool,' Maddie interjected. 'Doesn't that make them sleepy? We don't want them nodding off at the wheel.'

'Right,' Lewis stood, raising his arms, waiting for quiet. 'My thanks to each and every one of you—and the marron— for a well-executed vintage.' He waited for the laughter to fade. 'It's been a pleasure working with you all to achieve another great result.'

'You're a good leader, Lewis,' Roley raised his glass. 'We all love what we do.'

'Yeah,' Westy added. 'You're a rockin' boss and we are awesome.'

Bethany lobbed a crucified marshmallow at him, blowing on her fingers. 'Lewis is trying to be serious, and you're being very silly.'

Lewis laughed. 'All good. I'm done.' He raised his glass. 'To Kite and the people—and crustaceans—who make it great.'

'And a toast—ed marshmallow, and a big thank you for employing me at Kite,' Maddie decreed with a toothy grin.

A glass of red later, Lewis, unable to keep his eyes open, drifted quietly to his swag in the machinery shed. Westy disappeared not long after and finally Bethany, less surreptitiously, blowing kisses in all directions, retreated too.

Leaving Roley and Maddie alone by the fire.

As the energy of the others dissipated, the night closed in. Maddie and Roley locked eyes across the smouldering coals.

'France, eh?'

'We'll see,' Maddie shrugged. 'It doesn't feel real. Things are happening fast.' Half-smiling, she proceeded with caution. 'On the subject of things happening quickly, did you buy your girl a rock?'

'A ring?' Roley gave a short sigh and looked into the glowing embers. 'God, you know, not a lot of planning went into my proposal.'

'Oh?'

'It's all pretty stuffed,' Roley dropped his head. 'Y'know Maddie, I'm not great at this and…I might be a little pissed but I need to tell you.' He looked up.

Maddie nodded.

'The only way I can explain it, is to think of it like surfing,' he flicked her a look then stared into the fire. 'Vieve is like getting back from a surf. After a shower and a coffee or a beer I feel satisfied, content, that sort of thing.' Roley picked up a stick and started drawing in the earth.

'You…'

Maddie tensed.

'…you're like the moment I get to my feet and drop down the face of the wave. I use all my energy to trim and carve. I throw everything I have at it. I never want the ride to end. I'm in the moment and I feel alive.'

Maddie's brain fired to take in his words.

Roley drew his legs in. 'It's fucking exhilarating and exhausting and…I'll never stop wanting to be out there.' He broke the stick in two and threw the pieces into the fire.

Someone was moving through the dark. Their eyes caught quickly before they turned to look.

Bethany lugged her swag. 'Unless you've got earplugs, I recommend sleeping round the fire tonight. Someone's snoring like a bloody train in the shed.'

'And it's not Westy,' said Westy, following behind, balancing his swag on his head.

They laughed.

'Any idea of the time?' Maddie asked.

'After two,' Bethany replied, snuggling down.

'Well if you're joining us, better have more wine,' Roley's speech was slow and deliberate. 'Campfire rules.'

'Oh, go on then,' Bethany giggled.

'Rules is rules,' said Westy solemnly, sitting cross-legged on his swag, emptying a half-finished glass he found near Roley's chair and holding it up to be filled.

'So what's happening round the campfire?'

'We're just admiring the Southern Cross,' Maddie's speech slurred as tiredness and wine pulled at her reins.

They all looked up into the night sky. Away from the lights of town, the sky sparkled with starry jewels.

'Did you know, the five stars of the Southern Cross are believed to be between ten and twenty million years old?'

'Yeah. It's a baby as far as constellations go.'

'Westy, you just may be Stubbsy's orphaned son.'

'Go on Maddie. What else?'

'Within the constellation is the Kappa Cruch…Crucis cluster,' Maddie stuttered. 'The Jewel Box.'

'Ahhh,' Bethany cooed. 'What a cool name.'

'It's made up of around one hundred brilliant, multicoloured stars.'

They were quiet, humbled by the majesty.

'So, do you know about 'the fly' Westy?' Maddie quizzed.

'Nope,' Westy replied, shaking his head.

'One of Stubbsy's favourite bits. The Southern Cross is bordered by another constellation called Musca—the fly. Stubbsy always ends his commentary with something like: 'Australia, land of the flies. Too bloody right, it's written in the stars."

Maddie craned her neck looking up. On righting her head, the ground moved unsteadily around her. 'Move over Bethany, I feel the need for horizontalism.'

Bethany laughed, moving over in the swag. She was still looking up at the sparkling screen above, when Maddie plonked heavily next to her.

'The Southern Cross is beautiful, but life beneath the kite is pretty bloody amazing.' Maddie was asleep within a breath.

Chapter 21

Roley walked into the winery, squinting in the dark. Maddie was organising equipment on the back wall. She took a deep breath. 'Hi Roley.'

'So, it's real now,' Roley stated bluntly, hands on hips, 'Vintage in France.'

Maddie smiled. 'I only just found out. It's pretty exciting, they want me there now.'

'I'm sure you would have gotten round to telling me.'

Maddie moved to speak but Roley ranted on.

'I thought you had another week or two on your contract?'

Maddie looked at him. The words sounded childlike, a lukewarm affront thinly veiling something deeper. 'Seriously—my contract?' Maddie screwed up her face. She wanted to tell him to grow up and talk with her properly. Wasn't she a crystal bank of water, pulsing with power and thrill? Not his bloody mother, holding a tissue to his nose.

'Lewis spoke to Philippe. They want an assistant now to help with prep,' Maddie inclined her head. 'You must know Lewis has been stretching out the work for me here. He's been a bloody legend trying to get something sorted for me.'

Roley's arms dropped to his sides. 'I know. We've been talking.'

Maddie picked up a long extension cord and started looping it around the crook of her elbow and her open palm.

'We're going to miss you around here.'

Maddie stopped winding. Was that it? 'You know I'm coming back?' she queried.

Roley shrugged. 'Lewis said he'd offered you a position.'

She nodded. 'I'll have work overseas for around six to eight weeks, then I'll do a little travelling. I'll be back in three months tops.'

'I just expected you'd stay around. You seem to love the place so much.'

Something in his demeanour stirred feelings of familiarity, vague but disconcerting. This was Josh-like. Hadn't she left him behind? Maddie straightened. She didn't expect Roley to share her excitement, but she wasn't buying into any negative crap either.

'I suppose life is greater than its parts.'

Roley's face remained passive but a metamorphosis began under his skin. 'Life—is—greater—than—its—parts,' Roley sounded the words. 'Is that an Aunt Blingism?'

Maddie felt the hard edge, a direct hit to her diaphragm. She slowly sucked air to settle it—to think. He was struggling under the weight of his own situation. Maddie knew she was part of Roley's confusion. But that was his journey, his vehicle to steer.

Her naive, vulnerable self wanted to fix it for him. Even now, she could feel her consciousness lighting that well-worn path. She nodded imperceptibly, acknowledging and resisting. She had never felt so strong.

'No. Something I came up with on my own.'

Maddie burned to add more, but spelling things out, offering solutions was robbing him of the chance to exercise his own emotional intelligence. The pattern exposed, had to change. Finally, she understood, the next move had to be his. He needed to step up and take some responsibility going forward.

Still, her heart paused while she waited. Every cell of her being vibrated in anticipation that he would recognise this opportunity. Understand that opportunities were beyond being thin on the ground. Opportunity had run out, run dry, evaporated to a wispy vapour trail wafting between them.

Feel it, Roley. Trust it. Trust me.

'Facebook?'

She would have broken, but she'd already done that, weeks ago. And she'd pieced her fragments back together with that special emotional glue, not available in shops or online. Stronger than Araldite, its two parts—pain and experience—when mixed together mended all manner of severed emotional threads. With time, the bond promised to be stronger than the original. The trick was to not let it harden, flexibility was key.

Maddie inhaled, allowing her body to soften.

'Facebook's not my thing,' she managed evenly. She looked into his eyes. 'You'll just have to know in your heart that I'll be thinking of you.'

Her eyes flew from his. She looked around the winery; an austere, unsympathetic setting for the scene. She shivered as the chill inched from the concrete, through her boots, into her legs.

Silence in the strange half-light.

Less than a thudding heartbeat later, Bethany appeared around the barrels.

'Hiya,' Maddie smiled at her friend. 'Perfect timing.'

It was time to leave. To put some distance between them.

Maddie noticed the vehicle in her rear-view mirror, moving up fast. She pulled toward the left of her lane. The quicker this dickhead got past her the better. As it neared, Maddie noticed the flashing headlights and took a longer look in her mirrors.

It was a ute. Just pass me already, she willed. But the ute slowed as it caught her. Then it dawned. 'Christ. Roley.'

She slowed and pulled off onto the gravel shoulder. Roley pulled up behind.

She left her car and walked slowly back towards him.

Roley hardly waited for his ute to stop before vaulting out the door. Maddie watched as he made his way purposefully towards her.

He reached that distance where one would slow for the conversation to begin, and kept moving. When his toes met hers, he stopped, thrusting his arms around her.

Maddie felt awkward, pinioned in the embrace. She hadn't had a chance to raise her arms, to think.

She felt his desperation in this decisive, relentless clutch. Then she heard the hard swallow in his throat and under-stood this was the telling point. Her senses peaked. Last time she had been this close to Roley, so dreading the words to come, he had surprised her. Her anticipation now was a sharp tip of steel pressing on her sternum.

'I don't want to say goodbye to you.'

The words, spoken so close to her ear she felt the brush of his lips, settled. Transporting her back to that cocooned space where their souls entwined defiantly, despite everything, regardless.

She nodded as tears rolled from her eyes. They drew apart slowly, smiling softly at the sight of the other. Maddie brushed at Roley's cheeks with her fingers. Moving her face towards his, she felt his breath on her softly parted lips but her lips met the stubbly, skin of his cheek. Maddie opened her eyes to target his mouth. Roley gently deflected once more.

'I need to sort things, Maddie. I'm sorry, but…I need to put this right.'

Maddie dropped her head to his shoulder and nestled into his neck. They repositioned their legs, boots entwined for maximum contact—a hug to bridge time.

The air horn and cloud of grit from a speeding semi-trailer finally brought laughter and the end of their embrace.

'I'm seeing Vieve this weekend at her parents' place.'

Maddie shook her head slowly. 'I don't know what to say.'

Roley looked down at his boots. 'Neither do I. Consequences, eh? Maybe you could wish me luck.'

Maddie smiled. 'I don't believe in luck. It's like gods—something to throw your hopes and bad manners at expecting a happy outcome in return. I don't see the strength in that. How about I wish you honesty instead; the courage to find it and the faith to use it.'

Roley looked stunned. 'Think I just got caught inside.'

He smiled, pulling her into another embrace.

From her car, Maddie watched Roley make a U-turn and head south, back down the highway.

Eventually, she indicated, pulling out to continue her journey north, everything ethereal.

In the absurdly uniform vineyard rows either side of the highway, she noticed the tangle of bare canes and autumn leaves clumped around trunks. The cycle of life she had set her own to. New green leaves would be waving welcome atop long canes months from now. What else would be waiting, she couldn't know.

The strength of Roley's resolve had softened something deep. It felt like sharing a burden you didn't need to shoulder on your own.

It transported her back to her deck. She'd left Aunt Bling to find her mum. Her mother, quite unexpectedly, had put her arm around her and pulled her close.

'Maddie, whatever's happening in your life, always trust love is never lost. We store its gift in our soft structures. It tints memory's brush and infuses our future thoughts. It reverberates deep in our core and even death doesn't displace it.'

It was irrefutable proof. Her mother and her aunt were sisters after all. Maddie had hugged her mum like she couldn't remember doing for the longest time.

Emotion brimmed as she recalled the scene. It surged through her fascia, cleansing old patterns, creating space for new.

Maddie shook the image from her head. This place had worked her over but there would be time in the coming weeks to think. Right now, she needed tunes. She pumped the volume, slid on her sunnies and set ready to enjoy the ride.

Acknowledgements

Many people to thank.

Big shout-out to Arts Margaret River for supporting the annual Margaret River Readers and Writers Festival. The program offers workshops and opportunities to assist aspiring writers to navigate the publishing process which presents as a closed book—a hardback.

Margaret River Wine Association. Thanks Nick and Pip for allowing me to be a fly on the wall.

Generous local authors, Lily Malone and Danielle Costley. Your early edits steered me in all the right directions and your encouragement and support so warmly welcome.

Readers/friends—Bob, Tracey, Janine, Megan, Cindy. Whether it was a section, a chapter or the whole manuscript, your feedback was more valuable than you probably think. Also, Adam and Leif, surf-speak consultants.

Louis Kwan for the simple, stylish graphic. I was

desperate for a heart and you gave me three.

Maria Fitzgerald, for creative inspiration and making me laugh-always.

Sean Blocksidge, Margaret River Discovery Co. I suspect you love the Wilyabrup Cliffs too. Thanks for allowing access and manipulation of your beautiful photographs.

Julie-Ann Harper of Pickawoowoo Publishing Group. You happened along at just the right time and I am truly grateful. Thanks to Nicole, Evelyn, Eddie, Laila and all of your team for getting me over the line.

Mumu, kindling my curiosity in our myofascial system.

Jeepers, my beautiful four legged companion (since departed). I explored many ideas for this story walking the rails to trails with you.

And most especially, the wellsprings of energy and joy I share life with, Mark and Seb. It's been a ride! You administered quiet encouragement and reassurance when my confidence flagged and always, unwavering belief. Writing this has been all the more rewarding and fun for having you guys share the shotgun seat, messing with the throttle.

About the Author

Vikki Messenger made a sea-change to Margaret River before sea-changes were even a thing at a time when many gravitated to its beaches and wineries. Many stayed.

In those days an artistic undertone permeated the sleepy town with an organic vibe appealing to a younger set seeking something more.

Once Vikki discovered wine, made from grapes (who knew), tasted of every other thing on the planet she was hooked. The sensual beverage has delivered fun, friends and the only decent thing to drink with food ever since.

Vikki lives in Margaret River with her winemaking husband and their son.